DETOUR IN OREGON

DONALD F. AVERILL

INK START MEDIA
5710 W Gate City Blvd Ste K #284
Greensboro, NC 27407

CONTENTS

ACKNOWLEDGMENTS

Thanks to the Beaver Creek Lane readers for their comments and suggestions. Special thanks to Barbara Schroeder for her support, and to Sandra Reeves for her assistance with editing.

This book is dedicated to Robert Griswold.

CHAPTER 1

Hitchhiker

Daniel Newcomb arrived at a Boise, Idaho, I-84 truck stop at 6:07 a.m. He had ridden with Ricoh Starre, a veteran of the war in Iraq, who was shepherding a semi loaded with structural steel from Pocatello to Seattle. During the four hour ride, they hadn't said much; neither man was a morning person unless on the battlefield. Ricoh liked driving at night and slept in the afternoons. Dan napped most of the way between the two cities, hardly noticing the signs for turnoffs to towns near the freeway. Ricoh dropped Dan off, said good luck, and continued on toward the coast.

Dan entered the white-stuccoed, blue-trimmed visitor center, bought a paper, slid into a booth, and ordered breakfast. He flipped through the paper and stopped to read the comic section. After a few grins and a laugh, his pancakes, bacon, and coffee arrived. Well-muscled, six-feet-one, 192 pounds, Dan wore khakis, a white long-sleeved shirt, and a light Army jacket. His black shoes had a few scuffs, not up to military standards, but presentable. He continued reading the local paper while eating, washing things down with decaf. He was on his third cup and relaxing, occasionally looking up, massaging his weaker leg and watching travelers come and go. After reading the disappointing local job market news, Dan decided to move on. Nothing to keep him in Boise. He planned for his next meal to be in Portland, Oregon. He had spent just over an hour at the truck stop.

He pulled two one-dollar bills from his wallet, placed them on the table under the empty water glass, left the newspaper on the seat, and slid out of the booth. He stood, stretched, swung his backpack over his left shoulder, walked slightly limping to the sales counter, and paid his bill.

The girl at the counter handed him a receipt and some change, smiled, and asked, "Gum? Mints?" She seemed eager to spend more time talking with the handsome stranger, but didn't go so far to say when she got off work.

"Ah—yeah. Do you have any Superman comics?" He watched her glance at the magazine rack and look back.

She smiled, "Nope, just Spiderman. Sorry. Anything else?"

"Do you know of anyone going to Portland?"

Her smile wilted, but before the cute cashier could answer, a deep raspy voice from behind Dan said, "I'm going to Portland. Want a lift? I assume you mean Portland, Oregon, I'm not headed to Maine."

Dan smiled, turned, and stepped back from the counter, expecting to see someone shorter than himself, but the man speaking towered over Dan by at least five inches. Dan stepped aside. The man, sporting a beard of perhaps ten day's growth, moved slowly to the counter and handed the cashier a twenty, folded lengthwise.

Dan replied, "Yeah. That would be great. Thanks."

"You bet. As soon as I get my change, we'll be on our way. Get your things."

"I've got everything right here." Dan pointed at his backpack.

"That's it? Son, you travel light. Let's roll." The big man dropped a coin on the floor, but didn't try to retrieve it, he just moved toward the door.

Dan reached down, grabbed the quarter, and followed his ride toward the parking lot. As he went out the door, he glanced back at the cashier, smiled, and waved. The two men walked about 30 yards to a silver Kenworth semi with Sayers Moving painted in giant, blue, script letters on the sides of the trailer. Dan climbed into the passenger seat, dropped his backpack on the floor, and latched the seat belt. He watched as the big man pulled himself up into the driver's seat. The padded seat seemed too small for the driver, but he appeared to be comfortable, checking the mirrors for other vehicles and pedestrians. The trucker extended his massive right hand and said, "Name's Bert—Bert Sayers."

"Dan Newcomb. Pleased to meet you, Bert." Dan replied, shaking hands. "Here's the coin you dropped." Dan dropped the quarter into Bert's hand.

"Thanks. I thought it was a nickel." I have trouble bending down; knees are shot."

"Accident?" Dan queried.

"Kind of—college football. Halfway through my senior season, two UCLA linemen knocked me out of the game. I planned on having surgery after I graduated, but I've never been far enough ahead to do it; too many bills to pay. After surgery, I wouldn't be able to work for several months. My degrees in history and English aren't worth a shit. I should have pursued business or science—probably business. Science would be too difficult—doesn't interest me that much anyway."

"With bad knees, how do you move furniture?"

"I don't. I just drive. I call a team when I arrive at my destination, and they unload the truck. What do you do for a living?"

"Nothing—right now. I'm on my way to Alaska. I've been thumbing my way across the states to see the country. I was in the service; caught a bullet in Afghanistan. You might have noticed my limp."

"Hah! We're quite a pair; my bad knees and your limp. We'd make quite a track team—at the Special Olympics," he grinned.

Dan smiled, leaned back, and watched Bert maneuver the semi through an intersection and onto the ramp leading to the freeway. The transitions through the gears seemed effortless, and the truck moved smoothly onto I-84. Bert was wearing brown work boots that needed a shine, and gray pants. As the truck neared the speed limit, Bert relaxed, sat back, and rolled up the sleeves of his brown and black-plaid long-sleeve shirt. He looked like a truck driver—or a logger. His slight stomach bulge was undoubtedly due to too many hamburgers, or beers, and not enough exercise. If he had good knees, he could be a logger. Paul Bunyan crossed Dan's mind as he imagined Bert wrestling trees to the ground, he was almost big enough.

As the semi gained speed, Bert gave a quick glance at Dan and said, "So what's in Portland?"

Dan told Bert about Afghanistan and his stay at Walter Reed hospital. After being discharged from the service and the hospital, Dan had decided to hitch his way across the states on his way back to Alaska. From Portland, he would go to Seattle and then fly to Anchorage. He had always wanted to travel in the lower forty-eight. Moving from one truck stop to the next gave him the opportunity to see at least some of the scenery and meet a few people, hear their accents. Occasionally, Dan had stayed away from the freeway for a couple of days near a service station or car wash to earn some extra cash.

"I figured you were a vet," Bert smiled. "Your army jacket and short hair tipped me off. Thanks for serving in the military. Sorry you got shot, but I'm glad you got back in one piece. Going home to see your parents?"

"No, I just want to get home and get back to work. I'd like to learn to fly—maybe become a bush pilot. I think I'd like the adventure. My dad was a bush pilot."

"You said *was*. What's your dad doing now?"

"I think he's dead. He flew north of Fairbanks with a couple of hunters and they never returned. That's when I was seventeen—about eight years ago."

"So you don't know for sure he's dead?"

"No, but if he were alive, I think he would have contacted my aunt and uncle by now. We all knew flying into the bush could be dangerous."

"Wouldn't he get in touch with your mom?"

"No, my mom died of cancer when I was 14. She was only 45—that was a tough emotional time for me. Dad and I lived together in Anchorage until he disappeared. I used to worry about him crashing, and then it finally happened. I stayed with my cousins in Fairbanks for about a year and a half, until I finished high school."

"And then you joined the Army?"

"Not quite. I worked for my Uncle Max for eighteen months before I signed up. I went to Ft. Benning, Georgia, for training, and then I was sent to Afghanistan. I returned with a purple heart and a torn-up leg."

"Is your uncle your dad's brother, or your mom's?"

"My mom's. He's married to Mona, from England, and they have two sons. Try to guess their names."

Bert grinned and said, "Victoria and Elizabeth?"

Dan started laughing. "Good guess! But not very close. They're Earl and Duke. Earl is about 17 now, and I think Duke is 15, but I could be off a year. I don't remember birthdays. Do you have any kids?"

"I have a son—name's Gary. He's a junior in high school at Idaho Falls—plays basketball. This summer he's going to work wheat harvest outside Ritzville; that's about an hour southwest of Spokane."

"You know someone there?"

"Uh-huh. A friend of mine, Andy Anderson, has a ranch there. I want Gary to spend some time away from his girlfriend, and grow up a bit. I'd like him to go to college to find out a little more about what the world has to offer. All he knows now is sports and having a steady girl. Do you have a girl waiting for you?"

"Nope. I want to get established before getting serious. It might take a couple of years before I can make a down payment on a plane." Dan chuckled, "I have to learn to fly first."

Bert grinned. "That sounds like a good idea."

Dan and Bert sat in silence as the distance from Boise increased. They passed through a farming area where tractors were plowing, generating clouds of dust, irrigation equipment was being moved, and cattle were grazing. One of the dopey animals was scratching its hide on a barbed wire fence.

Bert noted Dan had seen the same thing. Bert smiled. "I've never scratched my back with barbed wire, mostly with door jams and fingernails, courtesy of my wife. I had a bamboo back scratcher, made in China, but I lost it. I think I left it in a motel room."

Dan leaned back and watched the fields and fence posts pass by as he recalled his mother scratching his back when he sat beside the furnace at home after breakfast. She'd scratch his back for a minute, kiss his forehead, and pat him on the back saying, "Get ready for school." Those minutes were portions of time he would never forget.

Dan's thoughts and the constant drone of the engine were relaxing. He closed his eyes and listened to the road noise. Suddenly in hand-to-hand combat, his opponent's knife was just about to cut into his neck when he jerked forward and twisted toward the door. He heard a loud noise, opened his eyes, and blinked.

"Hey! You all right?" Bert had been startled by Dan's sudden movements. The noise was from a passing truck's horn—the driver just saying hello.

Dan cleared his throat, trying to act as if nothing had happened, but then he decided to explain. "Sometimes, when I doze off, I have a recurring bad dream. It always startles me. A doc at the hospital said it will stop eventually. I hope it happens soon, it's a little embarrassing. I don't mean to scare anybody. Can we stop at the next rest area?"

Bert laughed. "Good idea, I've got to take a leak too." He pointed out the front windshield. "There's a sign; 11 miles to relief," Bert smiled. "Hang in there for about ten minutes."

"Don't exceed the speed limit, but that coffee wants out. I should have passed up the third cup."

As Dan watched the clock on the dash, each minute seemed like ten. When he saw the exit sign, he knew it would only be another couple of minutes before he could relax.

Bert's moving van exited the freeway, slowed gradually, and pulled into truck parking next to two other freight trucks.

"Let's stretch our legs a little, too," Bert commented as he put the engine in idle.

"Sounds good, I need to move my legs a bit. My bad leg needs some exercise. I've been sitting too much lately."

They had to walk about 40 yards to the restrooms. As they crossed through a grassy area where several people were walking their dogs, Dan and Bert saw a man yelling at his dog and pulling on its leash. It was a young cocker spaniel that apparently wanted to investigate the gravel near the truck parking area. A jerk on the leash spun the dog around. As the dog approached the man, he kicked it. The dog yelped and tried to get away.

Bert was about ten feet away from the man and said firmly, "Hey! Don't kick your dog. And, by the way, the dog doesn't understand when you yell at it."

"Did I ask for your input? Keep your trap shut. It's my dog! I'll do what I want."

Bert replied, "Just some advice, take it or leave it, but don't kick your dog."

Dan continued on to the restroom. It was a small building and a little crowded. Dan spent more than five minutes doing a two-minute task in the building, and exited after washing his hands and face. Bert was waiting outside. As they began walking toward the truck, they heard a voice from behind them.

"Hey, you big shit, I told you to shut up!"

Dan spun around just in time to see a lug wrench swinging toward Bert's head. Dan gave Bert a shove to the side and the lug wrench missed. "Keep that up and you're going to get hurt," Dan warned.

"I'll show you who'll get hurt." The man swung the lug wrench again, this time at Dan, and struck a glancing blow to Dan's shoulder. Dan quickly stepped into the man, grabbed his arm, and threw him to the ground. The lug wrench fell in the grass. Dan kicked it out of the way.

As the man scrambled to his feet, he uttered, "Lucky move, shit head."

"Look mister, I really don't want to hurt you," Dan replied.

"You're going to hurt *me?*" he snickered. "You're a punk, that'll never happen."

Dan realized he was going to have to knock this guy out or put him to sleep with a choke hold. The guy probably outweighed Dan by 20-30 pounds, but was several inches shorter. He rushed at Dan, but Dan stepped to the side and smashed the palm of his right hand against the guy's left temple. The man staggered, almost falling, but he regained his balance, and came at Dan a second time. This time Dan sidestepped and grabbed the guy from behind. Dan quickly got his left arm under the man's neck, locked it in with his right arm, and tightened his hold. The guy tried to shake Dan off, but in a few seconds went limp. Dan dropped the guy on the ground.

"That's my husband," a woman said as she knelt beside him. "I told him to let it go, but he gets angry easily—does stupid things. Is he hurt?"

"He's all right. When he's wide awake, tell him he's lucky I didn't break one of his arms, or his neck," stated Dan. "That wrench is a deadly weapon."

Bert had watched the whole thing. He walked with Dan back to the truck. "You sure moved fast! Glad you pushed me out of the way. It was over before I could react," he said. "Sorry I didn't help."

"Don't sweat it. When your life depends on it, you have to move quickly," smiled Dan. "I didn't want him to hit you; I don't know how to drive a semi."

Bert grinned and said, "I'm glad you didn't hurt that slob. Putting him out was good. I'd have kicked him in the nuts, too. But then we would have had to stay around and talk to the police. Let's hit the road."

When they were back on the freeway, Bert asked, "You like Superman comics?"

"Not really. I'd rather read a good adventure story, but I was wondering what Superman looks like now. When I was in high school, a girl I dated said I looked like Superman. The girl's name was Sandra. I don't recall her last name." Dan laughed and said, "I guess I could look a little like Clark Kent, if I wore glasses."

Bert commented, "Not with that crew cut, my friend. Maybe Sandra was yanking your chain. She probably wanted another date. How did you get that scar on your chin; was that also a wound from Afghanistan?"

Dan reached up to his chin with his right hand and said, smiling, "That's an old football injury. I tackled a guy without my helmet."

Bert laughed and said, "I wondered if you had ever played football."

"Yeah. I was kicked in the face, but I prevented a touchdown, I should have had some stitches, but I wanted the scar—macho back then," Dan grinned.

CHAPTER 2

Winter Home

An hour passed without much further conversation; neither man had much more to say. The few hours of conversation with Bert had probably exceeded all the talking Dan had had over the previous two weeks. As Dan watched the traffic from the truck cab, he noted the differences from observing vehicular movement from a passenger car. There were a few close calls when cars darted in front of the truck, but Bert anticipated the erratic car drivers' dangerous movements. From the vantage point of the seat in the semi, he could observe the approach of cars from both directions. Some relaxation was obtained when they were on the freeways; there was little potential for collisions with oncoming traffic.

Bert broke the silence, "What kind of music do you like, Dan?"

"Most anything except heavy metal and rap. I can't stand rap. I guess I don't even call it music. I like some country and some orchestral music—it all depends on the mood I'm in, but if I can't understand a singer's words, I lose interest. I like variety."

"There's a library of CDs in a case behind your seat. Pick something out for us to listen to. There's no rap or heavy metal there; I agree with you on that stuff."

Dan selected several CDs, loaded them into the player, and pressed random. The Bose speaker system in the truck was excellent. Dan and Bert listened for about an hour. As the music played in the background, they mentioned scenic places they had visited.

"Have you seen Multnomah Falls?" Bert asked.

"No. Where is it?"

"It's about thirty miles east of Portland; we'll drive past it," answered Bert.

"Can we see it from the freeway?"

"Briefly, but it's easy to miss. It's on the old Columbia River Highway, but I'll take you to it. It's a beautiful thing to see in a great scenic area of Oregon. There are several other falls on the old highway, too."

"Well, if you ever get to Alaska, I'll show you some beautiful scenery from the air."

"I've heard the mosquitoes are as big as birds," Bert smiled.

"Not quite that big, but I shoot them with a BB gun," said Dan. "They're so big, it's hard to miss. Sometimes it takes two BBs to bring one down."

Bert laughed and said, "Boy, you sure can pile it on! We'll stop and get some lunch in Pendleton. We're almost there."

As they left the Pendleton restaurant, Dan bought a map of Oregon and studied it as they continued driving toward Portland. Dan was amazed at the size of the Columbia River, and gained much respect for the wind surfers near Hood River. It was about three o'clock when they left the freeway at exit 31 and pulled into the visitor parking area at Multnomah Falls.

"I know you need to get into Portland, Bert. I want to stay here and look around for a while, so I'll say goodbye now. Thanks for the ride and everything. I'll let you know what I'm doing when I figure it out. I've got your card so I can contact you."

"Good luck, Dan. Thanks for the company and the excitement. Try to stay out of trouble! I wish you could meet my wife and son. Gary could benefit from knowing you."

Dan shook hands with Bert, climbed down from the cab, and slammed the door. He heard the engine rev, a toot on the horn, and watched as the big semi pulled away. Dan waved to the truck and gave a thumbs up. He heard two blasts from the horn, and watched Bert's truck pick up speed on the ramp joining I-84.

Standing in the middle of the visitor-parking lot, between the east- and west-bound freeway traffic, he looked high above at the jagged rocks, where the water began its journey to the ground below.

After getting out of the way of parking lot traffic, he put on his backpack, and walked toward the observation area so he could see the falls more clearly. He followed a concrete tunnel, perhaps a hundred feet in length, under the east-bound freeway traffic to a small foot-bridge over a stream of water from the falls. He could hear several languages being spoken by travelers as he moved toward the base of the falls.

Looking up, 500 feet above him, he could see tall trees poking into the blue sky, appearing to be growing out of the rocky cliff, where the water started cascading down the rock face and under a bridge that arched over a pool fed by the falls. Contrasting colors of the rocks; oranges, various shades of brown and gray-black, and the green trees, made Dan feel like he was part of an artist's painting. The spectacular waterfall reminded him of some of the mountainous areas in the back country of Alaska that his father had told him about. He scouted the area, but didn't want to go hiking, so he entered the Visitor Center. Hiking could be done later, after he found a short-term job. He'd work a few days before moving on to Portland.

He spent a few minutes looking at the displays of the Columbia River Gorge area and moved slowly toward the information counter. There was a pleasant-looking middle-aged gray-haired woman handing out literature to tourists. When the tourists moved away from the counter, Dan approached and asked, "Do you have any jobs available—maybe some janitorial work?"

The lady thought for a moment and said, "I'm sorry, but we have all the help we need right now. Check in the Gift Shop, they might know of something."

"Thank you."

Dan went outside and reentered the building at the Gift Shop and asked the same question to a young lady. The cute, twenty-year-old, without a ring, smiled, and said, "No. We don't need any help this season. You should apply next year in the spring."

She slowly turned away and then suddenly turned back toward Dan and said, "Oh, I just remembered, Mr. and Mrs. Sterling need a house sitter. They said anyone interested could call any time. They need someone right away."

The girl handed Dan a business card with a name and phone number on it. He looked at the handwritten information and began to think. *Was the job a short or long term commitment?* He didn't want to stay in one location for more than a few days; at most, a few weeks. He felt Alaska was calling him home. But, the only way to find out about the job was to make the call.

Dan dialed the number at the outdoor public phone. A very pleasant female voice answered. Dan asked her about the job, but she wanted to speak in person. She and her husband would be at the falls in about twenty minutes. Twenty minutes passed. Dan decided to wait for ten more minutes and then find a ride to Portland. About five minutes later, a nicely dressed, good-looking couple approached the Visitor Center. Dan met them in front of the building and asked if they were the Sterlings.

"Yes. I'm Terry, and this is my wife, Valerie," the graying gentleman put his arm around the woman's shoulders. "Sorry you had to wait so long. It took us a little longer than we estimated. We drove out from Portland on the scenic highway—lots of low speed curves."

"That's okay. It's nice to meet you. I'm Daniel Newcomb," he said as he shook hands with Mr. Sterling. Dan shook hands with Mrs. Sterling and noted that she was very pretty in spite of her age. She was a few inches over five-feet tall, and had short, curly, silver-gray hair. He assumed she was about 65, she had said they were retired.

"We want to spend some time in Arizona. We need someone to take care of our mountain property while we're gone," commented Terry. Terry wore glasses with black- plastic rims, was about three-inches shorter than Dan, and had wavy gray hair with a few small patches of brown. The pair made a handsome couple.

"Why don't we show you our place? While we're driving, we can get to know you a little," suggested Valerie.

"The white SUV is our car," Terry said as he pointed to the Jeep Grand Cherokee in the parking lot. Dan got in front while Terry helped Valerie climb into the back. Terry started the engine and they circled through the parking area and began moving on the two-lane scenic highway toward Portland.

As they drove through the lush green forested area, Valerie told Dan they had been retired for about 3 years. Terry had been a Boeing engineer, and Valerie had been a grade school principal in the Seattle area. They had retired early so they could enjoy traveling and avoid stress.

Valerie asked, "What do you do for a living, Daniel?"

"Please call me Dan. I just got out of the Army a couple of weeks ago." Dan told the Sterlings about Afghanistan and his parents. "I'm not sure what I'm going to do when I get home, but I like to fix things. I might start a repair shop of some kind and I want to learn to fly." Dan looked at Mrs. Sterling and smiled.

"Most everyone calls me Val. Terry could sure use your talents. He's been working on an old World War II surplus jeep for some time. He took it apart a couple of months ago—parts are all over the garage."

"It's not *that* bad, Val. I'll show it to you, Dan," added Terry.

They had driven on the scenic highway toward Portland for about ten minutes negotiating many low-speed curves. They crossed a bridge hugging the steep rocky hillside and Terry slowed, nearly stopping, and made a left turn off the paved road. Dan thought if he were a boy, he would have gotten carsick when traveling through all the bends in the road. The car shifted to a low gear to climb the steep hill on the dirt and gravel single-lane road.

The road wound around the hillsides and rose in elevation as they progressed. After another five minutes, they pulled into a clearing where a large log cabin and a two-car attached-garage were located. They drove to the cabin, parked in front of the garage in the gravel, and got out of the SUV.

Dan could hear sounds of a stream in the distance. He asked, "Where's the water?"

Valerie replied, "A really nice stream is behind the cabin, about 25-yards back. There's a bridge, but you could wade across; it's less than two-feet deep. It's pretty cold almost year-round—glacial runoff from Mount Hood. There's a drop of about eight-feet down to the water. You can reach the water, without climbing down, in several places downstream. Come on, we'll show you the cabin."

Terry unlocked the front door and flipped on a light switch. It was late afternoon, and the sun had been behind the trees for around an hour. It was cool in the shade, and in the cabin, which smelled a little musty. It had been closed up for several weeks.

As Val entered the cabin, she looked back, smiled at Dan, and said, "Follow me, I'll show you around. Terry, let's leave the door open."

Dan entered the cabin and scanned the living room. He could see the Sterlings had great taste. There was a large fireplace flanked with black granite and a hearth of gray-streaked white granite. Above the mantel was a mountain scene sculpted from sheet metal with a torch. A couple of thick carpets covered most of the light-oak floor. One wall had shelves full of books from floor to ceiling. After living so simply for so long, Dan was a little intimidated by the nice surroundings.

"Boy, this is great!"

"Thank you, Dan. Would you like to stay for dinner?" asked Val.

"Ah—sure." He grinned, "I don't have anything planned."

"How about a drink? We have beer, wine, or soft drinks," stated Terry.

"I'd like a Pepsi, or a Coke, if you have one," Dan answered.

Terry came back from the kitchen with two cans of Pepsi and said, "Let me show you my project while Val makes dinner."

Dan followed Terry into the garage. Dan was impressed by the variety of tools Terry had assembled. His talent as an engineer was evident. His efficient use of space allowed complete access to the metal-working equipment. Wood-working equipment could be rolled outside so sawdust wasn't a problem.

Terry said, "If you want, you can work on the jeep. I bought it from a friend. He used to collect old vehicles. I took out the battery, oil pump, lights, and started changing the wiring. I bought a new motor and transmission. Some of the stuff is still in boxes. All I ask is that whatever you do must be neat and, of course, it has to work," Terry grinned.

Dan smiled and replied, "That's the only kind of work I do."

"If you'd rather, you can work on a project of your own."

Val called from the house, "Hey, you guys—dinner is ready."

While eating, the Sterlings told Dan they would be gone for five months. He would be paid $500 a month. The utilities were paid and all his food was free. If he needed anything else, he could phone in an order. Terry and Val would return at the end of February. Following dinner, they sat and talked in the living room.

Dan retrieved a letter from his pack and handed it to Terry. "When I left the hospital, Captain Harwood sent me this letter. He said I could call anytime, 24/7, if I needed a reference. There's a number; it's in D.C."

Terry went to the kitchen and dialed the number. A couple of minutes later, Terry rejoined Val and Dan.

"So, would you trust me with your mountain home?" asked Dan.

"Not a problem, Dan. Captain Harwood says you are a first-rate young man, and he would trust you with his life. I think you deserve something in addition to our thanks for serving in Afghanistan," declared Terry.

Val grinned, "I second that thought."

Terry continued, "You mentioned wanting to get a pilot's license. I know someone that could help you. Phil Langford works at the Troutdale airport. If you need flying lessons, he's the person to see."

"Well, I was only going to be in Portland for about a week, but you've made me such a good offer, I'd be an idiot if I didn't accept. Thank you. I'll look up Mr. Langford."

"That's great Dan!" exclaimed Val.

She looked at Terry and smiled, "We can leave for Tucson next week; just as we planned. We're so lucky you showed up when you did, Dan. We were thinking we would have to postpone leaving for Arizona for a while. I'm afraid we started looking for a caretaker a little late, but I think we've found the right person."

"Thank you very much. You won't be disappointed."

Terry gave Dan a list of details about the cabin, utilities, and automatic food delivery. The Sterlings left a list of emergency numbers to call. Wind and ice, or occasionally a downed tree, could disrupt the regular landline service. Cellular phone service was a problem in the area, so they didn't have a cell phone at the cabin.

Terry stood up from the table saying, "Let me show you the emergency generator; it's in a shed behind the garage."

After Terry instructed Dan about the use of the generator, Val showed Dan the pantry in the back of the kitchen. Canned food for three months was on the shelves; but that was for two people. Dan probably wouldn't need to order much during the entire five-month stay. Fresh eggs, milk, and cheese were delivered to a locked steel box about a half-hour walk from the cabin. Val said bears, cougars, and coyotes couldn't get into the steel box. The owner of a small Corbett farm delivered the dairy products every two weeks. Val put the key in the drawer under the kitchen counter next to the refrigerator.

"If you want to order something, call the number on the tag attached to the box key. It will be delivered with the dairy products," Val explained.

"Any questions, Dan?" Terry asked.

"Just one. What do you do when there is opposing traffic on your road? There's only one lane."

"Well, we have the only cabin on this road, and there are several wide spots where two cars can squeeze by. Otherwise, someone will have to back up. We've never had any problems. Anything else?"

"Not that I can think of." Dan paused for a moment and then remembered something else. "Oh, wait. There is something else. Is there a gun in the cabin?"

Val answered, "I don't want guns around. If animals come to visit, we just wait and they go away. We're careful—we don't leave food outside. We burn all our garbage and take metal into our recycling container at our home in Portland."

"All right, I'll follow your procedures. I'm pretty self-sufficient. I'm used to solving unexpected problems," replied Dan.

Terry said, "Okay. Call us if you need to. We'll leave now. You can start investigating the cabin and the surroundings. We'll see you at the end of February. Keep the wild parties to a minimum, but have fun!"

"Thanks for everything. Enjoy your time in Tucson. See you next year."

CHAPTER 3

Visitor

Dan watched the tail lights of the Sterlings' car disappear into the trees and then walked around the cabin to check out the surroundings. He went to the bridge, took a look at the creek, and returned to the cabin, closing and locking the heavy front door made of rough-cut planks. He would check the outside more fully tomorrow during bright daylight. Starting in the kitchen, he began to investigate the cabin interior. Val had washed the dishes and left them drying next to the sink. A note on the coffee maker said it was set to start brewing at 6:00 a.m.

Dan pulled out all the drawers, opened all the cabinets, and made mental notes where everything was. The pantry was in good shape. No strange foods, just standard things he could eat out of the container or use as ingredients. He wasn't much of a cook, but he could follow directions. Several recipe books were stacked on the kitchen counter next to the stove. A large cylindrical container of black pepper with a Costco label got his attention. Dan thought it would take a decade to use that much pepper. The Sterlings must have gotten it on sale. He wondered if maybe they used the pepper to keep bears or other critters away.

The guest bedroom was next. What he thought was a large closet turned out to be a small computer room. Dan turned on the computer, and it immediately logged onto the Internet. He was surprised; he didn't need a password. There was a printer/copier, a 22-inch flat screen, and both keyboard and mouse were wireless. He pulled out a small drawer under the keyboard and found extra AA batteries. If he needed to have questions answered, he could use the Net for research. The adjoining room would be his bedroom. He opened his backpack and put his extra clothes in the chest of drawers. All his clothes couldn't fill up one drawer. He placed his toiletries in the bathroom on a shelf above the toilet tank.

After showering, he put on some pajamas and a heavy robe he found in the Sterlings' bedroom. Dan normally slept in his underwear, or in the buff, but his clothes were dirty, and it was a little chilly in the cabin. He hoped Terry wouldn't mind if he borrowed the pajamas. He found a pair of leather slippers, too small, in his bedroom. Dan tossed the slippers back onto the closet floor and put on a pair of clean socks. He would add slippers to his list of things to buy.

Dan sat down on the large brown-leather couch in front of the fireplace and mulled over his decision to stay for the winter. Six months of solitude might be too much to stand for most people, but being by himself would give him a chance to rid his mind of those bad dreams without the embarrassment that came when others observed his reactions. Tomorrow he would walk some trails, follow the road to the food storage box, and see if he had any neighbors nearby. Terry and Val hadn't mentioned any neighbors, and Dan hadn't thought to ask. Then he remembered Terry saying their cabin was the only one on the road. Apparently, the Sterlings' cabin was fairly well isolated, but surely there were other cabins in the area, accessible from other roads.

Dan walked over to the wall of books and started reading titles. There were many topics: history, crafts, education, engineering, and some novels—plenty of reading material for six months. Before he finished reading the titles on the first row of books, he stretched, yawned, and decided to go to bed. The time zone change had finally caught up with him. Tomorrow would be the day for exploring the garage and the forested area surrounding the cabin. He checked the front door, extinguished the lights, went in the bedroom, and slid under a comforter and sheet.

Dan was awakened by the gurgling sound from the coffee pot. A couple of eggs, some toast with Marion berry jam, and hot coffee took the chill off the morning. When he was dressing, he realized more clothes were necessary, especially a winter coat. He started compiling a list of his needs on a small notepad. He stuck the pad and a pen in his pocket and checked the thermometer in the kitchen window; it read 43 degrees. He found a plaid jacket and a sweatshirt in the bedroom closet. Undoubtedly, they were Terry's; a little small, but they should offer some protection from the chilly air. He took out the pad and wrote: heavy winter coat, jeans (3 pair), long-sleeved flannel shirts (2), and slippers.

Dan got the lock box key and started down the gravel road. Faint, sporadic noises of highway traffic and bird songs were the only sounds he recognized. Dan judged the highway sounds originated on the old Columbia River Highway. The forest filtered out the sounds from the freeway, and it was farther away than the scenic road by a hundred yards. Few vacationers travelling the scenic route would be in the area now. Tourist season was about over at the end of August, and it was late September.

During thirty-five minutes of walking on the narrow gravel road, Dan noted there were several pullouts, the road widened on both sides, but most often on the uphill side. At the edge of the last pullout on the downhill side of the road were two boxes mounted on large stumps. The gray box to the left had F. S. stenciled on it in dark-green letters. Dan assumed F. S. was for the forest service. The right box had Sterling stenciled on it in white letters. Dan opened the lock, lifted the lid, and looked inside. His order shouldn't fill the box; the volume was about six cubic feet. He closed the lid, locked the box, and headed back toward the cabin at a leisurely pace. Forty-five minutes later, Dan was back at the cabin. While walking back from the lock box, Dan had recognized two other sounds—the horn from a train passing by on the tracks adjacent to the freeway below, next to the scenic highway, and jet engines almost directly overhead.

Dan searched the Sterlings' library, found a book on weapons, and sank into the sofa. As his pulse slowed, he realized the past few weeks riding in trucks had gotten him out of shape. He looked at the title of the book he had selected, *History of Weapons.* Bored with the first chapter, which was about early man's hunting weapons, he checked the table of contents and turned to the section on crossbows. Diagrams of crossbows from the middle ages to the present were presented in great detail. Dan needed a weapon for protection from bears and cougars. For travel through the forest, it needed to be compact, but carry a lethal blow. Building a crossbow would make a good project. Terry's tools would enable a routine construction.

While he ate lunch, he sketched plans for a bow. He hadn't felt this much enthusiasm for anything in a long time. Dan left his dirty dishes in the kitchen sink, raised the garage door, and took a deep breath of fresh mountain air. When he removed his watch, it was 1:07 p.m. He found all the raw materials he needed and marked the metal pieces for cutting. Dan found a piece of oak for the stock that he roughed out with the band saw. He could sculpt the wood with chisels and sandpaper. With everything laid on the workbench, Dan put his watch back on, noting the time. It was a few minutes before five o'clock. Quitting for the day, he closed the garage door and went into the cabin.

Dan flipped a switch on the wall next to the fireplace and flames rose from around the metal logs. He sat down on the sofa and pulled his shopping list from his pocket to add a few more items—socks and underwear (6 sets), and three T-bone steaks. His four-mile walk in the morning, and the significant progress on his crossbow were major accomplishments for his first day.

While walking and working, Dan had considered himself lucky to have a job that only required minimal interaction with people. In the army, he had learned to kill with everything from a shoestring to a credit card. Now, those items could be removed from his weaponry. He hoped he could gradually let ordinary items become ordinary again. When he first came out of the hospital and was going through a checkout line in a store, he would look with suspicion at the person in front of him, watching the person's neck and arm positions. In a few seconds, he knew how to kill the individual with minimal effort. Living alone in the mountains would give him time for normal thinking to return.

Dan saw something he hadn't noticed before, a TV remote, resting on top of the mantel. He continued gazing around the cabin but didn't see a TV set. He picked up the remote and pressed the on button, hoping a TV screen would magically appear. Nope, nothing happened. He looked around again. Next to the switch for the gas fireplace was a switch labeled *S*. He flipped the switch and heard a whirring sound from above the fireplace. A large flat-screen TV descended from the ceiling. Dan concluded the *S* meant screen. The TV remote *ON* button brought the screen to life.

After five minutes of channel surfing, he found a movie channel without commercials. An old war movie was on—just what he didn't need. He turned off the TV and went into the kitchen. Not being very hungry; he opened a can of soup and got some crackers from the cupboard. Just as the beep on the microwave sounded, he heard scratching at the front door. The soup would have to wait. He opened the front door and looked out through the screen. A large German shepherd was sitting on the welcome mat. Dan estimated the dog must weigh at least eighty pounds. He opened the screen door and knelt on the floor about a yard in front of the animal.

"Well, hello! Who are you?" he asked.

The dog darted into the cabin, nearly knocking Dan over.

"Well, come right in," Dan uttered, a little surprised. "Make yourself at home."

Dan watched the dog walk from room to room, ending up in the kitchen, where the animal sat in front of the stove looking up at Dan.

"You must be hungry, big boy." Dan had seen a large bag of dog food in the pantry, but hadn't paid much attention to it; he hadn't seen a dog around the cabin until now. He cut open the bag and filled a cereal bowl until it was overflowing. He put the bowl on the floor, and the dog started wolfing the food down. The big dog was really hungry! Dan filled another bowl with fresh water and put it beside the nearly clean bowl. When the dog had almost finished lapping up the water, it turned and walked to the front door.

"Hey! Not so fast, buddy. Do you think you can just eat and run?" Dan had noticed the dog had a collar. But, while the dog was eating, he stayed away from the front end of the animal; a hungry dog had nipped him before. Dan slowly knelt beside the dog and saw "Henry" printed on the collar. There was a phone number, but the dog pulled away before Dan could make out the number. Henry wanted out and Dan wasn't going to argue. He opened the door, and the dog bounded away, vanishing behind the garage. Dan ran to the corner of the garage and caught sight of Henry crossing the bridge and moving into the darkness of the woods. He wondered if the dog was gone for good, or if maybe he had made a friend. Henry just might return; he knows where he can eat. Dan went back into the cabin to his lukewarm soup.

The next morning, Dan investigated the clearing around the cabin to see if he had missed anything during his previous survey of the property. A large, white, propane tank was behind the garage. Dan hadn't had the fireplace on very long the day before, just long enough to take the chill off, and he hadn't used the kitchen range, so not much gas had been consumed; the gauge indicated the tank was nearly full. Dan followed the trail to the creek and crossed the sturdy log bridge. The stream, about 10-feet wide, looked to be about a foot deep. The trail ended about twenty yards past the creek. Numerous small trees, shrubs, a few downed trees, wild blackberry vines, and pine needles, several inches deep, would make moving through the forest difficult. He'd check in the garage for a hatchet to help clear the way.

Dan's eyes followed the electrical power line from the house to the road. From the pole near the road, the power line disappeared into the trees. Dan went back into the cabin and dialed the number to place his order for food and clothing. A woman, sounding fairly young, perhaps a college student, answered.

"Hello. My name is Marlene. How may I help you? I see you're calling from the Sterlings' cabin," she remarked.

"That's right. Where are you?" Dan asked.

"I work at Warner's Department Store in Wood Village. I'll fill your order and see that it gets delivered."

"Thank you, Marlene. I'm Dan. I'm cabin sitting for the Sterlings."

"It's nice to hear your voice, Dan. The Sterlings said you would call when you needed things. What do you want to order?"

Dan read everything from his list, thanked her for taking the order and hung up.

After a quick breakfast, he raised the garage door and continued working on the crossbow. He was so engrossed with the fabrication of the bow, he had forgotten about lunch. It was about three o'clock when he heard a bark from in front of the garage. Dan looked up from the cluttered workbench and saw Henry sitting in the driveway.

"Henry! You came back!"

The dog barked and moved closer to Dan and sat down again. Dan knelt beside the dog and read the number on the collar. He stood, walked to the workbench, and wrote the number down on a pad.

"Are you hungry, Henry?"

Henry barked again and followed Dan into the kitchen. Dan had filled a quart-size Ziploc bag with dog food the night before and had laid it next to the saucepan. The large bag of food in the pantry would remain fresher if it wasn't opened repeatedly. He put some food in the saucepan as before, and went to the sink to get some water for Henry. Dan turned around with the water, but Henry was gone, and so was the plastic bag of food.

"Hmm. I guess he wants to eat elsewhere."

Dan picked up the phone and called the number he had written down. There was a recorded message. The number was no longer in service. The phone book indicated area code 218 was for northern Minnesota. Something must have happened to Henry's owners in Oregon, and the dog got stranded or ran away.

Dan covered the food and water with plastic wrap. When Henry returned, probably tomorrow, the food was ready. He didn't want to put the food outside; there were too many critters in the woods that might drop by for dinner. Bears, skunks, squirrels, and raccoons were to be expected, and perhaps coyotes.

After Dan's stomach protested its lack of food, Dan stuck a cookie in his mouth, a couple more in a pocket, grabbed a Coke, and went back to work in the garage. The crossbow stock and all the metal parts were ready to be filed, smoothed, and painted. Sanding the stock and finishing the metal parts took another hour, and then Dan painted everything black. He scoured the cabin and the garage for something to use as a bowstring, but nothing was obvious. Dan assembled the parts without a bowstring and then took a break for dinner. He thought he might have to travel into Portland to buy a bowstring.

After dinner, it was nearly dark outside so he closed the garage door. As he went back into the living room, he noticed a piece of filament tape on the kindling box next to the fireplace. He had once tried to break a piece of filament tape with his hands, but had to give up; it was too strong. He retrieved a roll of filament tape from a shelf above the workbench in the garage.

Dan removed the filaments from the tape, carefully braided them together, and by 10:00 p.m., he had a bowstring about four feet long.

Testing was next. He tied one end of the string to the middle of a piece of firewood and the other end around a broom handle. With both feet holding the firewood, Dan pulled as hard as he could on the broom handle using both hands. From his experience with lifting weights, he knew he could pull up with at least 500 pounds of force. The string didn't break; he had what he wanted. In the morning, he would make some arrows, or what the book called bolts. He had seen several pieces of lightweight steel tubing in the garage that he could make into bolts. Test firing was not far off.

CHAPTER 4

Secret Cave

Excited about progress on the crossbow, Dan skipped breakfast the next morning, except for coffee, and made bolts for the crossbow until noon. He had enough tubing to make eight shafts, and he used a small metal lathe to turn short metal rods into tips for the bolts. Dan pressed the tips into the tubing, and epoxied small plastic triangles for feathers on the shafts. He hadn't paid much attention to the gray, rainy day, but he was proud to have made eight, nearly identical, shiny arrows.

Dan had a quick lunch and got back to the crossbow. He attached the cord to the bow, and with some effort, drew back the string to the trigger mechanism. He put a bolt into position and went outside with the loaded weapon. Dan aimed at a nearby tree and pulled the trigger.

He was alarmed at the noise when the bolt was released. "Damn! That's loud." The bow propelled the bolt into the tree so deeply that he couldn't pull the shaft out with his hands. Using a pair of pliers, he extracted the bolt from the tree. He estimated the bolt had penetrated about two inches into the wood. Dan went back to the garage and looked up noise-level in the crossbow section of the weapons book. After attaching rubber silencers to the bowstring, most of the noise was eliminated. He shot three more times to optimize the positions of the silencers.

Drawing back the bowstring was not an easy task. The book described a method to pull back the bowstring by straightening the bowman's leg.

Dan made another cord from six feet of filament tape and attached one end to the bowstring. He made a loop in the other end for his right foot. After he shot a bolt, he extended his leg, and the bow was ready for another bolt. It took a little practice, but eventually, he could shoot four to five times in one minute with good accuracy. After extracting the bolts from his target tree, Dan returned to the garage. In the late afternoon, fog was creeping into the clearing reducing visibility. Cold and wet, Dan decided to quit for the day, feeling good about his progress.

Henry was waiting in the garage watching Dan's activities. After storing the bow and bolts on the workbench, Dan went in the kitchen, got the food bowl from the day before, and some fresh water. Henry ate like a hungry wolf and lapped up most of the water.

"Henry, you are so sloppy! You've gotten food and water all over the floor, but that's all right, it's just the garage."

Henry sat and looked at Dan. Dan reached out and scratched the dog between his ears and patted him on the back. "You're a good boy, Henry."

Henry whined and wagged his tail. He sat beside his water bowl, looking up at Dan.

"I wish you could talk, Henry."

Henry barked.

Dan said "Talk!" and Henry barked.

"So you know English; I was afraid you might only know German," Dan smiled. "You want some more to eat?"

Henry barked again.

In the kitchen, Dan put some dog food into a plastic bag as he had done before. He returned to the garage and placed the bag of food on the floor. Henry bit into the plastic bag, carried it from the garage, crossed the bridge, and disappeared into the light-gray fog that was beginning to obscure the closest trees.

Dan pondered Henry's actions and decided the next time the dog ran off with a bag of food, he would follow Henry. Maybe Henry had an injured companion or a mate. Dan was having a hard time believing someone intentionally got rid of such a smart and beautiful pet.

The next morning, it seemed to be colder than usual; the moist air was penetrating Dan's summer clothing, but the fog had lifted. Dan decided to remove the fake gas logs from the fireplace and get ready to burn wood. He might as well enjoy the warmth and noises of a wood fire. He stored the metal logs in the garage and turned off the gas to the fireplace. When Dan was working on his crossbow, he had seen an ax and a saw, big enough to cut through 18-inch diameter logs. Before he went outside after firewood, Dan put on a sweatshirt and Terry's flimsy jacket. He didn't think he would need a warm coat if he cut firewood. He expected to work up a pretty good sweat swinging the ax. Dan took the saw and ax from the garage, locked the cabin, and headed toward the stream.

After crossing the bridge he began to scan the woods for fallen trees. He didn't want trees on the ground; they would be dirty, wet, and full of bugs. Dan moved slowly into the underbrush and found a tree that looked promising for firewood. It was uprooted, probably a fatality of strong east winds, and leaning against a fallen tree, keeping it off the ground. The ax was effective for removing branches and roots, and he soon had about 20 feet of timber to cut into smaller pieces. Dan cut the log every four to five feet with the saw and then took a break. He had been right; he hadn't needed a heavy coat.

He tried to pick up one of the small logs and realized it would wear him out carrying them through the brush; they were just too heavy. He cut each small log in half and took another break. Dan nearly inhaled two cookies he had placed in Terry's jacket pocket. Something to drink would have been nice; he hadn't considered bringing water. Next time a bottle of water or a Coke would be included with the saw and ax.

Each log now weighed about 100 pounds. He lifted one up on his right shoulder and started toward the bridge. He had to be careful not to trip and break an ankle, or even worse, a leg. Dan was fortunate in one respect; the trip back to the cabin was downhill. Just as he finished moving the third of eight logs, Henry appeared.

"Henry! Did you come to help me?"

Henry stood motionless looking at Dan.

"That's okay. You have a fur coat. You don't really need a fire. Would you like to go for a walk, Henry?"

Henry barked.

Concluding that meant yes, Dan picked up one of the logs and carried it to the cabin. Henry followed closely behind wagging his tail.

Dan dropped the log at the side of the garage where he would cut and split it later.

"Before we go for a walk, I have to get the ax and saw. They'll rust out there with all this moisture." The ax and saw were retrieved and put in the garage. Dan already had the key to the lock box in his pocket. Dan's watch read 1:10 p.m., so the items he ordered should have arrived. The new friends started down the road to pick up the merchandise. As they proceeded toward the box, Dan could feel the temperature dropping, his nose and ears were getting cold. He made a mental note to order a hat or a hoody.

Before Dan and Henry had gone more than a hundred yards, snowflakes started filtering through the trees, slowly settling to the ground. Some of the snowflakes were very large; the air temperature was above freezing. Occasionally Henry would eat a snowflake as it tumbled through the air near him. Squirrels scurried across the road and scampered up trees, probably looking for bird nests to take home to the wife for soup. Dan smiled as he watched the little critters escaping from them, but Henry paid no attention. Henry seemed to know he and Dan were on a mission and he shouldn't be fooling around.

They made good time getting to the lock box. Dan opened the box, which was nearly full with bags of clothing. Trying to see in, Henry put his front paws on the box and strained to see in but the top of the box was too high. As soon as Dan retrieved the steaks from the bottom of the box, Henry dropped to all fours. Dan noticed Henry's interest in the meat and unwrapped one of the steaks. Henry sat down and cocked his head a little to the side, his tongue hanging out in anticipation of the fresh meat.

"Okay Henry, you've been a good boy."

Dan gave the unwrapped steak to Henry, expecting him to eat it immediately, but Dan was surprised again. The big dog sank his teeth into the meat, turned, and ran back up the road toward the cabin. Dan smiled and shouted, "Henry, you shouldn't eat raw meat!"

Dan left the other food in the box. It was colder in the steel box than in a refrigerator, so the food would keep overnight. He would get the rest of the order on tomorrow's return trip. Dan looked through the bags, found the coat, and put it on. The tags could be removed when he got home. Carrying three good-sized bags was going to slow him down a little, but at least he would be warm walking back to the cabin.

As he was relocking the box, a vehicle drove up and stopped across the road in the other turnout. Dan saw a man and woman, both in uniform, get out of their pickup. The man had been driving and was first to cross the road.

The uniformed man asked, "Do you have some ID?"

Dan wondered who he was dealing with, so he inquired, "Who's asking?"

"I'm Herb Edmond. This is my partner, Susan Lawrence. We're forest service rangers checking on people living in this area. We check once a month for problems with roads and utilities. We also check to see if burning procedures are being followed." Both uniformed officers showed Dan their ID.

Dan fished his wallet from his back pocket and showed his army ID to the rangers. "I'm taking care of the Sterlings' cabin for the winter."

Both rangers were dressed in heavy coats, and their baseball caps bore the forest service logo. Herb had shaved off what little hair he still had around the edges so looked completely bald when he removed his cap. He was about the same height as Susan, but probably weighed more than 200 pounds. With his round face, glasses, red cheeks, and zinc oxide on his nose to prevent sunburn, Herb reminded Dan of a circus clown wearing a ranger's uniform. He pointed up the road with his cap. "Did we see a dog with you a few minutes ago?"

"That's Henry. He showed up a couple of days ago. I've been feeding him. I called the number on his collar but got no answer. I guess I'll adopt him."

Susan commented, "If we are notified by the owner that the dog is lost, we'll have to take him from you. You understand?" Susan appeared to be about Dan's age, maybe a few years older. She was nice looking; her face was tanned, as if she had been a summer lifeguard. She was about five-eight and had short dark-brown hair with blond streaks.

"Sure. He's with me most of the time. He goes off into the woods sometimes though. I don't know where he goes; I haven't followed him. Say, can you tell me if I have any nearby neighbors?"

"Your closest neighbors are the Sandovals, Efren and Elaine. They're about a half mile through the woods southeast of you at a somewhat higher elevation. They usually move into town in October. The only road to their house comes in from the south, and it's closed after the first big snow. That road is snowed over from November to February."

The rangers shook hands with Dan and gave him their cards. Susan said, "Nice meeting you." She looked up to observe the falling snow. It had stopped. "Would you like a ride back to the cabin?"

After a moment's reflection, Dan answered, "Yeah. That would be great. My legs aren't in shape yet, and I've got these packages to carry uphill." He tossed the packages in the bed of the pickup and climbed in back with them. The rangers drove Dan to the Sterlings' cabin and said they would see him again next month. They commented that there might be measurable snow by then. Dan thanked them for the ride and waved as the pickup turned around and disappeared down the road. He took the clothing into the living room and dumped the bags on the sofa. The cabin was chilly, so Dan went back outside, carrying the saw and ax.

Dan cut a log in half and split the two stubby logs into wedge shaped firewood. After piling the wood next to the fireplace, he looked for some kindling. Burning wads of paper wouldn't ignite the firewood, so he gathered some dry pine needles from under nearby trees. In a few minutes, the fire was blazing and the cabin was warming up. He watched the burning logs, listening to the snapping and hissing noises, and removed his new coat.

Dan laid the contents of the bags on the sofa and checked everything against the receipt. After removing all the labels and stickers, Dan left the new clothes on the sofa, had dinner, read for an hour, and went to bed.

In the morning, the sun was out, the sky above was blue, a few wispy clouds could be seen to the west, but the cabin was cold. The tall pine and fir trees shielded the cabin from the sun until mid-morning. The temperature outdoors had risen to almost 40 degrees during the night. Dan put the new clothing in the washing machine and had breakfast while watching the weather report. After doing the dishes and drying his new clothes, he took some of the clothes from the drier and put them on. Impressed with the good fit, he planned to launder the borrowed clothes and return them to the bedroom closet.

Dan retrieved the logs he had cut the day before. Sweating from carrying logs, he took a few minutes to drink some water and eat a cookie. He split all the logs, piled most of the wood against the outside wall of the garage, and added to the supply next to the fireplace.

Dan was anxious to get the rest of the supplies from the lock box, so he ate a quick lunch and set out down the winding road. Henry wasn't around, so Dan made the trip alone. As he walked, he considered his decision to stay in Oregon until March. After a few minutes of thinking, he concluded it had been a good idea. By the time he was ready to resume his journey north, hopefully the bad dreams would be something of the past. Then he pondered Henry's actions. By the time he reached the lock box, Dan was sure Henry had a companion in the forest. He had thought briefly about it once before. Dan took the food from the lock box and began the return trip. When Dan was almost at the cabin, Henry barked and ran up to Dan, tail wagging.

"Henry! I missed your company on the trip to the box. Where have you been?"

Dan put the food in the refrigerator while Henry waited outside. When Henry saw Dan carrying a rubber ball found in the garage, he focused on the ball. Dan tossed it about thirty yards. Henry retrieved the ball before it stopped rolling and dropped it at Dan's feet.

"So, Henry, you like to play."

Henry sat down and looked at Dan, expecting to run after the ball again.

"Let's go for a walk!"

Henry barked twice. The dog seemed to be enthusiastic about going with Dan into the forest. They used the bridge to cross the creek, and continued into the woods where Dan had found the first firewood log. Dog tracks could be seen in bare spots among the clumps of long grass and pine needles on the forest floor. Dan couldn't keep up with Henry as the dog moved rapidly through the debris covered forest floor. Leaning trees were not an obstacle for Henry, but Dan had to climb over them. Tracking experience gained by Dan in Alaska helped him follow Henry's path through the dense wet undergrowth.

Dan had gone an estimated quarter mile when he came to a small clearing. He almost missed seeing it, but there was a small log-shack nearly hidden behind some large pine trees. The little shack was built against a rocky hill covered with smaller pine trees and some noble fir. No animal tracks were evident leading to the little building. Dan approached the small door of the shack after pushing approximately five feet of debris out of the way. It appeared no one had been there in many years. He guessed it had been a miner's cabin long ago. The occupant must have been fairly short, the door was little more than four feet high. Dan doubted whether the Sterlings or the Forest Service knew of the little structure; no signs of human presence were evident. Dan shoved the partly-opened small door into the shack, bent over, and stuck his head inside. The rough little building was empty except for a small potbellied stove and pine needles on the split-log floor.

Dan squeezed through the little door but couldn't stand up; the ceiling was too low. A bark from outside the structure caused Dan to call Henry. The big German shepherd entered the cabin, and began to sniff and scratch at the back wall. Surprisingly, Dan heard a bark from behind the wall. Dan dropped to his knees and looked closely at the wall. There was a horizontal board across the center of the back wall, but it was difficult to see inside the dimly-lit shack. Using his fingers, Dan could feel some space between the bottom of the horizontal board and the back wall where Henry had scratched. Dan pushed on the wall and the lower section moved, tilting back into an opening behind the cabin. A push on the wall section couldn't budge it. The rocks behind the building prevented the wall section from tipping back more than a few inches. However, Dan succeeded in sliding the section of wall, exposing a cave with a low ceiling about half the height of the cabin interior. Huddled together in the dark cave were two little puppies and another German shepherd, obviously the puppies' mother. Henry moved through the opening and sat down beside the other dogs, looking back at Dan.

"Henry! You brought the food here to your family!" Dan could see the remnants of plastic bags that had contained the dog food and a bone from the steak Henry had carried away from the lock box.

Henry barked, got up, and then sat back down next to the little puppies' mom, appearing to be proud of his family.

On his hands and knees, Dan started to crawl through the opening, but changed his mind when the female growled, got to all fours, and bared her fangs. Dan backed away from the opening.

"Okay, girl, I won't bother you and your little ones. I'll get you guys some food and water. Then maybe you won't growl at me." Dan replaced the section of wall and said, "Stay, Henry. I'll be back." Dan started to the Sterlings' to get some food and water. Now there were four mouths to feed. Dan was amazed to find the canine family behind the shack. They couldn't have gotten there through the little cabin, so there must be a rear entrance, a tunnel of some kind in the hill behind the building. He'd get Henry to show him the rear entrance to the cave.

Dan retraced the path he had taken from his cabin. It only took a few minutes to get a large bag of dog food and fill an empty plastic milk jug with water. He picked up two metal pie tins from the kitchen, grabbed the food and water, and returned to the little shack in 15 minutes. When he opened the sliding door in the back wall, the puppies were nursing. Henry was watching Dan very closely. Dan placed food in one pie tin and water in the other. He carefully put the food and water on the floor inside the cave against the back wall of the shack. He slid the back panel shut and left the cabin.

On the way home, Dan mulled over the details of the shack. A miner must have built the cabin in front of the cave on purpose. If someone attacked the miner, he could retreat and hide in the cave. That thought made Dan wonder if the opening in the rear of the cave was big enough for a man to crawl through. If so, the tunnel could be used as an escape route. The passageway looked large enough for Henry and maybe a small man, but someone as large as Dan might not be able to make it through. Once Dan found the outside opening, he would see if he could get into the cave from the rear. He'd need a flashlight.

CHAPTER 5

Flying Lessons

Nighttime brought two inches of snow to the woods. Dan looked at the calendar in the kitchen and tore off the page for September. It was the first week of October now. In the middle of the morning, Dan had opened the garage and was working on a knife. He needed something, besides a hatchet, for use in the woods to clear pathways. In addition, it could be used for offensive or defensive purposes, just like his crossbow. The survival knife was about a foot long, a little longer than normal, and would be carried in a scabbard attached to his lower leg under his jeans. Using a file, Dan had serrated one edge of the blade so he could use the knife as a crude saw. Henry came to visit Dan before noon.

"It's early for you, Henry. How's your family? We need to take them some more food and water, don't we?"

Dan had found an old blanket in the garage and had washed it. Oil stains suggested Terry must have been using the blanket on the garage floor when he worked on his jeep, but the dogs could use it now. After refilling the food and water tins, he would check for Henry's tracks in the snow and try to locate the back entrance to the cave. After that, he needed to get some more logs to split for firewood. Dan wasn't sure about remote life in Oregon, but in Alaska, away from a city, there was never too much firewood.

Dan used the blanket as a sack to carry the food and water. Dan and Henry went straight to the shack and opened the sliding panel to the cave. Henry entered the cave first. Dan folded the blanket so it was about two by three feet in size and placed it in the cave next to mom and the babies. The puppies weren't walking yet. Henry's mate didn't growl at Dan this time, but she watched his movements intently. Dan refilled the empty pie tins with food and water and restored the sliding panel to its normal position. Dan noted that the female also had a collar, but he couldn't read the name written on it; she was too far into the cave and the light was very dim. He would investigate the collar later.

Dan left the shack and called Henry. Dan watched the front of the log hut from a distance of about ten yards. It took about a minute before Henry appeared on the right side of the little shack, emerging from between two large trees.

"Okay Henry, how did you get here?"

Dan began following the dog tracks uphill through various patches of snow until they stopped at a bushy noble fir in front of some large rocks. The symmetrical tree stood about eight feet tall—a nice undecorated Christmas tree. Dan pushed back the boughs and could see an opening about 18 inches wide and two feet high. He tried to see into the gap in the rocks, but it was too dark, and the opening was completely concealed by the tree. When Dan returned, he had to remember to bring a flashlight.

Dan watched as Henry entered the opening. In about thirty seconds Henry reappeared. The big German shepherd must have gone through the passageway, turned around and come back.

"Good boy Henry! Let's find some trees to cut into firewood."

Dan and Henry scouted the area a hundred yards in all directions from the clearing around the Sterlings' cabin. They were able to locate seven logs that could be used for firewood. There were other downed trees, but ease of access was the critical factor that made a log desirable. Dan marked standing trees in the vicinity of the downed timber so the potential firewood could be relocated easily. As they moved through the woods, Henry led the way. The big dog usually took the easiest path through the undergrowth, rocks, and trees. Dan was tired after traipsing through the woods for two hours. His limping was becoming more exaggerated. They went back to the Sterlings' to get some rest and something to eat. It was the middle of the afternoon.

Dan made himself a cheeseburger and cooked a patty of meat for Henry. Re-energized, Dan found a flashlight in the garage and started back to the concealed opening of the cave. When they arrived at the noble fir, Dan pulled back the branches and was perplexed; there was no opening. If the snow hadn't melted, he could have seen his tracks.

"Oops—wrong tree."

Henry was standing in front of another, similar tree, watching Dan.

"Okay," Dan laughed, "I'm a dummy. I can't tell one Christmas tree from another." Dan went to Henry's tree, pulled the branches back, and directed a beam of light into the opening. He could see about six feet into the passageway, and then it constricted and turned slightly. Dan thought better of entering the tunnel. He didn't have anyone to pull him out if he got stuck. Henry went back into the cave and Dan returned to the Sterlings' cabin.

After eating dinner, Dan picked out a thick gray book, *Theory of Flight,* from the library. The first chapter was historical and he turned through it quickly. Chapter two grabbed his attention. He read quickly through the chapter on lift, and then breezed through control surfaces in chapter three. He stopped reading and stared into the fire. In the last couple of days he had begun to think about what the rangers had said about contacting Mr. Langford at the airport. He wouldn't be able to get much flying in if the weather turned bad.

Dan made a mug of decaf and went back to his book. He fell asleep during chapter four and woke up at 12:18 a.m. He blinked his eyes a few times, marked his place by sticking a pencil between the pages, and went into the bedroom. As he sat down on the bed to remove his shoes, Dan thought to himself, *I've got to get the jeep running so I can visit the airport.* But, before he removed his shoes, he went into the garage and started charging the jeep's battery, leaving it to charge overnight. Dan returned to the bedroom and went to bed.

Dan woke up and marked off another day on the calendar that had passed without a near death nightmare. Breakfast was over in about ten minutes. The garage was cold, so Dan built a fire in the fireplace and opened the living room door to the garage. He worked steadily, completing the wiring by noon. After lunch, Dan installed a new oil pump, put in new head lamps, and checked the charge on the old battery. The fireplace fire had gone out earlier in the day, but Dan had been so involved working, he had forgotten about it. He went in the cabin to warm his hands and heard scratching at the front door. "Oh, shit! I forgot about the dogs." He opened the front door to find Henry sitting on the porch.

Dan grabbed a bag of food and a gallon of water and followed Henry to the miner's shack. After feeding the dogs, Dan returned to the cabin and had dinner. In the morning, he would put the battery in the jeep and find out if the engine worked. If he could use the jeep as-is, he would install the new engine and transmission later on, maybe during the holidays. Right now, flying was nearly the most important thing on his mind, second only to caring for the dogs.

Up at 6:00 a.m., Dan started the day with Cheerios and coffee. He took a quick shower and was in the garage at 6:31. It took a few minutes to start the jeep but a squirt of ether in the carb helped the engine turn over. The engine labored at first and then settled into a satisfying rumble. Dan quickly raised the garage door and backed out onto the gravel driveway. The engine ran for about ten minutes before Dan shut it down and made a couple of adjustments. The engine restarted easily so Dan shut the garage door and locked the cabin.

He climbed in the jeep and started down the hill to the old highway which led to downtown Troutdale. He arrived at the airport at 7:45, hoping he wasn't too early, but someone should be around; planes fly at all hours. Dan saw the sign for East Winds Flight Academy and pulled into the parking lot next to the light-green metal building. Several small planes and a helicopter were parked at the side of the structure.

The interior of the academy was decorated with maps, pictures of airplanes and some wooden props attached to the wall above a business counter. Dan approached the counter and a man, about Dan's age, dressed in gray slacks and a white shirt, looked up from a map.

"Can I help you?" he questioned.

"I hope so. I'm looking for Phil Langford."

"Sorry, Phil's not here today. He's flying a state representative to Salem."

"Is there anyone else I could talk to about flying lessons?"

"Sure. Vic Reeves is working on an engine at the other end of the building. Just go through that door." He pointed with a pencil at a white metal door that was marked maintenance in large red letters.

"Thanks." Dan pushed on the handle and the door swung open to a spacious shop. There was an engine on a metal stand about 50 feet away. A man in overalls, sitting on a stool, his back turned toward Dan, was working at a bench a few feet from the engine. Dan stopped to look at the engine for a moment and then cleared his throat. The man turned around and smiled. Dan was surprised; it was a woman, maybe 50 years old, about five-seven with gray-blond hair. She had a bandanna over her short-clipped hair. She was pleasant looking—wore little makeup, had sparkling eyes, a straight nose, and a few freckles.

"I'm Dan Newcomb, are you Vic Reeves?"

"Yes, I'm Victoria Reeves. What can I help you with?"

"I want to learn to fly. The gentleman in the lobby told me to see you. He said Phil Langford isn't here today."

"That's Leland. He didn't tell you I was a woman, did he?"

"No, but that doesn't make any difference. I just want to learn to fly. When I get back home in Alaska, I want to get a plane and start a flying business—my dad was a bush pilot."

"Well, it sounds like you know what you want to do. How would you like to take a ride? I'm going over toward the mountain in about 15 minutes."

"Mt. Hood? That would be great! Can I help you with anything?"

Vic pointed, "See that box over there? Pull out a few of those bags and stick them in your pocket. We'll be taking the Cessna 180; it's the red and silver plane. You can look it over while I finish here. I'll be right with you. We'll talk about lessons."

Dan went out to the plane and walked around looking in the cabin and checking the landing gear. He was thinking ahead about having skis attached to a plane for landing on snow. He had to ask Vic about the price of a plane.

Vic joined Dan and did a walk-around to check the plane, something she never overlooked. Vic had never had an accident from either pilot or mechanical error, and she wanted to keep it that way. As she checked the plane, she explained what she was doing and what irregularities might be noticed in the pre-flight routine. Vic had Dan's rapt attention. Dan was soaking up everything she said.

"Still have those bags?"

Dan grinned. "Yes, ma'am, but I don't think I'll need them."

Vic exhibited a wry smile. "I wish I had a dollar for every time I've heard that." She stuck a dirty rag into her back pocket and unlocked the cabin doors.

Dan climbed in the plane and was confronted with a panel full of dials, gauges, and switches. He scanned the array, but was only able to identify a few of the instruments. Vic got in, got comfortable in the pilot's seat, and took a look at Dan. She could see a puzzled expression on his face.

"Don't worry. It's not as complicated as it looks. We'll take a little at a time. It will take a few hours in the air to get acquainted with everything."

Dan began to feel like he did when riding with Bert in his semi. Vic reminded him a little of his mother, but not quite as heavy; not that his mom was fat, she just wasn't a slim young woman any more when Dan was a teenager. Vic exhibited the same air of confidence that Bert had. She was in charge. When she got into the plane, she became part of it. Vic started the engine, wiggled all the control surfaces, and taxied to the runway. Dan smiled; the movement of the control surfaces reminded him of women swinging their hips to get attention.

As they moved down the runway, accelerating to about the same speed as a car on the freeway, they became airborne. The Cessna climbed in altitude and turned east-southeast, pointing directly at Mt. Hood.

"That was smooth, Vic—a wonderful feeling."

"Uh-huh. I always enjoy leaving the ground. I like the changing sounds when the plane lifts into the air. We'll circle around the mountain and come back down the gorge."

"How far is it to the mountain? It doesn't look very far."

"It's about 80 miles round trip—about half an hour."

Dan had numerous questions for Vic as they cruised toward Mt. Hood. He watched the altimeter and asked Vic why they were taking the current route.

"Well, as we leave the airport, we have to avoid the commercial traffic coming in from the East to Portland International; it's called PDX.

We don't want to tangle with a big jet—or any size jet that is descending to PDX. We can gain altitude as we approach the mountain. We'll circle Hood at about 10,000 feet. How are you feeling? No upset stomach?"

"I feel great. I've never gotten nauseated when travelling, but I've never been in a small plane before, either. My mom wouldn't let me fly with my dad. He promised her to never take me with him. It's way different than a military transport. Size does make a difference." Dan grinned and looked at Vic, but she didn't comment.

"What does your dad fly?"

"He was an Alaskan bush pilot. Dad flew into the back country with two hunters in his Cessna 170 and none of them came back. That was about—" Dan paused to think about the time elapsed, "seven years ago. It doesn't seem like it has been that long. I was busy in Afghanistan for nearly four years."

Vic glanced at Dan and said, "Sorry you lost your dad. Thank you for your military service, Dan. You've been through a lot."

"You're welcome. I've done some serious growing up in the last couple of years. Now, I want to start a business, but I don't have the funds to buy a plane. If you don't mind me asking, how much do you have invested in this plane?"

Vic thought a moment and replied, "Including the updating of instruments, around $60,000; I didn't buy it new. Okay, we're coming up on the mountain. We'll bank to the left, circle, and return to Troutdale through the gorge; there's no east wind today."

With that information, Dan knew he would have trouble getting a plane, unless he could find a used one to update, or rebuild a wreck, but even that would cost money. He would have to work for his uncle for at least a year before signing a contract to buy a plane. A regular income would be a necessity. He planned on using his house-sitting money for flying lessons.

They made a smooth landing, and Vic taxied the plane up to a hanger not far from the main office building. Dan helped Vic slide the doors open and roll the plane into the metal building. It had fluorescent lights and a long workbench with tools hanging from hooks on the back wall. Dan was in paradise.

Vic smiled and asked, "So, how was your first ride?"

"Fantastic. Now I know what I have to learn. I have some big obstacles to overcome."

"I'll tell you what. If you help me in the shop, I'll give you flying lessons, but you have to pay for the fuel."

"That sounds fair. I wanted to talk about rental costs and fuel." Dan was serious about stretching his dollars as far as possible.

"We can talk about costs while we work in the hanger. I'll go over everything with you so we can plan to get in as many hours of flight time as possible. I'll loan you some books to study to assist with your ground flight training. Hopefully, you'll qualify for your license before you leave for Alaska."

Dan didn't hesitate. "It's a deal. Thanks!"

"But I didn't tell you what we have to do in the shop."

Dan shrugged and grinned. "I don't care. Working with tools is second nature to me. My dad and uncle taught me everything they knew. I can fix almost anything—and I'm not bragging." Dan looked at his watch and then at Vic. "I've got to go. My dogs are waiting for me. Thank you for the ride. When do we start working?"

"We'll start on Saturday. I have three engines to overhaul and some instruments to install. The planes belong to people that don't fly during the winter. They have me do the maintenance during the periods they don't fly. I've been doing it for years, but I'm getting too much work for one person. I need help, and you can learn about the guts of the planes. As soon as we get a plane refurbished, we'll take it on a shake-down cruise."

Vic looked at Dan expecting to see some reservation, but Dan smiled. He was full of enthusiasm; he couldn't have anticipated a better deal.

"What time do you want me here?"

"Not too early, say 9:00 a.m.—bring a lunch; we'll work until dinnertime."

CHAPTER 6

Cabin Visitors

October 4, was a Tuesday. Henry came to get Dan, and they took food and water to the cave. Dan took a flashlight and read the name of the female, Duchess, from her collar. The pups, a male and female, were getting more active, and Dan was allowed to hold the little ones. They wiggled around in his hands, reminding him of handling worms when he was a boy. Dan estimated the puppies' age to be three weeks.

After reading about German shepherd puppies on the Internet, Dan decided to let the dogs have access to the shack. In the afternoon, he took a brace and bit from the garage and bored some one-inch holes through the shack's log walls so the puppies could see out into the woods. Dan gathered some pine cones, rocks, and sticks, and put them on the floor in the miner's hut. He figured the items would assist the puppies with investigations of their environment. Dan had yet to name the puppies.

After checking Henry's family on Wednesday and cleaning up the poop, Dan and Henry went to the rough logs they had located. Dan cut them to a size he could carry back to his cabin, and then cut the logs even shorter, split and piled the wood at the side of the garage. Tarpaulins found in the garage were used to keep rain and snow from getting to the firewood.

Their time together wasn't all work. Dan taught Henry how to play hide-and- seek. When Dan couldn't find Henry, he whistled three, short, high-pitched tones followed by one long low tone. Henry then knew he

48

could come out of hiding. Dan wished snow was on the ground so he could follow tracks. Henry always found Dan quickly; the dog's sense of smell gave him an overwhelming advantage.

Dan enjoyed interacting with all four dogs. He would sit on the floor in the shack and the puppies would climb over his legs and try to chew his fingers. They chased pine cones that he rolled across the floor. Dan found some canned dog food in the Sterlings' pantry and gave small amounts to the puppies. They would be eating solid food soon.

In addition to spending time with the dogs, Dan made a small, well-balanced throwing knife. He needed something to dig bolts from trees. Carrying around a pair of pliers didn't suit him. Friday evening, while he watched a football game, he made a sheath for the knife from a piece of leather found in the garage. He fashioned the sheath to fit on his back below his neck, an idea he had gotten from an army buddy.

Dan worried about the dogs. He didn't want them to be out in the cave during the really cold weather. When the east wind started howling through the gorge, it could get very cold. The large quantity of snow falling in the region during December and January would add to the undesirable conditions in the mountains. Fortunately, the elevation of the cabin was only about 1,200 feet; the cave about 70 feet higher. The lower elevations rarely had large amounts of snow, but occasionally the I-84 freeway, along the banks of the Columbia River, would be closed due to ice. Dan would make room for the dogs in the garage before the temperature dropped below freezing.

It was a damp, gray, Saturday morning; the east wind was gusting to about thirty mph. Dan took food and water to the dogs right after breakfast and was on time at the airport. He worked with Vic on a motor until six o'clock, and then drove back to the cabin. Henry was sitting on the porch, waiting for him. Henry wasn't used to Dan's absence from the cabin. Dan felt bad that he had been gone all day, but Dan had missed Henry as much as Henry had missed Dan. They hiked to the miner's shack so Dan could check on Henry's family.

On Sunday morning, Dan installed a doggie-door in the backdoor of the garage. He took out one of the lower panels of the six-panel door and attached a hinge at the top, so the panel could swing in and out. After he rehung the door, he showed Henry how to come and go from the garage. The bottom of the opening was too high for the puppies to escape. Most of the afternoon was spent arranging space for the dogs on the garage floor adjacent to the living room wall. Dan repositioned a large cabinet of tools and found another blanket to pad the floor. Now the dogs would have a warm cabin home when the weather got bad.

Dan worked with Vic nearly every day until October 22. Vic had planned all summer to visit her younger sister, Liz, in Amarillo, Texas. Vic had never met her brother-in-law, Ned Colwell, or her niece, Luella, a two-year-old. She was leaving the next day, Sunday, and would be gone for nine days. Dan didn't need the jeep during that time, so he decided to change the engine and transmission. The weather stayed nice, except for a couple of days of east winds. When Dan wasn't working on the jeep, he was caring for the dogs, or reading about aviation. One night when TV offered nothing of interest, Dan called Alaska and talked with Uncle Max. During their half-hour conversation, Dan told his uncle to expect him at the beginning of March.

During the week, Dan followed a routine. He was lazy in the mornings, but worked on the jeep after lunch, and took care of the dogs in the evening. Henry would come to get Dan about dinnertime, and they would go to the shack with food and water. Saturday was October 30, Halloween Eve. Early that morning, the sun had been out, and the east winds, although cold, had nearly stopped. The sky had become overcast, and the temperature was dropping. Dan usually worked on the jeep with the garage door open, but his hands, ears, and nose were almost numb, so he closed the door and opened the entrance to the living room.

He rubbed his hands together briskly to warm his fingers, so he could hold a match and light a fire in the fireplace. Dropping the new motor in the jeep was his next task, but he stopped working long enough to eat a sandwich. As he filled the coffee maker with water, he glanced out the kitchen window and watched some snowflakes swirling around, lazily dropping to the ground. When the last bit of sandwich was gone, he poured a mug of coffee and used it to further warm his fingers. He debated whether the warmth of the mug on his hands was a better use for the coffee than drinking the hot liquid. The same thought had occurred before when Dan was living in Alaska.

Almost as soon as Dan resumed working, he decided to hang it up for the day. Another mug of hot coffee was more desirable than wrestling with a cold engine block. He would resume work on the jeep tomorrow, Halloween day. Dan was pretty sure there wouldn't be any trick-or-treaters coming for candy, just Henry coming to get him. He turned off the lights in the garage and went in the kitchen to start dinner.

When Henry scratched on the front door, Dan had just put his dirty dishes in the kitchen sink. As soon as the door was opened, Henry came in and sat down next to the fire. Dan grabbed a bag of dog food and a gallon of water, put on his coat and gloves, and said, "Let's go, Henry, we need to feed your family." Dan didn't bother to lock his door; he would be gone for less than an hour. He hadn't seen anyone in the area for a month, except the two rangers, who had dropped by on Wednesday, and besides, rural people respected the property of others.

Dan had found another old blanket for the dogs. It had been under a toolbox in the back of Terry's jeep. He folded it and stuffed it in his backpack. When they left for the shack, two-inches of snow had accumulated on the ground, and the snowfall had increased enough to cut visibility significantly. Darkness was approaching as they entered the woods. Dan looked back at the cabin in the clearing. A photo would make a beautiful Christmas card showing the cabin with snow on the roof, smoke rising from the chimney, and firewood piled high against the garage. He imagined the smell of cinnamon rolls baking in the oven. That was something else to put on his list.

Henry led the way to the shack. They had found a path with fewer obstacles to climb over than before. The new path was a little longer than the original one, but easier on Dan's legs. He could hear the puppies playing as he approached the little hut. He opened the door very slowly; the little dogs waddled over to him and sniffed his shoes. Duchess was lying on the floor watching the puppies play. She got up and came to Dan when he entered the shack. She looked up at Dan, perhaps expecting some help. Dan smiled when he imagined Duchess wanted to ask him to baby-sit for an hour so she could get some sleep, or do some shopping at the mall.

"Good girl, Duchess. You're a good mommy." Dan scratched Duchess's neck and patted her back. Henry sat by the empty pie tins waiting for Dan to refill them. The last of the canned dog food was in the shack. He opened it with his throwing knife and scooped the moist food out for the puppies. More soft food would have to be ordered from Warner's, at least enough for a couple of weeks. As soon as Dan put the dry food in one pie tin, Henry started eating. Duchess joined him while the puppies were devoting their full attention to the soft food in the other pie tin.

Using the blanket from his backpack, Dan enlarged the bed for the dogs in the cave. They were already using the first blanket he had placed in the cave, but it wasn't big enough for four dogs. If the weather got any worse, it would be time to move the dogs to the garage. The hinged doggy-door was ready, so Henry and Duchess could come and go freely. The presence of the dogs should prevent other animals from staying in the garage, even if they came through the hinged door.

Dan backed out of the cave into the shack, and while on his hands and knees, cleaned up the floor. He uttered, "I'll see all you guys tomorrow," as he left the hut and closed the door.

Dan was about halfway home when Henry joined him.

"So, Henry, you're coming home with me today?"

Henry barked and got in front of Dan to lead the way. Dan wondered why Henry had left his family to go back to the cabin; Henry hadn't done that before. Had he heard or smelled something? Dan had been with the dogs for only 30 minutes. During that time the wind from the southwest had picked up and the intensity of the snow had increased. As they moved through the forest, the wind would occasionally dislodge snow from upper tree branches. The mini-avalanches covered the trail making it difficult to follow in the growing darkness. Henry would stop abruptly and wait for the blinding clouds of snowflakes to let up before continuing. Dan couldn't hear the birth of the avalanches, but apparently Henry could. Dan followed Henry closely, and when it was pitch-black, he reached down and grasped Henry's collar. After a couple of minutes of movement from tree to tree in utter darkness, they suddenly escaped from the forest into the clearing behind the cabin.

The cabin provided enough illumination to see the path to the bridge. Dan noted that the light in one bedroom was on. He must have forgotten to turn it off. They crossed the bridge and as they emerged from around the front corner of the garage where the firewood was piled, Dan suddenly stopped. There was a dark-colored pickup with a crew cab parked in the driveway. Though hard to clearly see into the cab, Dan saw a woman move in the front passenger seat, reaching toward the steering wheel. She beeped the horn twice. Dan assumed she had signaled someone in the cabin.

"Henry, hide!" Henry turned and ran toward the bridge behind the garage.

Dan walked a few yards to the front of the pickup. He stopped when the medium- height woman got out of the cab. Light from the cabin front window was enough for Dan to see she wore jeans, a plaid shirt that was too big, and a red hunter's vest. Dan thought it was a bit peculiar that she had on black flats; not practical footwear for the mountains. She had mussed-up brown hair, and although the light was dim, looked to be in her mid-twenties.

"Stand right there. Don't move," the young woman ordered as she pointed a handgun at Dan. She held the gun in her right hand and circled behind Dan. Holding the muzzle of the gun to his back, she checked his pockets. She found the flashlight in his backpack, but she hadn't detected either the throwing or the survival knife. "Okay, go in the cabin."

As Dan entered the front door, he pulled his right arm free of the backpack and let the pack slide down his left arm to his hand.

One of three men said, "Where'd he come from?"

"He was with a dog. They came around the garage. When I beeped the horn, the dog ran off."

The largest of the three men said, "Happy Halloween! Good evening, Mr. Sterling. Where's your wife?"

Dan quizzed, "What are you doing in my cabin?"

"Shut yur mouth! I'll ask the questions. Where's yur wife?"

The two younger men on the sofa laughed, and the third, larger, older man, doing the talking, was standing in front of the fireplace holding a rifle waist high. The rifle was pointed at Dan.

Dan replied, "I'm not married. The owners are in Arizona for the winter."

"Well, then, what's yur name?"

"Dan." Dan was going to say he was the Sterlings' son, but thought he'd better not lie. If they looked in his wallet, they'd discover he lied and it might make a bad situation worse.

"Woman, bring me that backpack, and get out of the way," the big man ordered.

Dan didn't like the odds. He glanced back at the woman, spun around and swung the backpack at her gun. She dropped the gun when the flashlight-laden pack hit her hand. Dan grabbed her arm, twisted it and was behind her. He reached behind his neck, pulled out his throwing knife, and threw it in one continuous motion. The knife slashed through the air and stuck solidly into the big man's left shoulder below his collarbone. Surprised, the man cried out in pain and pulled the trigger. The bullet passed through the woman's side below her rib cage and grazed Dan's left side near his waist. The young woman crumpled to the floor. Dan spun around and launched himself out the front door onto the deck. One of the other men fired a handgun; the bullet caught Dan's left calf. Dan rolled to his feet, vaulted over the handrail, and moved up the path to the creek as fast as he could go.

His calf hurt like hell and was probably bleeding badly, but he kept moving. He limped to the drop-off to the creek and slid down the bank into the water. Moving up-stream in the cold water, he fought to maintain his balance. Dan couldn't afford to disturb the snow on either bank of the stream. A trail of bloody footprints would be easy to track. The near half-moon, now above the trees, provided enough diffuse light through the thinning clouds for Dan to see the creek banks.

The cold water was just deep enough to wash the wound in his left calf. After moving about a hundred yards in the water, his legs were beginning to get numb. He exited the stream, avoided leaving a trail that was easy to follow, crawled under a large pine tree, and checked his calf. The cold water had stopped the bleeding. He was able to move about twenty yards under the trees without leaving any tracks in the snow. When he came to a downed tree that bridged the creek, he stopped and whistled for Henry to come out of hiding. He looked down at his injured leg; his movements had caused blood to ooze through his pants leg.

While he waited for Henry, Dan cut off his shirttail with his survival knife. After folding his handkerchief into a rectangular pad, he tied it in place with his shirttail. His side didn't hurt; the bullet had barely scratched the surface of his skin. Dan started moving across a rocky area about seventy yards from the miner's shack. He could hear Henry's breathing just before Henry joined Dan on the barren rocks.

"Good boy, Henry. Let's go."

Dan limped to the miner's hut. Once inside, he sank to the floor, out of breath. His eyes had adjusted to the faint moonlight in the cabin allowing him to just make out the puppies and Duchess on the blankets in the cave. Duchess raised her head to look at Dan and Henry, but the puppies were fast asleep. Dan extracted his flashlight from the backpack and turned it on. The lens was broken but the bulb still worked. He removed the bandage from his calf and could see that the wound needed stitches. He would have to keep the bandage on the wound to control the bleeding.

"Well, Henry, we need to go back to the cabin and get the crossbow. I can't do very much with this knife without isolating each man. There are three of them and they have guns, but I don't think I'll have to worry about the woman."

CHAPTER 7

Rescue

Dan and Henry left the shack and shut the door. Dan only used the flashlight when he had trouble remembering where he was on the trail. Following Henry was too slow, Dan had to return to the cabin quickly, while watching for signs of the three men. When near the clearing, Dan put the flashlight in his backpack. He crept to the back of the cabin and peered in the lighted bedroom window. The woman lay motionless on the bed. He wondered if she had died of her wound. Dan moved silently to the rear of the garage and slowly turned the back doorknob. The door was still unlocked, so he entered and took the flashlight from his backpack.

Dan whispered, "Henry, stay." Henry sat outside the door next to the propane tank. Dan didn't want to make a sound by bumping into anything, so he switched on the flashlight and found the crossbow. The bolts were still on the workbench where he had left them. He wrapped masking tape around the bolts and placed them in his backpack, then set the crossbow outside in the snow next to Henry. Dan moved to the door leading to the living room, stopped, and listened. He could hear the men talking.

"He got me good with that knife."

"Don't worry, Cliff, we'll go after the SOB in the morning."

"I think I got him in the leg when I shot through the doorway. I saw some blood on the front porch."

Cliff said, "That was a tough shot, Scooter. I might have got him when my shot went through the girl."

"He moved fast," Scooter commented.

The third man said, "That girl's in bad shape—lost a lot of blood."

Cliff said, "Don't sweat it. We'll leave her here and set the cabin on fire. Without help, she'll croak. We'll shoot that asshole that stuck me with the knife. Nobody will find them two until next spring, and then just bones."

"I've been wonderin', John. Where'd you find her?"

"At a coffee shop near the school. I talked with her for about a half hour and then asked if she wanted to have some fun. She didn't answer me. That was the night of our first motel stickup. I showed her my gun and told her to do what I said. We registered as man and wife, so it was easy to check the place out. She never knew what we was gunna do."

Scooter said, "Her first name's Ann, ain't it? What's her last?"

"I dunno. Who cares anyway?"

Dan had heard all he needed. He had to get Ann out of the house. A diversion would get the men into the driveway. Dan left the garage and sneaked around to the front of the garage where the pickup was parked. He slid under the truck and pulled his survival knife from the sheath on his right leg. It was easy to poke a hole in the gas tank with the tip of the blade. As the gas started dripping, he made another hole, and then a third, toward the top of the tank to let in air. He slid out from under the truck and scratched a match on the serrations of his knife. When the lighted match hit the pool of gasoline, there was a puff and the flame spread from the ground to the bottom of the gas tank. Dan quickly got to the back of the cabin and went in the garage to the living room door. He had to wait about thirty seconds before he heard one of the men yell.

"Hey! The damn truck's burnin'!"

There was a commotion as the men scrambled outside.

Dan went through the garage into the cabin to the master bedroom and closed the door. He sat on the bed beside Ann and checked her pulse. It was steady, but weak. She looked up at him and spoke in a whisper, "I put a pillowcase against the wound and used my belt to keep pressure on it."

Dan explained, "I heard the men talking. They're going to leave you here to die. Do you want to come with me?"

"Sure. But I can't walk. I'm kind of dizzy."

"That's okay, I can carry you, but we'll have to go out the window. Here, put this coat on." Dan gave her one of Val's coats and then helped her stand up against the wall. After sliding the window open, he jerked a blanket off the bed and tossed it through the opening. "I'll lift you to the window. Sit on the sill until I'm out. I'll get you down."

She whispered, "Okay."

It only took a few seconds for Dan to get outside and lift Ann from the window.

He wrapped her in the blanket, carried her across the bridge, and put her on the ground behind some shrubs. Henry had followed, and sat down beside the woman.

Dan said, "I have to get something—be right back." Dan went back to the garage, grabbed a pair of pliers, opened the electrical box and yanked out the breakers for the oven and the dryer, and picked up the crossbow. With the weapon slung over his shoulder, he rejoined Ann and Henry. He could hear the men yelling at each other. Dan picked up Ann and started toward the shack. The muscles in his arms were burning when they reached the shack, but not much time had elapsed. He knew the old route well, so didn't need to use the flashlight. Dan, breathing heavily, put Ann down beside the door and turned on his flashlight so she could see where they were going.

"There are three dogs inside, a mom and two pups. This is Henry, the dad."

As soon as the door was opened, Henry went in and entered the cave. Dan got in the hut and pulled Ann inside. Dan gave her the flashlight so she could see the inside of the tiny cabin.

Slightly smiling, she said, "How nice, you even have a stove."

"That comment means you're not going to die. Do you, by any chance, have a phone?"

"Yes. It's in my shirt pocket." Ann reached into her side pocket and pulled out what remained of a phone.

Dan saw the mangled cell phone and commented, "I think we know what saved you from a really bad stomach wound. The bullet must have been partially deflected by your phone."

Ann looked around and tossed the phone in the corner. "Well, I guess we won't be calling 911. I took it from Scooter when he escorted me to the pickup to warn them if anyone showed up. I tried to make a call, but I couldn't get a signal."

"The Sterlings told me there's no cell phone communication around here, but I was thinking there might be from the shack. It's somewhat higher up than the cabin is. You'd better turn out the light." Dan asked, "What's your name?"

"Ann Olson," she answered. "What's yours?"

"Dan Newcomb. I'm house-sitting for Val and Terry Sterling. They're in Arizona for the winter—snow birds. I've got to take care of those three turds in the cabin and then I'll get you to a hospital."

"And how will you do that? They all have guns. How can you fight them without a gun?"

Dan answered, "I just spent two tours in Afghanistan. I know how to fight in ways they've never even thought of. Those three guys are at a real disadvantage. I've got a crossbow and this," Dan pulled out his survival knife. "I also know this area very well; I've scouted every square foot within a hundred yards of the cabin."

"I wish I could help."

"You can. You can stay here in the cave with the dogs. I don't want any of them to get hurt. What can you tell me about those guys?"

"The big one is Cliff. He's kind of mean. John and Scooter do what he tells them. John is probably the smartest of all three, but he still does what Cliff wants. He's the youngest. He's the one who made me go with them to rob the two motels. Scooter is a follower; he never thinks ahead. He has long hair and wears a baseball cap."

Ann paused for a moment and then continued, "You know—I was just doing what they said. I was pretty scared. They said they would kill me if I didn't do as I was told. I believed them."

"That's about what I would expect. That's great information. They probably don't have any real training in the use of weapons for warfare. I expect they've only shot defenseless animals and people. Those facts might help me carry out my attack. Did they try to force you to have sex?"

"John did, but I told him I had chlamydia, and I didn't have my drugs with me. He believed me and must have told the others. They didn't try anything. By the way, I'm in my last semester of nursing school." Ann paused for a couple of seconds and then said, "Oh, the gun I had wasn't loaded. They were afraid I would shoot one of them."

"Well?"

"Damn right. I would have shot Cliff—right in his fat gut."

Dan smiled and then sat thinking for a couple of minutes.

"Okay, here's what we're going to do. You're going to have to get in the cave with the dogs, as far back as possible. I haven't named the puppies yet; maybe you can come up with some names. I was thinking Glittle for the little girl. I need one of the blankets, the flashlight, the pliers, and half the arrows in my backpack. Put the blanket in the middle, the flashlight and arrows on either side, and the pliers on top."

"I think I can crawl in the cave," volunteered Ann.

"Okay, then we'll get the backpack ready."

Ann slowly crawled backwards through the opening in the cabin wall and turned on the flashlight.

"What's in this box?" Ann inquired.

"What?" Dan frowned. "What box?"

"There's a small, blue, metal box on the wall about a foot above the opening. It looks like a lunch box."

"I never looked up there; I was always taking care of the dogs on the floor of the cave. Let me squeeze in there so I can get to it."

Ann picked up the puppies and inched her way back from the opening to give Dan enough room to get in the cave. Dan slid in on his back, extended his arms, and opened the box.

"Hey, we're in luck! It's a first-aid kit. I see sutures, needles, gauze, aspirin, tape, and tincture of iodine. The tape's no good; it's all stuck together—hard as a rock. The iodine solution looks okay; it's never been opened. Oh, great! Here's a candle." Dan paused and looked at Ann. "Do you think you can sew up my leg? We can use the candle for light. I don't want to use up the flashlight batteries, I'll need them later."

"Sure, and then you can stitch me up. Just watch what I do. I wish we had some antibiotics; the iodine has alcohol in it, so it'll hurt like hell. We'll have to do this fast, the candle won't last very long. Fill my handkerchief with snow; we'll numb the area."

Dan placed the two breakers from the Sterlings' cabin on top of the first-aid box, crawled from the cave, and filled the handkerchief with snow. When he returned to the cave, Ann sutured both entrance and exit wounds on Dan's calf. Dan was a little timid about sewing up Ann's side, but she reassured him it was necessary, especially the exit wound. The bullet had tumbled, ripped open her skin, making a jagged exit wound. Dan started a small fire in the potbellied stove and melted some snow in one of the pie tins so they could wash the blood and dirt from their skin.

When they didn't need the fire any longer, Dan extinguished it with snow to prevent smoke from divulging their position. Ann and Dan talked for a few minutes, and almost simultaneously, they fell asleep.

CHAPTER 8

Combat

The wounded sat side by side covered by one of the blankets and Henry lay at their feet. The two puppies were huddled together next to Duchess's belly. While Dan and Ann slept, the candle burned down, flickered, and went out. It was extremely dark in the cave. The small quantity of light from the moon couldn't penetrate through the clouds, trees, and the cracks around the cabin door.

Dan had set his internal clock to wake up about 5:00 a.m. He sat in the dark with Ann's head against his chest and began thinking out his plan of attack. He had to get the men out of the cabin to better his odds of success. Fortunately, he knew the cabin and the surrounding wooded area better than the three men did, and Cliff was already wounded. Dan wanted to get started before it was light out. Night fighting was one of his specialties.

"Ann," he spoke her name softly and gently touched her shoulder.

Ann stirred and opened her eyes. She was startled, thinking she was blind. "I can't see." Dan flicked the switch on the flashlight for a moment.

"Oh! That's better. I'm not blind. Are you going now?" she asked.

"Yes. I've got to take care of some loose ends," he answered smiling.

Although Ann couldn't see his smile, the sound of his voice was reassuring. She could hear him checking things and putting on the backpack.

"Stay here with the dogs. Don't let the puppies or Duchess leave the cave. I told Henry to stay, but he might hear things and leave the cave through the passageway in the back. Don't try to stop him; he doesn't know you and might bite."

"Okay. Come back as soon as you can. Bring me something from McDonald's," she laughed. "Be careful!" she insisted.

"I will. Make sure you stay in here, no matter what happens."

Dan crawled out of the cave and pulled the sliding door shut. He zipped up his coat, picked up his crossbow, and left the miner's shack. It was 5:10 a.m. when he pressed the button to read his watch. He moved through the forest slowly, sometimes feeling his way between known landmarks, the thin clouds allowing enough moonlight to illuminate tree trunks, but little else.

The snow had stopped falling in the early morning and was about six-inches deep in the clearing around the Sterlings' cabin. The gorge wind had swirled in the clearing causing snowdrifts about knee-high against the walls of the cabin. Dan would have to account for the wind when he shot the bolts from his present position. First in his plan was to take away the heat in the cabin.

Dan watched the rear of the building from behind a clump of trees at the edge of the clearing. The only snowfall was that being blown from the trees and small flurries from the cabin roof. He leaned the crossbow against a small pine as he watched smoke rising from the chimney. There were several inches of snow on the roof.

Dan's first task was to block the gas flow from the propane tank. That would cut off the furnace and the hot water heater. He couldn't detect any movement from the back of the cabin as he crept up to the cylindrical container. He took the pliers from his backpack and crimped the gas supply line.

His next target was the gasoline generator in the shed against the back of the garage. He brushed away the snow on the ground below the small door and slowly swung it open. It was pitch-black in the shed so he had to use the flashlight. He removed the main wiring to the generator, jammed it in his pack, and cut the wires behind the on/off switch to be sure it couldn't be started without extensive repairs.

The most difficult task was to plug the chimney with the blanket. Smoke should drive the scum out of the cabin. There was a small ladder, partially covered with snow, lying on the ground by the backdoor of the garage, but Dan didn't want to disturb it. It looked just big enough to get to the eaves of the roof. He looked over to the woodpile and decided he could gain access to the roof there. From the top of the pile of firewood he was able to get onto the garage roof. The chimney was just twenty feet away.

Dan moved stealthily to the chimney and took off his backpack. He started pulling out the blanket and the flashlight and the generator wiring fell in the snow on the roof. He didn't think it made a noise loud enough for anyone inside the cabin to hear. He shook out the folded blanket, wadded it up, and stuffed it in the chimney. He grabbed his backpack and flashlight and went to the edge of the roof above the firewood. Dropping to the ground, Dan rolled to his feet, and went in the generator shed. He waited to hear a reaction from the cabin. In a couple of minutes he heard some yelling from Cliff.

"God damn it, Scooter, do what I told you! Get on the roof and see what's blocking the damn chimney!"

Dan heard steps in the garage and the sound of the backdoor opening. He cracked the shed door so he could see what was happening. A man, apparently Scooter, wearing a baseball cap was picking up the ladder and leaning it against the eaves. He shook the snow from his hands and began climbing. For some reason, he hesitated after reaching the third rung of the ladder, Dan quickly opened the generator door and silently moved under the ladder with his knife drawn. He reached up through the rungs of the ladder, grabbed Scooter's left foot and cut through the back of his boot with the serrated edge of his survival knife. He rotated the knife a half turn and slashed through the hole in the boot, severing Scooter's left Achilles' tendon.

Scooter yelled, "God damn! Son of a bitch!"

As soon as Dan had made the slashing motion he ran for his crossbow at the edge of the clearing. It was difficult to see; the snow was falling again, much heavier than before. The thin clouds had been replaced with a mottled gray, nearly opaque, covering. The dim light at the early hour didn't help much, but Dan located the bow and loaded a bolt. Dan's watch read 5:45 a.m. He could still hear Scooter yelling for help from the top of the ladder at the edge of the roof. From what he heard, Dan reasoned that Scooter hadn't seen him.

From thirty yards away, Dan could make out two people, one on the ladder and one standing by the back door. The man by the door shot randomly into the woods three times and started helping Scooter get down the ladder.

The three shots from the rifle had only knocked some snow off the trees and hadn't come close to Dan. Dan aimed the crossbow at the two men and pulled the trigger.

There was a scream of pain followed by, "Shit! There's an arrow in my leg!"

It wasn't Scooter's or Cliff's voice, so the bolt must have hit John. Cliff would still be safely inside. He probably wouldn't help anyone but himself. Dan quickly reloaded the crossbow. Two bolts remained taped to the stock of the bow. The snow continued, but the sky seemed to be a little lighter. Dan thought his eyes were adjusting to the dim light, but then realized the sun must be rising. He could see a man limping badly, dragging a body in the snow toward the backdoor of the garage. Dan rose to one knee, took aim at the limping man, and pulled the trigger. The man staggered and fell headfirst into the snow drift next to the door.

"John?" Scooter tried to get a response from his companion. There was no answer. "Cliff! I think John's dead! Get your butt out here and pull me into the garage. I can't walk; my left foot doesn't work."

"I'm not coming out there! Save your own ass! Crawl or get on one leg and hop to the door!" yelled Cliff.

The count was one down, two to go. Dan decided to change his position to observe the front of the cabin. The larger windows might give him a better view of what Scooter and Cliff were doing, provided the blinds were still open. He got to his feet and moved back into the woods out of sight of anyone in the cabin. Moving through the woods was not difficult; much of the falling snow was accumulating on the limbs of the trees. Once in a while, a small quantity of snow would cascade to the ground. The tree limbs, somewhat lighter, would spring back up. This was occurring randomly in the trees, so Dan's position was not divulged.

Dan slowly circled around the clearing, keeping his eyes on the building. He had moved closer to the edge of the clearing, crouched down, moved behind shrubbery, and from tree to tree. He smiled when he saw the scorched hulk of the pickup sitting on wheel rims in the driveway. There wouldn't be much to salvage from the burned-out wreck. It was a total loss.

Just as Dan had picked a spot behind a large rock and tree, the front door opened. The muzzle of a rifle appeared and the gun discharged. The barrel wasn't pointed in Dan's direction. He looked to his left and saw Henry running across the clearing in the snow. One of the men had shot at Henry!

Dan had to risk exposing himself to gunfire. He stood up and yelled, "Henry! Hide!"

Henry made a sharp right turn and headed for the trees at the edge of the road leading to the cabin. Dan heard another shot and a yelp from Henry. Dan raised the crossbow and shot a bolt directly at the front door, then dropped back to the ground behind the rock, watching the doorway. The bolt stuck into the doorframe about waist high. Now he knew how much correction to make at this distance from the cabin. He loaded the crossbow and moved back into the trees so he couldn't be seen. This shaft was the last of the bolts that he had taped to the stock of the bow. He would get the rest of the arrows from his backpack after he found Henry.

Dan made his way to the road through the woods. When he reached some trees near the edge of the road, he whistled. Henry's faint whimper was the only noise he could hear. Dan waited, but Henry didn't come to him. He moved in the direction of the sound, crossing the open area where the road entered the clearing. He moved fast and could hear shots and the noise of bullets striking the trees close by.

Dan stopped behind a large tree and looked back toward the cabin. One man, evidently Cliff, was behind the burned-out truck with a rifle. Dan stood up and fired a bolt at Cliff, who was using the truck wreckage for cover. Dan continued moving behind the trees. About ten yards into the trees, he found Henry lying on his side, the snow tinted red near his haunches.

He crouched beside the dog and said, "Good boy, Henry. I'll take care of you."

Dan examined Henry and found a bullet wound in his right hip. There was no exit wound. Since Henry couldn't walk, Dan picked him up and began carrying him toward the shack. Hopefully, Ann could evaluate the damage and remove the bullet. If not, Dan was going to have to end this fast and get Henry to a vet.

Dan's arms began to ache when he was about halfway to the cabin. He didn't care; he had to save his friend and companion.

"I'm tracking you! I'm gunna put a bullet in you, you son of a bitch!"

Dan could hear Cliff's voice. He was probably about fifty yards behind Dan and Henry. Dan quickened his pace and began to recognize the area near the log hut. It was quiet at the shack when they arrived. Dan was able to open the door without putting Henry down.

"It's me Ann. I've got Henry. He's been shot." Dan put Henry on the floor and slid the rear panel to the side, exposing Ann and the dogs.

"I'm so glad you're back. I was worried when I heard the shooting. It's good to see you're okay."

"Can you look at Henry? He can't walk."

Dan took off his pack and reached in to get the remaining bolts. He searched the pack and then inverted it. The flashlight fell to the cabin floor, but no bolts.

"Damn! I must have lost the bolts in the snow on the roof! Quick, Ann, get in the cave and I'll put Henry in with you. Move into the passageway with the dogs. I'll cover the tunnel with the panel."

Dan suddenly thought of a way to make some bolts. He took out his survival knife and split a strip of pine from the edge of the sliding door. After cutting the pine piece in half, he trimmed off the rough edges and sharpened the ends of the two pine shafts. He hurriedly cut each shaft to about one foot in length and cut notches in the ends opposite the sharp points. As fast as he could, he loaded the crossbow with one of the hastily made bolts. He could hear the heavy breathing of Cliff and footsteps in the snow as the big man approached the miner's cabin.

Cliff shot into the cabin through the outer wall and yelled, "Get out here so I can see your mug when I shoot you in the head! I'm gunna splatter your brain all to hell."

Dan was in the cave behind the potbellied stove and the back wall of the shack. The cast iron stove afforded additional protection from Cliff's rifle shots. Two more slugs slammed into the cabin walls, penetrating the front outside wall, lodging into the back wall of the shack. Dan didn't make a sound.

Cliff yelled from outside the cabin, "I know yur in there! I followed yur tracks and the drops of blood! Where'd I get you, in the shoulder? I hope it hurts as much as that knife wound you gave me! Here, have a couple more!" Cliff shot into the cabin two more times. Dan remained silent. Cliff pushed the shack's door open wide with the muzzle of his rifle.

Cliff was bewildered when Dan wasn't in the cabin.

"What the hell! No one here?" He saw the opening in the back wall of the cabin where the panel was pushed back. "Come out of that hole, you son of a bitch! I shot yur dog, yur next!" Cliff realized someone had to be behind the cabin, so he shot two more rounds through the cabin's back wall, but they struck rock.

Dan yelled out, "Okay, I'm coming out. You got me in the shoulder!"

"Get out of that hole, God damn it! I wanta see you die!"

Dan yelled to Cliff, "You'll have to pull me out by my legs; I'm shot in both arms."

"Shit! Put your feet out through that hole and I'll pull yur ass out," Cliff bellowed.

Dan got on his back with his crossbow ready to fire. Cliff had leaned his rifle against the cabin wall by the door and was on his hands and knees. Dan had his legs extended into the cabin up to his knees. When Cliff started to grab Dan's left leg, Dan had a clear shot at Cliff's chest and pulled the trigger.

The pine shaft entered Cliff's chest above his left collarbone below his ear. Cliff flopped backwards against the front cabin wall, gasping for breath. About eight inches of the shaft had penetrated into his chest. Cliff couldn't talk; the expression on his face showed how perplexed he was. He just sat there for a moment, blinked, and looked at Dan.

As soon as Dan shot the makeshift bolt, he reloaded with the second shaft. Dan yelled at Cliff, "Don't do anything! Don't reach for that gun!"

Cliff reached for the rifle anyway; Dan pulled the trigger. The second shaft entered the big man's chest, pinning him to the wall. His arms dropped to the floor.

"Who—who the hell are you?" Cliff uttered. He looked at Dan and gasped, blood dripping from his mouth and nose.

"You don't need to know," Dan answered.

Dan scrambled out of the cave and knelt beside Cliff checking for a pulse. There was none. Cliff's eyes stared straight ahead.

"And you—you are dead."

CHAPTER 9

Clean Up

Even in death, Cliff was uncooperative. Dan struggled to drag Cliff's body outside. A handful of ammunition was found in Cliff's coat pockets. After putting the bullets in his pants pocket, Dan dragged the body away from the shack. He covered the corpse with snow so Ann wouldn't see the gruesome sight.

Ann called from inside the miner's cabin, "Are you all right, Dan? I heard you say you were shot in both arms."

"I'm fine. That was a little defensive lie. Cliff's dead. I put him in cold storage."

Ann stepped from the door of the shack and leaned against the wall to steady herself. She was holding Glittle in her arms. The male puppy was standing in the doorway and Duchess was right behind him.

"We have to get the dogs back to the cabin, but Scooter is still in there with a gun," Dan commented.

Ann stated, "I think Henry will be all right. The bullet is lodged in the hip joint and it's too painful for him to move. The bleeding has stopped."

"Can you take the gun and deal with Scooter?" Ann asked.

"Yeah, that's my plan. I found five rounds in Cliff's pockets. That should be enough to get Scooter to give up or die."

Dan grabbed the rifle and limped toward the cabin as fast as he could move. When he arrived at the Sterlings' cabin, he went around to the front as he had done before, staying out of sight in the woods. When he had a clear view of the front door and windows he put a slug through the front door to get Scooter's attention.

"Scooter!"

"What d'yah want?"

"Cliff's dead. I've got his rifle. You are way outclassed, buddy. I received sniper training in the army. Where would you like to be shot? In the head? It'll be fast that way; no trial." Dan had been shooting rifles since he was ten years old. He hit what he aimed at. Dan continued, "If you give up, I'll tell the police that you were cooperative. Maybe that will be taken into consideration when you're sentenced."

"Okay, don't shoot me. What should I do? I can't walk."

"Throw out all the guns and crawl out on the porch, face down, hands spread above your head. If I see you move, I'll kill you." Dan watched as two handguns and a rifle were tossed through the doorway near the entrance. Then Scooter crawled out of the cabin and lay motionless. Dan kept his rifle pointed at Scooter and moved forward to the porch deck. Once he was on the deck, Dan unloaded the weapons and put the bullets in his pockets. He threw the guns into the burned-out pickup.

"Stay right where you are!" Dan ordered. He entered the cabin and found a mess. Dirty dishes, cigarette butts and ashes were everywhere. Clean up would come later, after he had Ann, the dogs, and Scooter taken care of. He obtained a roll of twine from the hardware drawer in the kitchen and returned to Scooter. After tying him up, he put him in the cabin and tied him to the bed in the guest bedroom. Using the cabin phone, he called 911. The police would arrive in twenty to thirty minutes.

The snow had stopped falling and water was dripping from the eaves of the cabin. Dan picked up a hatchet from the garage and started back to the miner's shack. Along the way, he found two long tree limbs suitable for making a travois. In less than ten minutes he was back at the shack. Ann had moved the dogs into the cabin, and they were all resting on the blankets. When Henry saw Dan, he wagged his tail and looked up, but couldn't get up. Henry whined and Dan went to him.

"Good boy Henry. We'll take care of you pretty soon. Ann, you did a good job getting the dogs out of the cave and into the cabin."

"Thanks, but they cooperated. They seemed to know Henry was hurt. His family is staying close beside him."

"I'm going to make a travois so we can all go to the cabin at one time. I tied up Scooter and put him on one of the beds. I guess I shouldn't have wasted time providing for his comfort. The police should be at the cabin when we get there."

"What can I do to help?" Ann asked.

"I'll need one of the blankets. Here's my knife to cut some twine. We need three pieces about four feet long. Use the knife as a ruler; it's a foot long. I'm going to look for another limb to hold the long pieces of the travois separated at the bottom." Dan gave Ann the knife and a roll of twine from the cabin. Dan took the hatchet and removed a two-inch diameter limb from a nearby tree. He took a section four feet long and assembled the travois. "Okay, everyone, you're all going for a ride."

Dan helped Ann and Henry get on the travois. He placed the puppies on Ann's lap, picked up the leading end of the travois and started pulling. Duchess followed beside the triangular, wheel-less cart watching the puppies and Henry. Fortunately, the trip to the cabin was downhill. Dan didn't have to exert much energy to keep the travois and riders moving at a slow walking pace; in addition, the snow allowed the travois to slip over the ground with relative ease.

As they moved toward the cabin, Ann asked, "What did you feel when you killed those men?"

"Nothing. If I hadn't killed them, they would have killed us. They were the enemy. Kill or be killed. There's no time to think about it. When it's over, you forget as much as you can, but sometimes you have bad dreams, at least I do."

The Sterlings' cabin was a beehive of activity when Ann, Dan, and the dogs arrived. Two ambulances were in the driveway. Two men were carrying John's body from behind the cabin to one of the ambulances. Scooter was being put in one of the three police cars. A uniformed policeman and a man in a suit, wearing a heavy coat, were approaching Dan.

"Are you Daniel?"

"Yes, sir. I called 911," answered Dan.

"I'm Deputy Sheriff Seth Andrews, Multnomah County detective," stated the slim man in the suit. "This is Deputy Calvin Benson," Andrews gestured toward the other man.

"I'm Dan Newcomb. I've been taking care of the Sterlings' cabin while they're in Arizona."

"Who put the arrows in the dead man?" asked Andrews.

"I did," answered Dan. "There's another body in the woods. He's also got arrows in him. I'll take you to the body."

"Where's your weapon?" asked the detective.

Dan said, "You mean the crossbow? I left it at the miner's shack where the body is. Here's my knife; I cut his foot with it." He pointed at Scooter. Dan handed his survival knife to the detective.

Andrews held up the knife and said, "That's quite a blade."

"Could you have someone take Ann to the hospital? She has a stomach wound and probably needs some antibiotics," Dan requested.

"Sure. Cal, take the woman to Legacy-Mount Hood in Gresham. I'll talk to her later."

"Yes, sir." Cal walked to his police cruiser and began moving it closer to Ann.

Dan bent down, looked at Ann and said, "Ann, as soon as I get finished here and take the dogs to a veterinarian, I'll come to the hospital to see you. I'll have someone look at my leg, too."

"Okay, I'll see you later. Thanks for saving me!" She reached out and took Dan's hand.

Dan smiled. "My pleasure. Take care of her, Deputy." Dan watched as Ann got into the cruiser. He turned to the detective and said, "Detective, I'll take you to the other body. You'll need a couple of men to bring him back here. He's heavyset, probably weighs over two-fifty. I covered him with snow. He's a bloody mess."

Andrews signaled to an ambulance crew. One of the EMTs approached and talked with the detective.

Dan looked around and then added, "It looks like the snow is melting and the sun's going to come out. In spite of how it started, I guess it's going to be a nice Halloween. Kids should have fun tonight."

Dan and Detective Andrews started walking toward the creek behind the cabin. Two men from one of the ambulances followed carrying a stretcher.

"Did you know there was a reward for the three men and the woman?" quizzed the detective.

"Nope. Ann wasn't part of the gang, she had to do what they wanted. Those guys kidnapped and threatened her."

"Well, we'll get this sorted out soon. Let's get the other body and the crossbow.

We'll need the crossbow for evidence. It'll be returned to you in a few days with your knife. We found a knife with blood on it in the cabin. Is that yours too?"

"Yes. That's the one I threw at Cliff when he was going to shoot me. Detective, I need to take care of the dogs. Can someone take me and the dogs to a veterinarian before I go to the hospital? Henry, the male dog, has a bullet in him and can't walk."

"Sure. We'll take you and the dogs in an ambulance to a vet. There's one on the way to the hospital. We need to get that bullet."

"I know, for evidence," smiled Dan.

"Yep!" the detective grinned. "We'll be here for a couple of hours helping the medical examiner and the forensics people. I'll see you later at the hospital."

CHAPTER 10

Hospitals

Dan and the four dogs were taken to the veterinarian. The staff told Dan what they would do for the puppies and Duchess. After a cursory exam, they said Henry would have to be anesthetized to remove the bullet. The operation on Henry would be expensive, but the reward money would more than cover the bill. Dan would also have his pay from the Sterlings for the first month of cabin sitting to cover expenses if necessary.

He would have to buy some things for the cabin that were damaged in the war of the woods. But, he thought almost everything that was damaged could be fixed using materials that the Sterlings had in their garage. After Dan got the dogs settled, the ambulance transported him to the hospital. A doctor checked his left calf, said the sutures were fine, and gave him a prescription—antibiotics for ten days. Then Dan went to see Ann.

Before Dan went to the third floor, he visited the men's room. As he washed his hands, his image in the mirror made him wish he had gotten a haircut and shaved. He looked like a ditch digger that had been living on the streets for several days. He could smell his armpits, so he washed his shirt and underarms to eliminate the odor. After drying his shirt with the warm air from the hand dryer on the wall, he re-dressed, then took the elevator to the third floor. As he approached the nurse's station, a nurse came out of a patient's room and walked directly toward Dan, smiling.

"Are you Daniel?" she asked.

Dan replied, "Yes, ma'am. How did you know?"

"I'm Mary, Ann's nurse."

Mary was an average-looking woman, in her forties or fifties. Dan, like most young men, had trouble estimating the age of women more mature than Ann.

"Ann described you perfectly. Is it all right for me to call you Dan?"

"Sure. Where's Ann? Is she okay?"

"She'll be just fine. She's in room 312. I just took her something to eat. She said you guys hadn't eaten in two days. She said something about McDonald's, but I think she was joking. Follow me, I'll take you to her."

Dan smiled, remembering that Ann had jokingly asked Dan to bring her something from McDonald's when he returned from the fight at the Sterlings' cabin. Dan followed the nurse down the hallway to room 312. Mary stepped in the room and motioned for Dan to come in.

"Ann, I brought you a visitor."

The hospital bed was tilted so Ann could eat and watch TV simultaneously. As soon as she saw Dan, she clicked the TV off.

"Hi Dan!" Ann said enthusiastically. "Come sit on the bed beside me," Ann said as she patted the bed.

For a moment, Dan was tongue-tied. He barely recognized this woman, but he immediately recognized her voice. So many things had been on his mind the last two days he had never taken a good look at Ann. She had put on some makeup, and her brown hair was actually reddish-brown and been washed and combed. She was just short of beautiful!

Dan finally spoke, "Wow! You look great!" He quickly added, "How are your wounds? Have you called your mom?"

"Hey! Slow down! Thank you. Mary gave me some injections to prevent any problems with the healing process. I feel pretty good except it hurts when I laugh or move around. Please don't make me laugh, and stay in one place so I don't have to move. I called my mom and she'll be here tomorrow. She has a load to deliver in Portland, and she wants to meet you."

"Your mom has a load to deliver?" Dan grinned, "She's transporting drugs?"

"No, silly. My mom and dad have a trucking business. She's delivering TVs to a department store. She's little, but she drives a semi like it's a passenger car. My dad got hurt and stays at home in Boise. He does the books and answers the phone." Ann looked at the nurse and said, "Mary, do you think we could get something for Dan to eat?"

"Sure. Let me call the food service people. They always have extras. I'll be right back."

"Dan, I'm worried about the medical expenses. I don't have any money, and I don't want my mom and dad saddled with hospital bills. They have their own expenses to worry about."

"Hey, don't worry. There was a reward for those three idiots. The detective said I would get $10,000 for their apprehension. Apparently they were responsible for several other holdups in addition to the two motels. They shot a service station employee, but she gave the police a good description of them. We can use the money for your care and Henry's operation."

"Oh, thank you! That's awesome. How is Henry doing?"

Dan looked at his watch. "They're operating right now. I'll know in a couple of hours."

"I thought of a name for the male puppy," Ann commented. "Don't laugh, 'cause if you do, then I will, and it will hurt."

"Can I smile?" Dan asked smiling, "Okay. What's the name?"

"Nomah!" she blurted out. "It's the last part of the county, Multnomah," Ann smiled. Dan returned the smile, "Well, that's interesting. I was thinking Nomah for Multnomah Falls. Maybe it's true, great minds do think alike."

"I'm glad you like the name, even if you already had thought of it. I think Nomah is a cool name. It's almost biblical. I like Glittle, too. I think Glittle and Nomah are great names for the puppies."

Dan nodded and said, "I agree."

Mary returned to the room carrying a food tray. "Here you are, Dan. I'll put it on the bed so you and Ann can continue to talk."

"Thank you, Mary," Dan replied.

"There's a Deputy Sheriff, Seth Andrews, here to talk to both of you," informed Mary. She stepped into the hallway and directed Andrews to enter the room.

The detective stepped inside and said, "Go ahead and eat, Dan. I'll start with Ann. Tell me, Ann, how did you meet those guys?"

Ann told the detective the whole story about meeting John and the men forcing her to help with the motel robberies. Then they made the mistake of driving to Oregon and going to the cabin where Dan lived.

After talking with Ann, the detective started asking Dan questions. Dan had finished eating and started telling the story from his viewpoint. Dan was very good at remembering minute details. He had conducted many reconnaissance missions for the army in Afghanistan. Details could mean life or death for his buddies.

As Dan related his part of the story, both Ann and Deputy Sheriff Andrews were engrossed in the plot he had used to overcome the three men. As Dan finished his narration of the events, the detective rose to his feet and thanked them for their cooperation. He shook hands with them and said they might be called to testify if there was a trial. But, since Scooter had confessed, they probably wouldn't have further involvement.

"Remember, Dan, you'll receive a reward check for $10,000. The money is from all the merchants that were robbed as well as Crime Stoppers. I hope you both recover from your wounds without any complications. Good luck!" The detective backed out of the room, waved, and walked toward the elevator. Andrews suddenly turned around and returned to Ann's room. "I forgot to tell you, Dan, the crime scene tape will have to remain for a couple of days. I'll send a man to clean it up after we're sure we have all the information we need. See you later."

"Okay, Deputy. Thanks."

Mary returned to Ann's room and picked up the food trays right after the deputy sheriff left.

Dan asked, "Mary, is there anyone that could give me a ride back to the cabin? I have to fix a place in the garage to play house for a couple of days. I'd like to get started. I also need to go to the vet's and check on Henry and his family."

"Who's Henry?" Mary quizzed.

"My dog. He got shot. He's at the veterinarian having the bullet removed."

Mary smiled, "Was this a group thing? All three of you got shot,"

"Well, we heard you were a good nurse, but we wanted to see for ourselves," Ann quipped and grinned.

Appearing more serious, Dan commented, "Mary, you're not supposed to say anything that will make Ann laugh." Then he smiled.

"To answer your question, Dan, we have some volunteer drivers that can ferry you around. We need to schedule them in advance though."

"As much as I would like to stay here with Ann, I really should get back to the cabin and make sure nothing freezes. I don't need anything else to repair."

As Mary left the room she said, "I'll see if I can get someone right away. Let me check—be right back."

Dan turned to Ann and asked, "When will you be able to ride in a car?"

"I'm not sure, but it will probably be several days. What were you thinking about?"

"I've been working on Mr. Sterling's jeep, and it'll be running again in a day or two. I was thinking you might stay in the cabin for a few days before you go back to Seattle for school. I was hoping you could help me clean up the place. You could also help me with the dogs and we could get better acquainted, but I want you to heal properly. Maybe you should remain quiet for a week or so."

"I think I'll have to drop out of school this semester. I've already missed a week, and it will be at least another week, maybe two, before I can get back to school. I might not be able to catch up, and I don't want to ruin my grades with a bad semester. I'd be happy to help you with the cabin and the dogs, but it will depend on what the doctors say. Henry will need special exercises to rehab his hip. I could be his special nurse."

"Let me have your number and I'll call tomorrow when your mom is here. Say, what are your parents' names?"

"Beverly and Ben. I'm sure Mom will want to talk to you. Just call the hospital and tell the receptionist the room number; it's 312."

Mary returned to the room and said, "I got a ride for you, Dan. Mr. Nyman will take you home. You can make arrangements with him for additional taxi service if you need it. He's waiting for you downstairs near the admissions counter."

"Thanks, Mary, and thank you for the food. Take good care of Ann for me."

Dan turned to Ann and said, "I'll call you tomorrow." He held Ann's left hand between his hands and said, "Take care." Dan turned to leave the room.

"Oh, Dan. Give me your number so I can call you at the cabin."

Dan wrote down the Sterlings' phone number on a pad next to the room phone. He had to get the number from his wallet. He didn't think anyone would be calling him so he hadn't memorized it.

"Hey, the number ends in 312! That part is easy to remember," stated Dan. "Bye Ann."

"Bye, Dan. Don't forget to call."

Dan waved as he left the room. "Don't worry, I won't forget. Bye."

CHAPTER 11

Bad News

When the elevator door opened, Dan stepped into the lobby looking for a man he imagined to go with the name Nyman. No one, other than hospital personnel, was standing near the admissions area. There was a small group of nurses near the front entrance, but no one else was in the lobby except for the middle-aged female receptionist.

Dan began moving toward the foyer at the hospital entrance. As he approached the automatic doors, a mature man with glasses and gray hair stood up and waved to get Dan's attention. He had been sitting on a concrete bench between two pillars, out of sight from the elevators. The gentleman was a little less than six feet tall, nicely dressed in navy-gray slacks, and a white shirt with the sleeves rolled up. He wore a Red-Cross volunteer pin on his collar.

"Mr. Nyman?" Dan asked.

"At your service, young man. My first name is Ronille, but I go by Ron or Don. My middle name is Donald. Ronille sounds too affected."

"It's nice to meet you Ron. I'm Daniel Newcomb. I go by Dan," he smiled.

They shook hands and Ron asked, "Well, Dan, where would you like to go?"

"I need to check on my dogs at the vet's down the street from here."

"Okay. I know the place. It's about a quarter of a mile east. They have a very good reputation. How many dogs do you have?"

"Four; male and female adults and two puppies. Henry, the adult male was shot and he's having surgery to remove the bullet."

"I hope he'll be okay. What kind of person would shoot a dog?"

Dan walked ahead expressionless. "He's dead."

Ron stopped in the parking lot at a dark-blue SUV, unlocked the door with his key, opened the door, and pressed the door unlock switch. Ron looked at Dan and smiled. "I like to save the batteries on my remote. Remotes are expensive." Ron and Dan climbed in the car and headed toward the animal clinic. "Where are you working, Dan?"

"I'm not really working. I'm housesitting for Val and Terry Sterling at their cabin near Multnomah Falls. I got out of the Army about six weeks ago. I was on my way back to Alaska and decided to stay in Oregon for five months. The dogs were abandoned; so I adopted them."

"Good for you. My wife adopts cats. We've got six of them now. They've all been to the vet so they can't multiply." He grinned, "The operations are guaranteed." Ron slowed down and made a left turn and parked in front of the animal hospital. "I'll wait in the car for you. Come and get me if you need help with the dogs."

Dan had gotten out of the car and was walking toward the front door of the animal clinic. He turned and said, "Thanks, Ron. I'll be back in a few minutes."

The receptionist behind the counter, dressed in loose-fitting green medical garb, stood and asked, "May I help you?"

"Yes. I'm Dan Newcomb. I brought in some dogs this morning. One had a bullet in him and was to undergo surgery. Can you tell me how he's doing?"

The woman answered but didn't smile. "You'll have to talk to Dr. Lester; she's in charge today. Please take a seat. I'll tell the doctor you're here." The receptionist withdrew from the counter, entered a room behind her, and closed the door. When she opened the door, sounds of barking penetrated the waiting room. In about ten seconds, an examination room door opened and a studious-looking young woman wearing glasses, a white lab coat, and carrying a manila folder spoke to Dan.

"I'm Dr. Lester. Please come in so we can talk."

Dan had a feeling that something had gone wrong. He entered the exam room and asked, "How is Henry?"

"Please have a seat, Mr. Newcomb." Dr. Lester's face, devoid of expression, said a lot more than she realized.

Dan had experienced the doctor's mood before, when one of his army buddies was killed. He sat down on a black-vinyl cushioned bench and looked up at the doctor.

"I'm sorry to have to tell you this, but we couldn't save Henry."

Dan couldn't believe what he had just heard. "What? I thought the bullet could be removed without any problems. What happened?"

"There was a piece of bone in the hip joint, not a bullet. The bullet caused extensive internal damage that no one could repair. We kept him anesthetized so he passed without any pain."

Dan's eyes welled with tears and his throat tightened so he couldn't speak.

The doctor saw his discomfort and handed him a small box of tissues. Dan wiped his eyes, swallowed with some difficulty, tried to clear his throat, and managed to say, "Can I see him?"

"Sure. All the equipment has been disconnected. Come with me."

Dan followed the doctor into an operating room. Henry looked like he was sleeping.

"I'll give you some time with Henry." Dr. Lester stepped out of the room and shut the door.

Dan moved slowly over to Henry and put his hand on Henry's shoulder, half expecting his special friend to jump down from the table ready to go for a walk. Dan realized this was the last time he would ever see Henry. His eyes overflowed with tears, which began to trickle down both cheeks.

Dan hadn't cried since his mother had passed. He could hardly get words to form, but he choked out what he could. "I'm so sorry this happened to you, Henry. You were a great companion. Don't worry about Duchess and the puppies. I'll take care of your family. If there is a heaven, I know you'll be there. If I get to heaven, I know you'll be waiting for me, listening for my whistle. Goodbye, Henry."

Dan placed both hands on Henry's body and sobbed. Dan's shoulders shook as he remembered the things he and Henry had done together. Dan had hoped Henry would enjoy living in Alaska, investigating new things. All those ideas were now lost. Dan wiped the tears from his eyes, slowly turned away from Henry, and left the room.

Dr. Lester approached Dan and said, "Are you all right?"

"Yes. What should I do about Henry?" Dan wiped the tears running down his cheeks with his sleeves.

"There are several options. You can bury him on your property with or without a casket. You can have him cremated. We can give you his ashes."

Dan thought for a moment. He couldn't bury Henry on the Sterlings' property without their approval. After Dan left for Alaska, what would be the point of the grave? Sterlings had never known Henry. Dan didn't want to carry an urn of ashes around as he traveled. The hospital would dispose of the ashes from the cremation.

"I think cremation—you dispose of the ashes," stated Dan, his voice noticeably quivering.

"All right. We'll have to send you a bill for the cremation; the amount depends on body weight. I'm sorry for your loss."

"Thank you, Doctor. Can I take the other dogs with me now?"

"Sure. Duchess was a little dehydrated, but we've given her fluids. The puppies are doing fine. They've had good care. I'll give you a schedule for their shots and checkups for the next six months. Oh, yes, we gave them all a bath."

Dan was able to force a smile and said, "Thank you, Doctor."

"I'll bring the dogs to you in the waiting room."

Dr. Lester escorted Dan to the waiting room where Ron was waiting. Ron approached Dan and said, "I was concerned that it was taking so long. I decided to come in. I'm sorry they couldn't save Henry."

"Thanks, Ron." Dan paused and wiped tears away. "Can you help me with Duchess and the puppies? I'd like to take them back to the cabin."

"Not a problem. I've transported many animals in my car."

One of Dr. Lester's assistants brought Duchess into the waiting room on a leash and the puppies were together in a small animal carrier. The assistant said, "You can return the carrier at your convenience."

Dan asked, "I'd like to get some food for the puppies, enough for two or three weeks. When I run out, I'll return the carrier and get some more food." Dan paid for the food, and the two men put the dogs and food in the back of the SUV.

Ron followed Dan's directions to the cabin. The trip took about twenty-five minutes. Dan noticed the unpaved portion of the road was strewn with ruts. He couldn't believe the ambulances and police cars could have messed up the road so badly. When the two men arrived at the clearing where the cabin was located, the cause of the torn up road was evident. There were several large vans from TV stations parked next to the cabin and a half-dozen passenger cars.

Ron spoke first, "What in hell is all this?"

CHAPTER 12

TV News

Reporters from three local TV stations seemed to have free rein of the Sterlings' property. Dan could see people milling around in the cabin and the garage.

"Ron, this is private property. Look at those idiots! They've gone behind the crime scene tapes."

"Stay in the car Dan. I'll take care of this."

Ron got out of the car and walked over to the front porch of the cabin. Dan watched from the car as the TV people gathered around Ron. In a couple of minutes, Ron came over to the car and motioned for Dan to open the window.

"I've negotiated a contract for you. Only one of the TV stations will be allowed to stay. The interview will be shared with the other stations. They will have to fix the damaged road and pay for the veterinarian's bills. If they don't give you a written contract to sign in about ten minutes, there will be no interview, and they'll be prosecuted for trespassing and sued for damages. What do you think?"

Dan smiled. "Thanks, Ron. That sounds good to me. I had no idea you were so well informed about contracts and legal matters."

Ron smiled, "Well, I learned a lot during forty years in the clothing business. One of the reporters should have a contract for you in a few minutes. You and the dogs stay in the car. I'll wait out here."

Ron leaned against his car and watched the personnel from two of the stations pack up and depart. A couple of minutes later, a well-dressed, pretty young woman, carrying a clipboard, approached the car. Dan lowered the window.

"Are you Daniel Newcomb?" she asked.

"Yes. I've been told we have a contract to sign before I give you an interview."

"That's correct. I'm Cindy Hernandez, reporter for TV7. We have prepared a contract for you to sign. May I join you in the car?"

"I have to take care of some things. Can you interview me as I begin checking things around the cabin?"

"Sure. Let's do that," the reporter answered and smiled.

Ron reviewed the contract and nodded to Dan that it was acceptable. Both Dan and Ms. Hernandez signed the paper on the clipboard. Cindy introduced Dan to her cameraman, Armando Lopez.

While Dan settled the dogs in the garage, the questions started. As Dan began answering, he found the blanket from the chimney, the generator wires, and the four bolts on the garage bench. The breakers he had left in the shack had been reinstalled in the electrical box. The police had kindly helped Dan start repairs to the cabin. As Dan related the story, he was able to repair the gas supply line and start restoring the generator wiring. Duchess followed Dan closely as the reporter asked about the skirmish at the shack.

"Can you show me the miner's shack?"

Dan glanced down at the reporter's feet and said laughing, "You'll never make it in those high heels. Do you have a pair of regular shoes to wear?"

"I have some sneakers in the van. I'll put them on."

When Cindy returned, Dan couldn't help but laugh. The sophisticated looking, nicely dressed reporter, wearing sneakers, created an odd sight. It was obvious her first concern was getting the story. Dan was relieved; he wouldn't have to carry Cindy if her high heels got stuck or broken.

Dan, Cindy, Armando, and Duchess walked to the little hideout. Duchess stayed very close to Dan and occasionally whined. When they arrived at the shack, which had crime scene tape across the open door, the reporter stuck her head in the opening and observed the blood stains. Dan watched Duchess search the miner's hut and the cave behind it, undoubtedly looking for Henry. Dan knelt beside Duchess and put his right arm around her neck. He talked quietly to the dog. Armando was capturing everything with his camera.

"I know girl. I miss Henry too. We'll spend some time together later. Henry and I used to go for walks. Maybe you would like that." As Dan stood up, he wiped his eyes, and looked at the reporter. "I think you have the whole story now. You can call me if you need any other information. Let's go back to the cabin."

During the interview, Ron had started cleaning up the pickup wreckage. It wasn't marked as off limits. He had put on a pair of gloves and had begun moving what he could of the wreck away from the entrance to the garage.

Cindy thanked Dan for the interview. The TV crew packed up their equipment and left for their next assignment. Dan was grateful when the TV people were gone. In spite of having a signed contract, he doubted they would live up to the agreement. But now, he could finish repairing the generator. He could start cleaning up the interior of the cabin as soon as the crime scene tape was removed.

Duchess remained at Dan's side as he finished the generator repairs.

"Let's check your puppies, Duchess."

Duchess followed Dan to the dog beds in the garage where the puppies were curled together sleeping. Ron had given them some soft food, and after eating, they had fallen asleep. Duchess checked out the puppies and returned to Dan's side.

Ron came into the garage and said, "I have to go now, Dan. I've given you about all the help I can here at the cabin. Call me tomorrow when you need a ride. I'll leave my day open so I can take you anywhere you like."

"Thanks, Ron. You have done a great job. Thank you for helping get the TV people out of here. I'll let you know when I need a ride. If I don't have the jeep running, I'll need a lift to the Troutdale Airport. I'll let you know if I don't need a ride."

Ron gave Dan a salute and got in his car. He drove slowly to the gravel road and disappeared down the lane into the trees.

"Come on, Duchess. Let's go for a walk."

Dan left the light on in the garage, but closed the doors so the puppies wouldn't wander away from the building. He closed and locked the cabin door and off they went. Dan wanted Duchess to see where they picked up food and other items, so they began walking down the road to the lock box. Almost all the snow had melted, and Dan guessed the temperature was in the high 40s. The early snowfall in the area might indicate a cold and blustery winter was coming, but he wanted the rotten weather to wait until he was able to fly. High winds and snow made poor flying weather.

Duchess kept close to Dan as they walked down the torn up road. Dan talked to Duchess and told her of the experiences Henry had on the trips to the lock box. He couldn't prevent his eyes from tearing as he recalled their hikes and investigations of the nearby woods. But talking to Duchess was cathartic, refreshing his spirit. The time seemed to pass quickly and they arrived at the box. Nothing was expected, but Dan opened the box and looked in anyway. A package in the bottom of the box had an envelope attached. Dan removed the envelope and opened it. It was a birthday card with, *Happy Birthday! I thought you might like this to wear in the winter—Marlene*, handwritten in ballpoint.

Dan's birthday was in February, and he thought it was a little strange that he would be receiving a present from someone he had never met; only talked with on the phone. He opened the box and found a long-sleeved, plaid, flannel shirt. Dan had an uncomfortable feeling. As he relocked the Sterlings' box, he frowned, and stuck the shirt package under his arm. He would return the shirt at the first opportunity he had to drive into Warner's.

"Well, Duchess, I'll have to call Marlene and tell her I can't accept the shirt. Let's go home." Dan reached down and patted Duchess on the back. Duchess looked up at Dan, wagged her tail, and they started back to the cabin.

It was time for dinner when they reached the cabin. Dan opened the front door and ducked under the yellow police tape. He had decided to enter the house in spite of what was printed on the tape. He had to get something from the pantry to eat, feed the dogs, and get things he needed to set up housekeeping in the garage for two days. After opening the door to the garage and moving the items he needed onto the hood of the jeep to serve as a kitchen counter, he blocked the living room-garage doorway with two cardboard boxes. The dogs had to stay in the garage.

He prepared dinner on a hotplate and ate with a fork, his only utensil. Beans, mixed vegetables, cheese, and bread were his dinner fare. He made coffee with the empty bean can and strained off the grounds with a paper towel. Dessert was replaced with time on the porch with the dogs. Glittle and Nomah wandered about while Duchess and Dan watched, keeping the little ones from falling two feet to the ground.

The dogs had a place to sleep, but Dan had to improvise. It was easy to remove the passenger seat from the jeep, which doubled as a pillow. He found an old air-mattress and a sleeping bag stored above the ceiling joists in the garage. Dan and the dogs were set for the night. It was almost like camping out, except they had a roof over their heads, and heat from the house.

In the morning, Dan's body ached, but he wasn't sure whether it was a result of the uncomfortable sleeping conditions, or the physical activity of the previous day. He made sure the dogs had water and let them out of the garage while he had French toast and coffee. He had rescued some syrup from the pantry; bread, eggs, and milk from the kitchen. Then he called Marlene.

A woman's voice asked, "May I help you?"

Dan didn't recognize the voice so he asked, "Is Marlene there?"

"Marlene doesn't work here anymore."

"Could you give me a number where I could reach her?"

"I'm afraid not. We can't give out personal information."

"Okay. Thank you."

Dan hung up the phone and began to wonder what had happened. Did Marlene quit or was she fired? If he was to talk with her again, she would have to initiate the contact, but he was curious to find out what had happened. He returned the puppies to the garage, hoping they had relieved themselves outside. He should have been watching them, instead of trying to talk with Marlene. Dan felt that staying out of the house was unnecessary, so he went into the living room, started a fire, and turned on the TV. All the local stations had the same story.

Cindy, the TV reporter, had made her interview available to the local stations so Dan was on all the Portland channels. He was made out to be the hero of the woods, capturing three thugs wanted in Washington State, and saving their hostage. Dan watched critically and was frustrated with the misstatements of the facts; he wasn't shot twice, and there was no old miner who lived in the shack. He turned the TV off and added some good-sized logs to the fire. The three logs should burn for at least an hour. About ten minutes after the story had aired, the phone rang.

"Hello."

"Guess who this is."

"Marlene," Dan answered. He recognized the voice.

"That's right! I just saw you on the news. I didn't know you were so handsome! When I heard your name, I realized you had to be the guy I knew from taking your phone order. Did you get the shirt?"

"Yes. Thank you. But my birthday is in February. Besides, we have never met and I can't accept the gift. I'm going to return the shirt to the store."

"Oh, please keep it. You mean a lot to me. You're the only hero I know!"

"I'm no hero, Marlene. I tried to call you at the store, and they told me you don't work there anymore. Is that true?"

"Yeah. I got tired of that job. Most of the time, I just sat around and waited for the phone to ring. It was pretty boring."

"What are you going to do now? Don't you need a job?"

"Not really. I've saved some money so I don't need a regular job. I just work when I find something interesting to do."

"Well, I've got to hang up, I have to call the cabin's owners."

"Can I buy you dinner? I can meet you wherever you like."

"Thanks, but I'm afraid not. I don't have a car and all my time in the next week is going to be set aside for repairing the cabin. Besides, my girlfriend and her mother are coming over for dinner." Dan's patience was wearing thin, so he lied about having a girlfriend.

"Well, okay. I hope I can meet you face-to-face sometime soon."

"Look, I really have to be going. Thanks for the call and the shirt. Bye."

"See you later, Dan."

Dan hung up the phone. He wasn't quite sure what to think of Marlene. The things she said had made him feel a little uncomfortable. If only he hadn't given that stupid interview. But, then again, maybe it was best to have gotten the episode finished.

He called Sterlings in Arizona and related what had happened. They assured him that as long as the cabin was still standing, everything was all right with them. He promised them he would fix the cabin so they wouldn't even know anything had happened. Since most of the damage was cosmetic, he could fill holes and apply new finish. Terry and Val were concerned about Dan's welfare, and he assured them he was okay.

Following the talk with the Sterlings, Dan went to the garage to check on the dogs. The puppies were asleep, and Duchess was sitting beside the door into the house. She whined, so Dan moved a box and let her come into the living room. She sat next to the sofa where Dan had been relaxing. Dan tried to find a movie on TV but couldn't find a free one. Duchess began walking around the room sniffing the furniture and the floor, stopping next to the fire. She curled up on the hearth in Henry's place.

Dan looked at Duchess and said, "I know, girl. I miss Henry too. Let's go out on the porch." Dan stood up and put on his jacket, walked to the front door, and looked back at Duchess. She sat on the hearth staring at him. He motioned to Duchess, and said encouragingly, "Come on, girl! Come outside with me."

CHAPTER 13

House Guests

When Dan opened the door, he could feel the warm, humid air outside. The temperature had gone up at least twenty degrees since the day before, and it had started to rain, the drops crashing sporadically on the roof. There was a gentle breeze and the smell of the wet forest was refreshing. Dan left the door open and sat down in the rocking chair on the porch. Duchess walked slowly out to Dan and sat down beside the rocker, staring into the trees. Dan reached down and stroked her head and neck. Her eyes looked sad; he knew what she was feeling. They both wanted Henry to suddenly appear from around the corner of the garage, or come running from the trees.

They sat quietly for about ten minutes as the impacts of the raindrops on the surroundings became louder and constant. The muted background noise from the stream had faded, hidden in the sound of the rain striking the roof. The nature sounds were soothing, almost hypnotic. The ring of the phone brought Dan back to full consciousness from the sleep-like state. He rocked forward, stood, went into the living room, and grabbed the phone.

"Hello."

"Hi, Dan. This is Beverly, Ann's mom. I'm at the hospital with Ann. How are you doing?"

"Oh. Hi, Mrs. Olson. I'm fine. You got here earlier than expected. How is Ann? How are you?"

"We're both okay. I was very worried when I was told she was shot. Ann is feeling much better now. The doctor said she could leave tomorrow, but she can't be active for about a week. She can move around, but she can't do anything strenuous. Would you like some guests on Tuesday?"

"That would be great! Should I pick you up from the hospital?"

"If that's okay with you."

"No problem. I'll be finished with flying lessons about four in the afternoon. I'll arrive at the hospital about 4:15. We can have dinner here at the cabin. Could I please talk with Ann?"

"Okay. Here she is."

"Hello, Dan. How are the repairs coming along?"

"Hi, I've done a few things, but I'm not supposed to be in the house. I slept in the garage with the dogs last night. Duchess is sticking close to me. I know she misses Henry. Did you know Henry didn't make it?"

"Yes, Mr. Nyman told me. I'm so sorry, Dan. I thought the bullet was on the surface of his hip bone, but it had done more damage than could be seen."

"You couldn't tell, Ann. I have to admit I cried when I found out, but I was able to see him and say goodbye. There were only two other times I was ever that sad, when my mom and dad died. How are you feeling?"

"I'm just tired, but Mom being here has helped my spirits. I'll see you on Tuesday. Get some pizza and beer, okay?"

"What? No McDonald's?"

"Nah. Canadian bacon and pepperoni—with lots of cheese. I need to replace some of the fat I lost during the kidnapping."

"That should do it. I'll pick you up tomorrow. Bye, Ann."

"See you later, Dan."

When he had mentioned flying lessons to Ann, he realized he had forgotten to call Vic and cancel today's lesson and work. He called the airport and talked with Vic.

"I heard what happened, Dan. I didn't expect to see you today. Anyway, it's not a good day for flying. We don't need to have freezing rain causing us problems. How are you doing?"

"I'm okay. I'm taking it easy today. I'll see you tomorrow. Okay?"

"Sounds good. You take care."

"You too. Bye."

"Bye, Dan."

Dan looked around the cabin to see what he could straighten up, but decided to respect the wishes of the deputy, except for the kitchen and the sofa. The walls, windows, and ceiling would have to be wiped and washed to remove the smoke residue. Duchess followed Dan around the house as he inspected the surfaces. She finally curled up beside the fireplace.

Duchess's behavior was a little annoying, but Dan understood that she missed Henry, so he couldn't get mad at her. He felt sorry for her, but what could he do to comfort Duchess? As he mulled over the situation, he suddenly realized that Duchess probably thought Dan would bring Henry back. She had always seen Dan with Henry. How could he tell Duchess that Henry was never coming back?

When Ann arrived, Duchess would have another person she knew at the cabin. He didn't know how long it would take before Duchess resumed her normal activities. Dan didn't know much about her regular life, he had only been around Duchess when she was in the cave with the puppies. Maybe Beverly or Ann would know something about Duchess's feelings. Dan would be willing to bet that Beverly was going to have an enjoyable time playing with the puppies.

It had been about 45 minutes since he had talked with the Olson women. Duchess had suddenly gotten up from the hearth and was on all fours watching the front screen door. Dan looked toward the entrance and then heard a car pull up in front of the garage. A car door slammed, so he started toward the door to see who his visitor was. The cabin door was still open from earlier when Duchess had joined him on the front porch. Just as Dan emerged from the cabin, he saw a woman he didn't recognize coming up the porch steps. Duchess had followed Dan to the porch and stood in the door growling.

"Hi, Daniel! I'm Marlene. I told you I'd see you later."

Dan looked back at Duchess and said, "It's all right girl."

Marlene was about the same height as Ann, about five-seven, but she was much heavier. She wore white shorts and a blue sweatshirt; her short dark-brown hair was a little mussed up and she held a small black purse in her left hand. She carried keys in her right hand. She wasn't pretty, but she wasn't homely either, just average looking.

"Can I give you a hug?"

Before Dan could answer, Marlene had wrapped her arms around him, pinning his arms to his sides.

"I guess so," he answered too late, but was relieved she had not grabbed his ass.

"How did you find me, Marlene?"

"I can find everything with a computer. I did a search for Sterlings' property and found the cabin location. It was easy to drive up here. The road isn't very good though." She paused, glanced at Duchess, and then said, "Your dog doesn't seem to like me."

"Duchess is just protective. She has two new puppies in the garage. She's a little wary of strangers. She didn't like it when the TV crews were here." Dan nervously looked across the clearing to the road, wishing someone would come by and rescue him from this person. Unfortunately, no one was expected.

"Come in the house and sit down. Are you going to look for a new job?"

"No, I don't think so. I think I might try to find something in Seattle near the University of Washington—maybe working with computers."

They sat on the sofa watching Duchess return to her spot near the fireplace. She circled around and dropped to the rug beside the hearth. Dan was trying to think of something to say to Marlene when the phone rang.

"Excuse me; I'd better get that call. It could be my house guests, or the cabin owners." Dan picked up the wall phone and answered, "Hello."

"This is Deputy Sheriff Andrews. By any chance, is Marlene there?" Before Dan could answer, Andrews added, "Don't let her know I asked."

Dan turned so he wasn't looking at Marlene and said, "Yes."

"Okay, I'm on my way. I'll be there in about ten minutes. Try to keep her there if you can, but don't make her mad. She might be dangerous. She could have a weapon."

"Okay, Sheriff, I'll expect you next week. I'd like to get my crossbow and knives back as soon as possible. I don't have any other weapons for protection from bears and mountain lions." Andrews had already hung up so he didn't hear what Dan had said. Dan continued, "Next Monday would be fine. Goodbye."

"Was that the police?" quizzed Marlene as she stood up.

"Ah, yeah. Deputy Sheriff Andrews said my knives and crossbow would be returned next week."

"Oh. Well, I guess I'd better go."

Dan thought quickly and said, "I'm expecting some guests. It might be hard to pass them on the road coming up from the old highway. You probably noticed how narrow and chewed up the road is. You might get stuck, or even drive off the edge. Maybe you could wait until they arrive. They should be here in the next ten minutes. When I heard your car, I thought they had pulled into the driveway."

"Well, all right," Marlene replied nervously, looking around the cabin.

"Let me show you the puppies." Dan took Marlene into the garage where Nomah and Glittle were huddled together asleep. Duchess had followed them to check on her little ones.

"Gosh. They sure are cute," remarked Marlene.

Dan could hear the crunch of wheels on gravel as a car arrived outside. He heard two doors slam. He had expected the police would park on the road and walk to the cabin, so not to announce their presence, but it must be the police. Dan thought: *Why did the police want Marlene?*

Dan looked at Marlene and motioned toward the living room. "Let's go back in the cabin. I want you to meet my house guests." When Marlene and Dan entered the living room, Duchess was standing at the front door wagging her tail. Dan estimated it had been about ten minutes since the call from Andrews. There were two loud raps on the door frame.

"Come in, Detective."

"Hi, Dan. I'd like you to meet Officer Lori Manning."

The officer stepped forward and shook hands with Dan. The officer said, "Nice to meet you. You did a good job with those criminals."

"Thanks, Officer. Glad to meet you. How can I help you?"

Andrews motioned toward Marlene and said, "I have a warrant for your arrest, Marlene. You'll have to come with us. The US government and the State of Oregon have both issued warrants for your arrest;

Internet and IRS fraud. You have a right…" After Andrews finished reading Marlene her Miranda rights, Officer Manning handcuffed her and escorted Marlene to the patrol car and drove off.

"Detective, what did Marlene do?"

"That's the name she gave you. Her real name is Wanda Simmons. She'll be staying in a jail cell until trial arrangements are made. She's wanted in Colorado for identity theft. She is nearly a genius with computers, and hacked into company files and stole personal information. However, she made a mistake while working for Warner's. Their computer system has tracking programs, and when they found out she had been stealing information from employees' records, they fired her. Colorado law enforcement notified the Fairview police when Wanda used a social security number of a woman in Colorado. The Troutdale authorities received information from the Fairview police and the search was on for Wanda Simmons, alias Marlene Coglin. You delayed her at the cabin for just the right length of time, Dan. Thanks. I think she was just about to leave."

"I'm glad I was able to help."

"You've had two days of catching crooks," added Andrews. "Ever consider becoming a police officer?"

"Nope. I like the outdoors and animals. I wouldn't be very good at paperwork, and I really don't appreciate people shooting at me. When I left Afghanistan, I thought the shooting was over. I hope you have the keys to Marlene's car—the jeep won't run. I've got to fix it in the morning so I can pick up Ann and Beverly. I've got to get up early. Oh, yeah, I have to cancel my flying lessons for a few days, too."

"Officer Manning told me she would leave the keys in the ignition of Marlene's car. I guess I'd better check." Andrews walked out to the car and looked inside. He gave Dan a thumbs-up; the keys were there. The detective climbed in, started the engine, lowered the window, and yelled, "Goodnight. Thanks again," and drove off.

CHAPTER 14

Ann Says Goodbye

Ann and Beverly stayed with Dan for three days, during which time he postponed the flying lessons and working with Vic. Early the first day, the crime scene tapes were removed, and while Ann rested in the cabin, Dan showed Bev the property, taking her to the shack and cave where the dogs had been living.

It rained hard the second day, Wednesday. They passed time with board games, TV movies, reading, naps, and conversation. Dan kept logs on the fire and brought the puppies in from the garage. Glittle and Nomah seemed to have a fondness for Ann, perhaps because of her gentle nature. Ann was becoming more active, had begun to laugh at the puppies' antics, and Dan's terrible jokes. Assisted by prescription medication, Ann was able to tolerate pain from laughing.

Beverly spent most of the day in the kitchen making oatmeal, chocolate chip (no nuts), and peanut butter cookies. While she was waiting for cookies to bake, she found a book about Alaska in the Sterlings' library. Every once in a while, she would read something to Dan and ask, "Is that really true?" In the afternoon the rain stopped, but by evening, the fog was so thick, visibility was limited to about ten yards. The surrounding trees couldn't be seen from the cabin porch. It was like living in the center of a hollow egg.

In the late afternoon, Bev and Dan cleaned ceilings, walls, and windows in the morning, removing soot and a few old spider webs.

Ann washed table and bed linens, curtains, and everyone's clothes. After dinner, they watched a movie and went to bed early, tired from the day's activities.

Bev got up early the next morning, Thursday, and began to pack, readying for the return trip to Boise. When Ann heard noises from the kitchen, she got up, dressed, and joined her mother.

"Where's Dan, Mom?"

"He took the dogs for a walk. They had been cooped up in the garage and house too long. He said he wouldn't be gone long. Put on a coat and go outside. You'll probably see him coming up the road."

Ann slipped on the parka Bev had brought from Boise and went out on the porch. It was cool, but damp, and everything smelled fresh. She smiled when she heard Dan calling to the dogs. Then, he appeared from the trees with Duchess, dropped to his knees on the road, and clapped his hands. Glittle and Nomah came running up to him. Still learning how to maintain their balance, the puppies bumped into each other, falling and rolling over. Glittle stopped for a hug, but Nomah only slowed momentarily and continued on, following Duchess. He scrambled up the steps to the porch, where he began pulling at Ann's jeans.

"What are you doing, Nomah? You little rascal." Ann crouched down and picked Nomah up, holding him next to her body. Nomah squirmed as if to say, "Put me down!" Ann was afraid she might drop him, so she lowered him to the porch. She watched Nomah jump from the porch and run to Dan, biting at his pants. Dan picked up both puppies and put them in the garage with Duchess.

"Where did you go, Dan?"

"Good morning! I took the dogs down the road about 30 yards and came back. I thought I might have to chase the puppies, but they stayed on the road with their mom and me. They are pooped out from the exercise and seeing what they think is a never ending forest. I believe they are overwhelmed. You were still asleep or I would have asked you to come along. How are you feeling today?"

"Pretty good, but I'm not looking forward to that long trip home. I'm going to miss you, Dan, but I'll see you for New Year's. We can keep in touch by phone and email. Give me your email address so I can write you. Okay? Mom already has your phone number and you have ours. Will you promise to call me?"

"I promise. It will be awfully quiet around here when you and Bev are gone. I'm planning on finishing repairs to the cabin, and then I'll try to finish working on Terry's jeep. It's running, but I can do better.

"You have a lot planned, and you are taking flying lessons, too. You're going to be busy!"

"Hopefully, the jeep will be finished by Thanksgiving. I'm also going to try to train Glittle and Nomah to do a few things, but they might be too young. You know, I'm going to miss you, too. Let me know where I can pick you up when you come back for New Year's.

"I'll probably ride the bus, but I'll let you know."

"Does your mom want to get out of here right away?"

"Yeah. We'll go as soon as we eat and get things packed in the jeep. I'll call as soon as we get home. I know I'm going to cry as we drive away." Ann stepped up to Dan and they hugged each other.

Dan bent down, kissed Ann, and said, "I'll probably shed some tears, too. I hate to say goodbyes to people I really like. I guess I'm not very manly."

"That's another thing I like about you, you're honest about everything."

Bev yelled from the kitchen. "Hey! Come in and have breakfast, you two. We've got to get going, Ann."

"Okay, Mom, we're coming."

As soon as breakfast was over, Dan volunteered to clean up the dishes so the ladies could pack their things in the jeep. As he washed dishes, he thought about how much he would miss the company of Bev and Ann, especially Ann. Dan was astonished; the packing only took a few minutes.

Ann came into the kitchen, paused with her hands behind her back, and attempting an English accent, said, "Arthur, if you have finished polishing the silver tea service, please drive us to the truck stop."

Dan almost dropped the plate he was drying when he started laughing. Ann smiled and began laughing too. "Wait 'til you hear my Alaskan accent—what do you think?"

"Well, say something."

"I did—the words froze so you couldn't hear anything. It gets that cold in Alaska, you know."

"That was terrible! You need to work on your jokes, Dan."

"Sorry about that, but I can't do accents. Are you ladies ready to go?"

"Uh-huh. Mom is already in the jeep."

It took almost thirty minutes before Dan and the women pulled into the truck stop. Beverly pointed to a blue semi that had big, white, B & B lettering on the trailer. Dan parked beside the truck, which dwarfed the jeep.

Bev unlocked the doors and climbed in the cab. She started the diesel engine as Ann and Dan put the ladies' clothing behind the seats. Dan accompanied Ann into the visitor center where Ann bought a handful of snacks. Bev and Ann both gave Dan a hug, and as Bev got back in the cab, Ann kissed Dan and said, "Thanks again for saving my life—call me!"

"You are very welcome, and as we say in Alaska —." Dan mouthed, "Good bye. I'll miss you," but he didn't say the words aloud.

Ann laughed and said, "I think you're just a little crazy, but I like it." She climbed into the cab and slammed the door. Ann leaned out the window and gave a last wave as the truck began to move, black smoke puffed from the exhausts above the cab.

Dan watched the truck roll slowly toward the freeway ramp and grinned when he heard two beeps from their horn. Dan stood beside the jeep with a lump in his throat until the truck was out of sight. He returned to the cabin in silence, thinking of being alone again, but happy that he had the dogs to care for. He looked at the calendar and realized he hadn't had any nightmares for a week.

The Olsons had driven on I-84 for about 20 minutes when Bev saw the sign for the turnoff to Multnomah Falls. It seemed to Bev that the Sterlings' cabin was directly south of the highway, so she gave two long bursts of the semi's horn. Ann jumped and looked questioningly at her mom.

"What was that for, Mom? Did you recognize someone in another truck?"

"Nope. That was for Dan. I'll bet he heard it, too—our last goodbye. I hope we see him again."

"Geez, Mom, I think you like him more than I do."

"What's not to like, Annie? He's nice looking, smart, loves animals, is responsible, and most importantly, he saved your life."

"I know all those things. But Mom, he wants to be a bush pilot—his father was killed doing that. I'd be worrying all the time. Look at all the problems you and Dad have had since he got hurt."

"Remember, dear, it took you several years to figure out you wanted to be a nurse. Dan has been in the military for four years. Give him some time to decide what he wants to do with his life. Didn't he say he wanted to get established before he got serious about romance? I remember he said it will take a while before he can get a plane, maybe even a couple of years. He might lose interest in flying and do something else. Besides, you have to finish nursing school before you run off to parts unknown."

"Yeah, I guess you're right. This detour has put me behind in my classes for a quarter. Now I won't finish until next fall. In the meantime, he might find someone else, get serious, and get married. Sometimes, I think I'm afraid to fall in love. There is so much disappointment if it doesn't work out. I wonder if I just feel close to Dan because he saved my life."

"Don't rush it, Annie. Sometimes, an imagination creates a situation that might never happen. Concentrate on your training, and things will happen as they're supposed to."

"You believe things are predetermined? I had no idea you would think that."

"Well, think about this, Ann. You were kidnapped and ended up in the mountains with a nice young man that had ridden in trucks from Washington, D.C. to Multnomah Falls, Oregon. You two happened to be in the same place at the same time and you have feelings for each other. What are the chances of that happening? Was it a coincidence? It sure makes me wonder. Maybe Dan *is* your soul mate."

"Maybe you're right, Mom, but right now, I'm going to take a nap. My brain is going into overload. I'm really confused." Ann curled up in the passenger seat and pulled a blanket over her legs.

Dan had located another dead tree leaning against a rocky area between some living firs. Just as he started trimming off the dead limbs, he heard two, long, truck-horn blasts in the distance. He wondered if Beverly and Ann were passing by on I-84. He would have to ask Ann if Bev had sounded the horn when they passed by the falls. Of course, it might have been another truck signaling to someone else.

It had only been a little more than an hour since the women had left the cabin. Dan was already missing Ann, but he was relieved she hadn't seen him react to one of his bad dreams. Maybe she would never have to know about them, but he didn't want to keep anything from her, either. Dan had never felt so close to a woman in such a short time. She was as gentle as a mother with her new baby, but as tough as a marine.

The log Dan had recovered was nearly thirty feet long, so he had to cut it into manageable lengths to carry back to the cabin. It took him almost an hour to cut the log into eight shorter pieces which he could manage. It was nearly two-hundred yards back to the cabin, but he had to get the fuel back before the persistent rainy weather began. He carried the ax and saw to the garage, feeling good about his progress. He would bring the wood back to the cabin the next day. In the meantime, he had to get lunch and feed the dogs. Dan wanted to spend the afternoon working with Duchess and the puppies. He had to remember to be very patient.

It was about five in the afternoon when the phone rang. Dan frowned as he answered the phone. It couldn't be Ann; it was too soon for her to have reached Boise.

"Hello?"

"Hi, Dan. This is Detective Andrews. If you're going to be there tomorrow, I'll drop off your weapons."

"Hi, Detective. I'll be here in the morning. I'll be in the woods bringing firewood back to the cabin, so I'll be coming and going. I've got a flying lesson in the afternoon."

"Okay. I'll bring your weapons around 10:00 a.m. You'll need to sign for them."

"All right, I'll be here then. See you tomorrow."

CHAPTER 15

A Foot of Snow

Ann called at 8:17 p.m. and talked with Dan for a half-hour. Just as they were about to hang up, Dan remembered to ask, "Did you sound your horn as you went by Multnomah Falls?"

Ann laughed and said, "You heard us! Mom thought you might. I wasn't sure about it. That was our last goodbye to you. I'm missing you already. Shall we call each other every other night? What do you think?"

"Sounds good to me. If we call every day, we'll run out of things to talk about. I'll call you day after tomorrow in the evening at eight o'clock. Okay?"

"Okay. Bye, Dan."

"Bye, Ann. Tell your mom hello for me."

The next morning Dan was up early to start a fire and feed the dogs. They played on the living room floor and fell asleep in front of the fire as Dan ate breakfast and watched the early morning news. While they were sleeping, Dan made his first trip into the woods to retrieve the logs. He carried back the biggest log, cut it into three pieces, split it, and piled it under the garage eaves.

Then he took the dogs for a walk around the tree line near the cabin. The puppies tried to chase a squirrel, but the little rodent was too quick for the uncoordinated little dogs. All they could do was emit yips.

Nomah and Glittle quickly lost interest in the squirrel and chased each other, growling, and wrestling around on the porch. Duchess wasn't very cooperative with Dan, showing little interest in learning things Dan had taught Henry. Dan put the dogs in the garage and continued retrieving and splitting logs.

Detective Andrews returned the two knives and the crossbow on November 4 as he had planned. The two men drank coffee and munched on Bev's cookies. Andrews stayed about twenty minutes and drove away with a couple of cookies in his jacket pocket. Dan carried back two more logs, split them, ate lunch, and left for the airport.

That evening, the weather report indicated the cold weather would arrive a day earlier than had originally been forecast. The next morning, November 5, Dan brought back the last of the logs, stacking the firewood at the side of the garage. When he finished, he estimated he had enough wood for about a month, maybe a little longer, if he conserved.

He could cook and heat the cabin using the fireplace. The propane was to power the generator if the electric power failed. Then he could decide when to have lights and TV. It would be easy to skip watching TV and spend time reading. The only programs of interest would be NFL games; Alaska didn't have a collegiate football team, so he didn't have a favorite university team, but he was starting to become a fan of the two big Oregon university teams, the Ducks and the Beavers.

At 7:00 p.m., Dan called Ann. It was 8:00 p.m. in Boise.

"Hello Dan. How are you doing at the cabin? How are the dogs?"

Dan brought Ann up to date on the visit by Detective Andrews, the firewood, and the dogs. Ann asked about his wound and said she was healing rapidly. She was feeling much better and had gone out for coffee with a classmate from high school. He worked for a home security firm, and business was very good. He had bought a house and was looking for someone to help him decorate. Ann volunteered; she didn't have anything to do until classes started in January.

"Well, you'll have fun doing that. You won't have to worry about smoke damage and bullet holes. Are you going to call me in a couple of days?"

There was a long pause before Ann said, "Sure. Bye."

"Bye, Ann."

Dan wondered what had caused that long pause. If she wasn't serious, and really didn't care that much for him, he hoped she would just say something. The sooner he knew, the better. He didn't want to continue thinking about them being together if they didn't share the same feelings for one another. He sat and looked at the phone for several minutes before cleaning up the kitchen and going to bed.

The alarm woke Dan at 6:00 a.m. He had been dreaming, but it wasn't his usual nightmare. He had been piloting a bush plane in the back country of Alaska and had to land on water. The plane had flipped over, he was struggling to get out of the inverted, sinking airplane. The ice-cold water was sapping his ability to get to the surface; he was running out of breath. He sat on the bed thinking, *reading that book about aircraft crashes before going to sleep was not a good idea.* The cabin was cold, so he built a fire, opened the door to the garage, and the dogs rushed in. As soon as Dan started preparing breakfast, the dogs, led by Nomah, joined him in the kitchen, waiting patiently for their food and water.

Patience didn't survive for long; Nomah and Glittle were underfoot as soon as they smelled the uncooked bacon. Dan filled the dog dishes and water bowls. It was amusing to watch the animals attack their food. That's when Dan realized he had fed the puppies only once the previous day. He had to remember to give the little ones two meals a day. They were burning lots of calories with all their activity and were growing like weeds.

They wouldn't be little much longer. Dan wished he had a camera to record their growth, but he had other priorities for his money. When the Sterlings returned, Dan was going to fly back to Alaska. He hoped the ticket wouldn't be too expensive. Alaska was beckoning, but the trip was still three months away. The calendar was going to be covered with black *X* marks by the time he was ready to leave.

Cooking bacon over the fire in the living room fireplace was not easy. Dan needed a grill of some sort to hold the cast-iron skillet over the burning logs. His mouth watered when he thought of French toast and pancakes cooked over the fire, but he had to check to see how much syrup was available in the pantry. Without syrup, Dan's breakfasts in the cabin would be ruined. If snowed in, he couldn't get more syrup. Dan had to laugh at himself, thinking of a pregnant woman's cravings, sending her tired husband out late at night to get what she craved. In that case, open-all-night convenience stores were a blessing.

Dan opened the door to the pantry and scanned the rows of cans and boxes. He spotted a box labelled maple syrup, but was anything in the box? He stepped into the little room and opened the container and found four-unopened plastic bottles of syrup. Dan was set for at least a month, probably 'til Christmas, before having to reorder, even if he ate pancakes every day. After today's flying lesson he would make a metal support for the skillet. Tomorrow morning would start with pancakes; he could almost taste them.

The afternoon passed quickly. Vic had Dan take a written test sample and then had him help her install a new altimeter in one of the planes. After dinner, Dan felt content sitting on the sofa reading, but after a few minutes, his mind began to wander, so he placed a pencil between the pages, and laid the book on the floor. It was time to make a trivet to support the skillet over the fire.

The dogs were asleep in the garage. The sounds from outside the cabin had changed; there had been a shift in wind direction. Dan opened the front door, listened, and looked at the tree tops swaying in the wind, now coming from the southwest instead of the east. With a cold front coming from the north and the warmer humid winds from the southwest, Dan suspected that snow would be falling before long.

He donned his coat and gloves, and went in the garage. While searching through a bin of metal odds and ends, he extracted a piece of heavy screen, and a metal rod about four feet long. The dogs were awake now, so he put them in the house. A half-hour later, he had a tall trivet to support his skillet over the fire. A hacksaw and welder had been put to good use.

Visions of hot cakes smothered in maple syrup came to mind as Dan stepped over Nomah to get to the fireplace. Installation of the trivet over burning logs was supposed to be easy. Unfortunately, the burning logs were not cooperative, and as soon as he began moving the logs, all three dogs became active; Glittle and Nomah wanted to play. Duchess had moved to the kitchen and had begun lapping water from her bowl as Dan moved the puppies away from the fireplace. Nomah wouldn't give up, so Dan shut the wire curtain shielding the fire and said, "Come on, let's go outside."

Duchess recognized the words and moved to the front door, the pups close behind. Opening the door was a bit of a problem with all three dogs trying to get out simultaneously. Dan slowly swung the door open, pushed out on the screen door, and the dogs ran from the cabin, jumped to the ground and ran behind the garage. Dan grabbed his flashlight, shut and locked the door, and followed Duchess, Glittle, and Nomah over the bridge and into the woods. The dogs headed for the miner's shack with Dan trying to keep up.

When Dan got within 30 yards of the shack, he could hear Duchess growling and the puppies yipping. As Dan neared the shanty, he knew immediately why the dogs were barking. They had discovered a skunk, and it had taken refuge in the shack; the odor was as foul as Dan had ever detected from Alaskan skunks. Now, he began to worry about the dogs getting sprayed. Getting the stench out of a dog's fur was not in his plan for the day.

He removed his coat and held it like a Spanish bullfighter would hold a cape. In place of a sword, Dan held the flashlight and a good sized branch and nudged the skunk into the cave behind the shack. As soon as the skunk was out of the dog's reach, Dan closed the door and wedged it shut with a pine cone. Pepe would have to exit the tunnel through the rear entrance, or eat his way through the logs in the door. Dan put his coat back on after giving it a sniff.

"Come on, Duchess, let's go home!"

As soon as Dan and Duchess turned away from the miner's shack and started back to the cabin, Glittle and Nomah followed in little bursts of running, then stopping to sniff objects along the way. When Duchess crossed the bridge behind the cabin she stopped, put her nose in the air and waited for Dan to catch up. Glittle and Nomah ran across the bridge and headed to the front of the house. The last of the sun's rays had vanished.

"What do you smell, girl? Is it a change in the weather?" Duchess whined and followed closely behind Dan to the front door where the puppies were waiting. As the door was opened, Nomah stuck his nose into the cabin and scampered into the kitchen. Dan had to laugh. "Could you be hungry, Nomah?" Dan fed the dogs and sat down on the sofa, picked up his book, and read a few more pages. After a few minutes of reading, he got up, warmed some coffee in the microwave, and got two of Bev's cookies from the big, pink, ceramic pig on the countertop. As he went back to his book, he glanced outside—it was snowing—large flakes were beginning to cover the ground near the porch.

Snow fell all evening, and when Dan went to bed at midnight, the snow was still coming down. He built up the fire, looked at the puppies sleeping on the sofa, and noticed Duchess's slow breathing as she slept on the floor in Henry's place next to the fire. She still missed her mate, but no longer searched for him outside. She had finally realized Henry wasn't coming back.

Dan got up at 6:00 a.m., looked out the bedroom window to see nothing but white. Tree limbs were sagging under the weight of the snow. It was still snowing, however, the white crystals were falling in tiny, swirling-flakes instead of the huge ones that had dropped from the sky the night before. Dan put on slippers, a robe, and went into the living room. All three dogs looked up and watched Dan stir the coals, add three more small logs to the fire, and put the trivet in place. It was November 7—Ann should call today.

He could hear the thumps on the living room floor when he went in the kitchen. Glittle and Nomah had jumped down from the sofa and joined Dan. "I think you guys had better go outside for a few minutes." He let the puppies out on the front porch and they just stood there looking at the snow. The first two steps were hidden, so the white stuff was about a foot deep. Dan put on his coat, got a snow shovel from the garage, and dug a path to the driveway. Nomah and Glittle both made some yellow snow and ran back up on the porch. Duchess was next. She came out, walked to the driveway, then bounded through the snow, and disappeared around the side of the garage where the firewood was stacked. She apparently wanted some privacy for her bathroom break.

Before feeding the dogs, Dan took off his wet slippers and coat. After pulling on a pair of thick argyle socks, he made pancake batter. The skillet was sprayed with cooking oil, placed on the trivet, and loaded with three islands of batter. He flipped the pancakes with a spatula, keeping close attention so they wouldn't burn. Dan wanted to enjoy his first pancake breakfast without massive carbon deposits.

Back in the kitchen, Dan placed three large, triangular shaped pancakes on a dinner plate, sat down, smeared a slab of butter on the stack, and added an adequate amount of maple syrup. He got up to get a mug of coffee, and when he returned to the table, he decided more syrup was needed. Pretending to be a little boy again, he smiled, and looked around the cabin. If his mother were watching, she would scold him for using too much syrup. He couldn't see her, so he poured syrup over the stack of pancakes until it puddled on the plate. His father had never said anything about the syrup. Now he was ready to eat!

He was about half-way through his stack of pancakes when the phone rang. Vic was calling to tell Dan to stay home. Travel was too treacherous with all the snow and ice on the roads. She said she would call back when they would be able to continue at the airport.

CHAPTER 16

Isolated

The pancakes tasted better than the ones he had at Shari's back in Boise. Maybe it was the ambience. He was on his own; he could lick his plate if he wanted, and he had three dogs for companions; each having a distinctive personality, which Dan imagined to be like having three children. Cooking over the fire in a warm cabin blanketed with over a foot of fresh snow seemed to make the pancakes taste better than any restaurant food he had ever eaten. However, there was an adjustment to make. Next time he would prepare bacon first.

Of even more importance than pancakes and dogs, in the not too distant future, after the nightmares had vanished, and when he had a dependable income, he hoped to have a wife with whom he could share his adventures. At the moment, Ann was his only love interest. She was smart, fun to be with, and good looking. Dan smiled and looked at his dirty dishes.

After cleaning up the dishes, Dan picked up the phone to call in an order for eggs, whole wheat bread, and butter. After Bev made all those cookies, the eggs and butter were running low. *Huh! No dial tone.* The snow had probably broken a tree limb which knocked down the phone line. Dan tried the light switch and the power was off, too. He hadn't noticed the lights being off. Reflected light from the snow and the light from the fire had illuminated the interior of the cabin without using artificial light.

It was time to get the generator running so he could check the weather report. But before he dressed to go outside, Dan looked through all the drawers in the kitchen, bedrooms, and garage trying to find some batteries for a small multiband radio that he found in the master bedroom closet. He only found a few discharged batteries and they were the wrong type. He needed a rectangular nine-volt battery.

After getting ready to go outside in the falling snow, he put more logs on the fire. The dogs seemed content to lie on the floor and watch Dan move around the cabin. It took him about five minutes to get the generator running. He flipped a switch labeled *house*, went back inside, and turned on the TV. After the system rebooted, he selected a news/weather broadcast and found out the extent of the storm. Elevations above 4,000 feet had received from 20 inches to two feet of snow, and above 8,000 feet, the new snow was over three feet deep.

The old Columbia River Highway was closed and would not be open for at least a week. The narrow winding road was difficult to plow for fear of damaging the decorative concrete, rock bridges, and abutments that were constructed in the 1930s. But, as soon as roads were cleared of snow and debris, crews would be fixing power and communication lines. Forest service personnel, on snowmobiles, would be patrolling roads leading into the mountainous areas.

Dan felt fortunate. He had everything he needed to last at least two weeks, maybe longer, if he conserved propane. He couldn't imagine running out of firewood or food; the wood he had cut and split would last at least a month, and the pantry was full. He had plenty of syrup; he only needed eggs. Dan might have to hike to the nearest neighbors, about a half-mile away, to borrow eggs. The Sterlings had made a map showing their neighbors' homes. The owners' names were listed and each site was circled in ink. There were snowshoes in the bedroom closet, and Dan could leave the dogs in the garage with food and water while he was gone. But first, he would see how long he could last without venturing out.

Dan sat down on the sofa and scratched Nomah's back. Nomah rolled over against Dan wanting more attention. It was amusing how Duchess and Glittle slept so soundly, even when Nomah was making noises with Dan. Dan thought of what his father would be saying, "*They are typical women, letting the men work while they sleep in. No wonder they live longer than men.*" Dan smiled as he watched the sleeping dogs and rubbed Nomah's back. He wondered if some day he would make that comment.

He switched off the television, and turned off the generator. He could read without artificial light until late afternoon. Chapter eight of his book was about navigation with problems to work at the end of the chapter. He read for about ten minutes and put the book down, realizing that Ann wouldn't be able to call him. That meant he would not hear her voice for at least a week, maybe longer.

It was the first time in his life that he saw the advantage of having a cell phone. *Oh, that's right, cell phones won't work here.* It might be too late. Dan had already felt Ann's interest in their relationship had waned, perhaps beyond recovery. As soon as he could call Boise, he would talk with Bev. She would give him the facts about Ann.

The below-freezing temperatures lasted for eight days. On November 14, the sun broke through the clouds and the snow began to melt. Dan went out to look around for damage to the cabin, but everything appeared normal. The dogs were happy to get out of the garage, running in and out of the snow for about ten minutes. Glittle and Nomah chased snowballs tossed in their direction, but Duchess had little interest in the snow. Dan figured she had seen plenty of snow in her lifetime in Minnesota.

As Dan was going back in the cabin, he heard engines. The sounds grew louder and two snowmobiles glided over the snow and stopped in the driveway, still covered with about six-inches of snow. The drivers, a man and a woman, shut off their engines and walked over to the porch. It was Susan and Herb, the two rangers he had seen twice before.

Dan shook hands and said, "Glad to see you. I haven't seen anyone in over ten days." Duchess started barking, so Dan said, "Just a minute," and let the dogs out of the cabin. Duchess sat down on the porch after sniffing both rangers. Glittle and Nomah were extremely excited, wagging their tails, their bodies seemed to be moving at random. They couldn't keep still. Susan dropped to her knees and began petting the puppies. She wore a cap, earmuffs, a heavy coat, and had removed her gloves to pet the dogs. Susan's attention caused Nomah and Glittle to settle down

"What are their names? They are so cute."

"The smaller one is a female named Glittle and her big brother is Nomah. Their mom is Duchess."

Susan replied, "Oh, I remember. Their daddy was shot. I'm so sorry he didn't make it. Are you going to take them with you to Alaska?"

Dan suddenly realized he hadn't thought out the difficulties associated with taking *three* dogs on an airplane to Alaska. "You know, I'm not sure. I'll probably take Nomah, but I don't know about Duchess and Glittle."

"Well, I'm looking for a dog. I'd love to have Glittle," Susan smiled. "I'll give you my number. Please call me if you decide to only take Nomah with you."

Herb spoke up, "*I* don't need a dog, but is there anything *you* need?"

Dan smiled and answered, "I could use a dozen eggs." Dan expected a laugh, but Herb walked over to his snowmobile and opened a case behind the seat. He walked back to Dan and handed him a dozen eggs.

"Here you are. Complements of the State of Oregon. Anything else?"

"No thanks. But thanks for the eggs. I didn't think you'd have eggs with you. I was going to hike over to my neighbors to see if they had some to spare. Let me get you guys something." Dan went to the kitchen, put a dozen cookies in a plastic bag, and returned to the porch. Herb was petting Duchess. Her tail was wagging and she licked Herb's hand. Dan handed the cookies to Susan and said, "These were made by Beverly Olson, the mother of the girl that was kidnapped. They're very good. Once you start eating them, you won't want to quit." Dan smiled and continued, "They're like potato chips."

Herb commented, "Good thing you didn't hike over there, Dan. Efren and Elaine Sandoval aren't home. We were just there. Their cabin is locked up tight. I've been thinking about your dog, Duchess. I might know someone that could use a friend. My mother lives alone and she might be interested in a pet. I'll tell her about Duchess. Here's my card. Give me a call before you leave for Alaska."

"I'll do that, maybe before Christmas. A dog for Christmas—might be a good present, but I'll have to think about splitting up the dogs. The pups haven't been anywhere else, but maybe they'll adjust quickly.

They're all very smart. Say, do you have any idea when the phone line and power will be fixed?"

Herb replied, "We'll turn in a report tonight. A crew should be out here in a day or two. Most of the downed lines in the city are repaired. Suz, give Dan your number. You can write it on the back of my card." Herb handed his card to Susan, who wrote on the back and handed it to Dan. Herb watched Dan stick the card in his coat pocket.

"Well, we'd better get going. It was nice talking to you. Enjoy the eggs. Ready, Suz?"

"Yep. Don't forget to call me about the female puppy, Dan. I'd really love to have Glittle—she's beautiful."

"Okay. Thanks for coming by, and thanks again for the eggs." Dan and the three dogs were on the porch by the door. They watched the rangers start their snow mobiles, and Dan waved as the rangers drove away. Dan turned, opened the door, and the dogs ran into the cabin. Dan laughed. "You know where it's warm, don't you?"

Dan put the eggs in the refrigerator and replaced the snow and water in the bottom freezing compartment. Most of the snow in the compartment had melted. He had thought of putting the frozen food outdoors, but animals might be attracted, so that idea quickly evaporated.

CHAPTER 17

Conversations

Two days after the rangers had visited with Dan, a power company truck stopped at the cabin to announce the power had been restored. Dan was already aware of that because the lights had come on 30 minutes earlier. Just after the power company truck left, the phone rang. A computer voice informed Dan that the telephone line was now working. The communications company was sorry service had been curtailed, but falling tree limbs sometimes caused interruption of service, especially in rural areas.

A few minutes after the phone company's call, the phone rang again. Dan thought it was the company again, but it was Vic. She was postponing the flying lessons until after Thanksgiving; she would be out of town.

Dan looked at his watch; it was 3:35 p.m. in Boise. He dialed Ann's number.

"Hello, Dan."

Dan recognized Bev's voice and asked, "Hi, Bev. Is Ann there?"

"No, Ann is with a high school friend. She's helping him decorate his house. They've been pretty thick the last couple of weeks. Ann tried to call you but the phone was disconnected."

"I wondered about that. The phone line and the electrical power were down for about ten days. We had more than a foot of snow and some broken limbs knocked down the wires. They were just fixed today."

"I'll tell Ann what happened. Ann and her friend spend too much time together, in my opinion. I don't care for him much, but Ann thinks he's wonderful. To tell the truth, I think Ann might not go back to school in the spring. She might get married before she finishes with nursing school. I can't say much; I don't want to cause any ill feelings. She's our only offspring. Just so you know, her friend's name is Josh Springer. Something about him bothers me, but I can't figure out what it is."

"Well, Bev, I appreciate your candor. I've been thinking about Ann and me in Alaska, but I didn't think she would find someone else so quickly. I thought she would finish nursing school before she got serious—at least that's what I'd hoped. By that time, I'd have had a job and known better what my future holds. Oh! I think I've found some people to adopt Glittle and Duchess. I'm going to take Nomah with me to Alaska."

"I'm sorry to tell you about Ann. You know, I think you two would have been a great pair, but I can't select who Ann marries. Maybe that's a good thing. I just hope Ann's not making a big mistake, but I guess time will tell. I'm glad you've found good homes for the dogs. Keep in touch and let me know when you leave for Alaska. Okay?"

"Okay—Mom. I'll keep in touch. Have a nice holiday season. Give Ann my best wishes. Bye."

"Bye, Dan. Enjoy the holidays with the dogs."

"One last thing, Bev. Your cookies are really good."

"Thank you. I'm happy you like them. Bye."

Dan hung up the phone, sat on the sofa, and pondered. *Why had Ann gotten away from the things we discussed? Maybe it was something I said, or did, or didn't do. Was she just looking for security?* He closed his eyes and shook his head, trying to get Ann out of his thoughts. He needed to concentrate on getting his pilot's license, take care of the dogs, and plan the rest of his trip to Alaska. He had to develop plans A and B, or maybe plan C, if insurmountable problems arose with the other plans. Now Dan was just putting in the time at the cabin until the Sterlings returned, except for some tune-ups on the jeep. Maybe he would find a girl in Alaska, someone a little more settled and not easily drawn away from her goals.

Dan wondered if his desire to become a bush pilot was genetic, his father loved dealing with life on the edge of danger, but he had always been careful, and then—he never came back. How would Dan find enough money to buy a plane? He had to be patient. He would start by working for Uncle Max and begin saving for a plane. How long it would take to make a down payment? Would he buy a new plane or a used one? Maybe he was getting ahead of himself—first, he had to learn how to fly, but Vic said he was making better than average progress.

Dan kept thinking about Herb Edmond's mother and her desire for a pet. Duchess would be an ideal animal, but were the puppies old enough to be separated from their mother? As soon as he got time off from the airport, which should be in about a week, he would take a trip to the animal clinic. He had to get the answers to several questions. He could call the clinic, but perhaps it would be better to see the vet in person; besides, the dogs needed some shots.

He placed an order for dog food, bacon, eggs, and some grape jam, and called the animal clinic to make an appointment. The next day, Dan put the dogs in the jeep and drove to the lock box. Surprisingly, the dogs were well-behaved, staying in the jeep until they arrived at the box. Nomah jumped out first, followed by Glittle and Duchess. When Dan opened the box, the three dogs wanted to see what was in it. Dan picked up Duchess and let her look in the box, then Nomah, followed by Glittle.

On the way back to the cabin, Nomah tried to get into the grocery bags. He must have smelled the bacon or the dog food. Dan put away the food and called the Department of Motor Vehicles to obtain a temporary license for the jeep. The appointment at the animal clinic was the next day. They were given shots, weighed, and blood was drawn to check for problems. Nomah weighed 36 pounds, Glittle, 26, and Duchess, 75. Glittle was a little light for her age, but Nomah was slightly above the normal curve for a male. The vet asked if Nomah was eating Glittle's food in addition to his own. Dan hadn't noticed, but said he would watch for signs of competition for food.

Dan ordered a turkey, cranberry sauce, and pumpkin pie for Thanksgiving. The dogs followed Dan into the kitchen every time he checked on the status of the cooking bird. The odor from the cooking turkey was something they had never experienced. On Thanksgiving Day, Dan watched football, read more about airplanes, and fed the dogs their regular food—spiced with turkey giblets. After eating, he took the dogs on a walk to the lock box, back up to the miner's shack, and returned to the cabin. They were all tired after the exercise and took a nap.

Eight days after Thanksgiving, on Friday, December 5, Dan decided to call Herb Edmond to ask if his mother still wanted to adopt Duchess. Dan dialed the number on the card Herb had given him.

"Hello."

"Hello Herb. This is Dan Newcomb. Do you think you could bring your mother out to see Duchess?"

"Sure can. How about tomorrow? Saturday's my day off. We could drive out and let them get acquainted. Would 1:00 p.m. be all right?"

"Sounds good to me. I'll be watching for you. Thanks."

"Thanks for calling, Dan. I think my mom will bond with Duchess. What about Glittle? Should I get Susan to come out, too?"

Dan reflected for a moment. "Ah—yeah. That's a good idea. We'll see how they all get along, and I can tell them about the recent visit to the vet. Say, what's your mom's name?"

"It's Rochelle. See you tomorrow. Bye."

"Bye, Herb."

Dan had put off the inevitable long enough. Glittle and Duchess had to be provided with good homes, and Dan had confidence in the rangers and their families. Both dogs would be with loving people, who would take good care of them. Dan felt an emotional tug at his heart when he thought of Glittle and Duchess being gone. He would have to spend more time with Nomah, teaching him things he would have to know when living in Alaska. Dan had been thinking about an exercise program to develop Nomah's strength and endurance. Sunday would be a good day to start Nomah's new training.

Dan hung up the phone and started considering what the next three months would be like for Nomah without Duchess and Glittle. He reviewed everything he knew about the two dogs so he wouldn't forget to mention anything to their new owners. Dan was finally able to go to sleep around two o'clock Saturday morning. When he got up, he watched the dogs as they ate. It would be their last day together.

It was going to be difficult for him to say goodbye to Glittle and Duchess. He had some of the same feelings when Bev and Ann drove away, but this was different; the dogs had become dependent on Dan, and he truly loved them. He had originally thought the dogs would spend the rest of their lives with him, but maybe it was better this way; he wouldn't have to suffer three losses when they passed. Dan resolved to give Nomah the best care possible; he wanted Nomah to be with him for a long time.

A white Suburban arrived in the driveway at precisely 1:00 p.m. Dan put down his book and walked to the front door. Nomah was already there, ready to investigate the noises. Glittle joined her brother, but Duchess stayed beside the fire. Dan opened the door just as Herb was reaching for the door knocker, a brass ram's head.

"Hi, Ranger."

"Hi, Dan. I'd like you to meet my mother, Rochelle."

Dan opened the screen door, letting the dogs out. They were so excited they began jumping on both Rochelle and Herb. Rochelle picked up Glittle as she reached to shake hands with Dan.

"Pleased to meet you, Mrs. Edmond. Sorry about the dogs; they get very excited when people come by. We don't have many visitors out here. Come in and meet Duchess.

She's being lazy today—enjoying the warmth of the fire. I think she's aware that something is going on. Have a seat."

"Thank you Dan. Call me Rochelle. This is a very nice cabin. Herb told me it belongs to the Sterlings. How long will you be here?"

"Until February, but I don't want to postpone finding owners for the dogs until the last minute. I want to make sure they are in nice homes before I leave. Say, Herb, what happened to Susan? I thought she was coming with you."

"She told me to tell you she'd be a little late. She wanted to buy a pet carrier for Glittle so she could secure the dog in the back seat of her Honda."

Dan sat down next to Rochelle and called Duchess, who slowly got up and walked over to Dan. Dan had Duchess sit and shake hands with Rochelle. Rochelle dropped to her knees on the rug and put her arms around Duchess.

"Duchess, you are so pretty. How would you like to come live with me? I have something for you." Rochelle opened her purse, pulled out a small plastic bag of doggie treats, and held one out to Duchess. She sniffed it, took the treat, and returned to the hearth to chew on it. Glittle and Nomah came over to Rochelle, tails wagging. "Oh-oh! I think I started something." She smiled at Dan and asked, "Can they have a treat, too?"

"Sure. They'll all love you."

CHAPTER 18

Goodbyes

Dan was impressed with Rochelle. She was quiet around the dogs and didn't appear to be disappointed in Duchess's apparent lack of interest in her. Rochelle scratched Nomah's neck and ears and gave him a tap on the rear. She repeated the procedure with Glittle; both puppies lay down at her feet, tails wagging. Rochelle suddenly stood up and said, "Dan, could you show me the miner's shack? Maybe we can take the dogs."

"Sure, good idea. They need to get outside and run around. Wagging their tails doesn't use much energy."

As Herb, Rochelle, Dan and the dogs were moving from the porch toward the garage, a little blue Honda pulled up and parked next to the Suburban. Susan waved and said, "Sorry I'm late," as she slid out of the driver's seat. "Hi, Rochelle! Hi, guys. Hi, dogs." She laughed and said, "I think I got everybody."

Everyone said, "Hi, Susan," as she joined the group.

Susan asked, "Are you going somewhere?"

Dan replied, as the puppies started jumping at Susan's legs, "We're going up to the shack to give the dogs some exercise. They need to run off some energy."

Susan looked toward the tree line behind the garage, pointed, and said, "Up there?"

"Uh-huh," Dan answered and smiled.

"I'd better change to my boots then; just a sec."

"Oh! Me too," Rochelle remarked.

Rochelle walked quickly to the Suburban, opened the backseat door, climbed in, and changed her shoes to a pair of nice-looking cowboy boots. Susan had put on her regular work-boots. Both women wore pants, Susan jeans and Rochelle brown slacks; probably too good to wear out in the forest, but she didn't seem to care. They both wore light jackets over heavy sweaters.

Herb looked at Dan and shook his head as if to say, "I don't believe it." He whispered to Dan, "Why didn't they wear boots from the beginning? Did they think there were sidewalks up here?"

Dan smiled, looked back at Herb and said, "Boots aren't very sexy."

Herb laughed and said, "Let's go, ladies. Dan, lead the way."

Dan crossed the bridge, with Susan close behind, followed by Herb and Rochelle.

Herb grabbed his mother's arm a couple of times when it looked as if she might lose her balance. The pups ran ahead of Dan, seeming to know where they were headed. Duchess stayed back with Herb and Rochelle. Duchess understood where the treats came from.

Susan, Dan, and the pups moved rapidly until they were out of sight of Herb and Rochelle. Rochelle was getting out of breath, so she stopped for a moment. She said, "Herb, you go ahead. I'll be along. Duchess and I will enjoy each other's company. She'll lead me to you. She'll smell and hear her puppies."

"You sure, Mom?"

"Yes. You go ahead. We'll be right along."

Herb increased his speed, and was out of sight in about ten seconds. Duchess sat beside Rochelle waiting for the gray-haired lady to begin moving forward again. As soon as Rochelle began to walk, Duchess followed. Duchess seemed to know Rochelle needed to move more slowly than the others. Rochelle looked down at Duchess and said, "You are a very nice girl, Duchess. We're going to be very good friends, aren't we? Here, I have something for you." Rochelle removed a treat from her jacket pocket and gave it to Duchess. Ten minutes later Duchess and Rochelle joined the others at the miner's hut.

The skunk was gone and so was the odor. Dan related the skunk story, told how he and Ann had avoided being shot, and where the dogs were when he originally discovered the little shack. They looked around for about five minutes and started back to the cabin. As they walked, a small plane passed overhead. Susan and Herb looked up, smiled, and Herb said, "That's Vic Reeves's plane."

As Dan watched the plane disappear, he said, "You know the pilot?"

"Yep. Vic sometimes helps us with rescues. Sighting from the air can guide us to a stranded hiker. I'll have to introduce you."

"That's not necessary, Herb, she's been giving me lessons for the last few weeks."

"Shoot, I wasn't going to mention that Vic was a woman. I wanted to see what happened when you found out."

Susan commented, "Herb's a bit of a tease, always trying to get people in trouble. When we first met, he told me he had put in for a transfer—didn't want to work with a woman. I got mad at him and he confessed that he was just kidding. He found out that he shouldn't mess with me."

Herb was grinning. "Yeah, Suz let me know I had to watch my step with her."

When they arrived back in front of the cabin, Susan looked at Dan and said, "Do you think I can take Glittle home with me? I bought a carrier so she can ride safely in the back seat." She looked at her watch and then continued, "A gentleman friend of mine is going to help me get the house ready for Glittle. He's supposed to meet me at 3:00 p.m."

Herb grinned and said, "Is it Tom, Dick, or Harry?"

Susan grinned, but said defiantly, "None of your business, Herbie." Susan walked over to Dan and whispered, "His name is David Nestrom; we've been dating. He's a Portland policeman."

Dan replied, "I don't see why you shouldn't take Glittle with you, but you'd better keep her on a leash for a week or so—until she gets used to her new home. If she runs away, she might get hurt trying to find her way back here. This place has been her whole world up to now."

"I understand; I'll take good care of her. Does she need any shots?"

"I'll get the vet's records for you. They're in the cabin." Dan went to the kitchen table, picked up Glittle's veterinary report, and gave it to Susan. He had also prepared a bag of food for Glittle so Susan could continue with the same feeding schedule Dan had been following. Dan suggested she check with the vet if she wanted to change to a different brand of food.

Susan thanked Dan, picked up Glittle, put her in the Honda, and returned to give Rochelle a hug. After saying goodbye, Susan got in her car and drove away. Dan could already feel a hollow in his heart. *What would it be like when Duchess was gone?* He would just have to adjust to the new situation; he had done that plenty of times in the military, but this was different. He had grown to love his dogs.

"Well, Dan. I heard what you said to Susie. I'll be careful with Duchess, too, but I think that these two old ladies should get along fine. How old do you think Duchess is?"

"The vet told me Duchess was probably six or seven. I guess that would place her in her mid-40s as a human."

"Oh, she's just a youngster, then. I'm 63, going on 80," Rochelle laughed.

"Mom, you don't look a day over 70."

Rochelle grinned, "You'd better be careful, Herbert. I'll train Duchess to take a chunk out of your posterior." She looked at Dan and smiled, "I call him Herbert when his jokes aren't funny."

Dan gave Duchess' vet report and a large bag of food to Rochelle. She shook hands with Dan, thanked him, and gave him a hug. Herb helped Dan load Duchess into the Suburban and gave his mom an assist into the back seat with the dog. Herb shook hands with Dan and said, "Thanks for everything, and make sure you continue to work with Vic. She's top notch. Maybe you'll be able to fly before you get back to Alaska."

As the Suburban drove away, Dan could see Duchess looking out the back window as if to say goodbye, wondering where she was going. Dan wiped his eyes and turned around to Nomah, who was sitting on the porch by the front door, and said, "It's just the two of us now, Nomah. I've changed my mind. We'll rest tomorrow, and on Monday, we'll start a whole new routine. Let's go inside and get warm by the fire."

CHAPTER 19

Nomah Visits the Airport

Sunday was breakfast experimentation day. When Dan made the pancake batter, he added some orange juice instead of milk. The pancakes tasted fine, just a little more zest than they had when he used grape juice. That earlier experiment produced olive drab pancakes—army issue, but he didn't tamper with the eggs and bacon. Dan wondered if vitamin C was destroyed when the pancakes cooked. Something to research on the Internet.

Nomah and Dan hiked through the forest to see the Sandovals' place. Their day of rest would start in the afternoon. When they reached the house, no one was home, as the rangers had said. It was a nice looking, cinder block building covered with a rock veneer. It had a steel roof, much better than cedar or composition shingles because it was located among a stand of several large pine trees. The falling needles were a mess to clean off a roof, unless it was made of steel.

The excursion through the rough, hilly area between the Sterlings' and the Sandovals' mountain homes had been quite a workout. Dan found a plastic bowl on the porch and gave Nomah some water as he looked over the area around the cabin. The downed trees were covered with moss, as were the rocks, making walking a bit dangerous. In addition, wild blackberry vines, ready for trimming, grew everywhere. The thorns easily punctured Dan's pants. Apparently, the Sandovals hadn't been to their cabin in some time. A blue plastic tarp covered a large stack of firewood.

After the water break, Dan and Nomah made their way back to the cabin for lunch. As Dan was finishing lunch and cleaning up the kitchen, he realized that Nomah was awfully quiet. Dan walked into the living room and found Nomah sound asleep by the fire. The morning's activities had worn the puppy out. Dan sat down on the sofa, picked up his book, and started reading.

The cold steel blade sliced through his neck. Too late to react, there was nothing he could do about it. He tried to turn to see who his killer was, the blood oozing between his fingers as he attempted to stop the flow. His last thoughts were: *I'm going to die, the enemy has won. I'll never get back to Alaska.*

Dan suddenly woke up in a sweat and jumped to his feet. Nomah had gotten up from the hearth and stood looking at Dan. "It's all right, Nomah. I had another bad dream. Damn! I thought I was over those. You can tell when something is wrong, can't you? Maybe when I get involved with flying, those crazy dreams will go away for good—course, if I worry about falling out of the sky, they might come back, even more often." He smiled, knowing Nomah couldn't understand.

Dan sat back down on the sofa trying to clear the images from his thoughts—changing fighting to flying. The morning's exercise and saying goodbye to Duchess and Glittle Saturday afternoon had taken their toll. Nomah approached Dan, slowly wagged his tail a couple of times, and jumped up on the sofa. He curled up and laid his head in Dan's lap. "I think you're missing Duchess and Glittle, aren't you? Me too." Dan scratched Nomah's neck and ears and said, "Good boy, Nomah. We'll be all right, we just have to stay busy. We have each other."

Monday morning, December 7, Pearl Harbor Day, was going to be a nice day for flying. Dan remembered seeing a medium-size flag in storage in the garage. He used a step ladder to reach the flag staff holder mounted on the end of the garage above the door and inserted the pole. After putting the ladder away and walking toward the jeep, he turned and saluted the flag. Dan had never been very religious, but he said a short prayer for those people who had died in 1941.

The sun was out, a slight east wind was stirring the flag. The weatherman predicted three days of dry, sunny weather, although the high temperatures would only make it to the mid-40s. Dan watched birds searching for morsels to eat and items to line their nests. He sat in the rocking chair on the porch as he sipped his morning coffee. Nomah pushed the screen door open and sat beside the rocker.

"I'm going to leave you in the garage today, big boy. I'll try to get home early so we can take a walk."

Nomah yawned, looked up at Dan, and then lay down on the porch, apparently watching the birds, just as Dan was doing. After breakfast, Dan and Nomah played fetch with a stick for a few minutes before Dan got ready to drive to the airport. After putting Nomah in the garage with enough food and water for the day, Dan drove to Troutdale to see what Vic had planned. She was already at work when Dan arrived. They worked on an engine until 4:00 p.m.

As Dan drove back to the cabin, he began to wonder how Nomah was going to react to being shut up in the garage for hours at a time. Before Dan reached the cabin, he had decided to take Nomah to the airport on Tuesday. It wasn't right to leave Nomah alone for most of a day. He'd take food, water, a blanket, and a rope to keep Nomah from roaming around the airport. He made a mental note to get Nomah a good, strong collar. A piece of clothesline rope would serve as a temporary collar; it was soft, yet strong.

When Dan pulled into the gravel driveway, he could hear Nomah barking. Dan went in the cabin and opened the door to the garage. Nomah ran into the living room, circled the sofa, went into the kitchen, reversed direction, and jumped all over Dan.

"You're a bit excited, huh? Sorry I was late, Nomah. Tomorrow, you go with me. Okay?" Dan dropped to his hands and knees and wrestled with Nomah for a minute, then they went outside to play Frisbee. Nomah, however, didn't understand the game. When Dan tossed the disk, Nomah ran after it, got it between his teeth and ran away from Dan. Nomah seemed to love to frustrate Dan. When Dan approached to get the Frisbee, Nomah would run with it.

Dan wondered if Nomah was getting back for being locked in the garage all day. Nomah understood keep-away all too well. Nomah would run with the Frisbee, drop it, and wait for Dan to approach the disk. Nomah would bark, grab the disk and run away. Dan had to use treats to entice Nomah to return the disk. It would take a couple of days to get Nomah to play Dan's game.

Tuesday was supposed to be another nice day. When Dan woke, it was foggy, but by time to go to work, the fog had lifted, the sun was bright, but it was still cold in the mountains.

Dan gathered items for Nomah, put him in the jeep, and drove to the airport, arriving 10 minutes early. He waited in the jeep with Nomah for a few minutes until a white Ford 150 pickup drove up and parked next to the maintenance building. Vic locked her pickup, came over to the jeep, and saw Nomah sitting in the passenger seat.

"Oh! Is this Nomah? He's beautiful."

"Thanks. I guess I should have asked you if it was okay to bring him with me."

"It's okay, but will he be afraid of the planes? The engine noise can be pretty loud, especially at takeoff."

Dan thought a moment and said, "As long as he's near me, he'll be fine. I brought a blanket, food, and water."

Vic grinned and replied, "For you or the dog? I told you to bring a lunch, but we won't have time for a nap."

Dan laughed. "I like your sense of humor. I was afraid you might be serious all the time."

"Well, when I'm flying, I'm serious, but when I'm on the ground I can afford to joke around—a little bit. Let's get to work. We'll fly again tomorrow if that's all right with you."

Dan hadn't expected what he'd heard. "That sounds great!"

Vic smiled and replied, "I expected you to say *awesome*."

Dan laughed, and responded with a little swagger. "That expression is more for teenage girls than for a man of my experience."

Vic looked at Nomah, then Dan, and said, "I expected your dog to bark after that statement."

Dan grinned, nodding his head, "You're right. Nomah knows the truth when he hears it. He should have barked, but he's a little timid in the presence of a lady."

When Dan and Nomah got home, they had dinner and went outside. It had been dark since five o'clock, so they sat on the porch and listened to the incoming jets pass overhead on the way to PDX. The night sky was clear, the lights from planes, stars, and a crescent moon provided faint illumination to the trees surrounding the cabin. The only sounds were from jet engines and a train passing through the gorge hundreds of feet below.

There hadn't been an east wind for nearly ten days, and the weatherman on channel 12 had mentioned it looked like there wouldn't be a white Christmas. The day-time temperatures would be hovering in the mid-forties for at least the next week. Dan still had a plentiful amount of firewood for the slightly below-freezing nights.

After a half-hour on the porch, Dan and Nomah went into the cabin. Dan started a fire, sat down, and picked up one of the texts Vic had loaned him. The pop and crackle of the burning logs and the quiet surroundings reminded Dan of the long winters in Alaska. He put the memories out of his mind and started reading. Two hours with the text seemed to fly by before his yawns signaled it was time for bed. It had been a long day.

CHAPTER 20

Ground, Air, and Sea

Dan put some finishing touches on Terry's jeep during the evenings after returning from work with Vic. He touched-up the paint on the hood, changed the oil and filters, and tidied up the shop. Time in the cabin shop would now be limited. Thursday and Friday, Dan worked inside the cabin patching damaged areas he had missed earlier, and applied new finish over the tinted wood filler. Unless one knew where to look, the patches couldn't be seen.

Dan ate Cheerios, Wheaties, and oatmeal for breakfasts during the week, but went back to regular pancakes Saturday morning, December 12. He had had his fling with fruit juices in the pancake batter.

Rochelle Edmonds, who adopted Duchess, invited Dan and Nomah to Christmas dinner. Herb came with his date, Sari Martine, a Forest Service secretary, and Susan brought her fiancé, David Nestrom, and of course, Glittle. The three dogs were together again, probably for the last time, before Dan and Nomah would leave for Alaska. The dogs played together most of the afternoon, while Rochelle, Sari, and Susan got ready for Christmas dinner. When dinner was being served, Duchess wanted in the house. Rochelle let her in, expecting her to go to her blanket next to the fireplace, but Duchess lay down beside Dan at the dining table.

"I think she misses you, Dan," Rochelle commented.

Dan remarked, "I'm beginning to feel like a mother that couldn't take care of a new baby and gave it up for adoption. Duchess has a better home than I could give her—she just doesn't understand that."

When Dan said good night and drove off with Nomah, Duchess followed the jeep until it exited Rochelle's property. She sat for about ten seconds, watching the jeep disappear, and slowly returned to the porch where Rochelle waited.

Except for Christmas and New Year's, Dan spent at least six hours a day at the airport working with Vic until the end of January. Dan had accumulated almost all the hours of ground-training and three-quarters of the necessary flight-time for his private license. Vic was impressed with how quickly Dan had adapted to flying. She found it uncommon the way Dan diagnosed problems, and she recognized Dan possessed a sixth-sense of the causes of noises while flying. Dan knew almost as much about the construction of the planes as Vic did.

Vic had helped Dan obtain funds from a veteran's organization to assist with fuel costs and rental fees. The first week in February, Dan came to work expecting to be helping Vic with airplane maintenance, but when he walked into the hanger, Vic said, "You are soloing today, my friend."

"Really?"

"Uh-huh. Let's get you a rental. It will have insurance for an unlicensed pilot. Come on. Oh, you'd better tie up Nomah, he can't go with you."

Dan followed Vic into the flight office and signed paperwork for his flight.

Vic paid the fees, and Dan promised to pay her back from his wages. Dan didn't get nervous until he was back on the ground. He felt a little light-headed as he walked back to the shop. He had done everything correctly, in fact, almost perfectly. He was elated.

"How was it, Dan?" Vic was smiling as Dan entered the maintenance area and went over to Nomah, sat on the floor, and hugged his dog.

"I descended a little too fast. I had to goose it a bit just before I hit the runway, but it was fun. I just wish you had warned me that I would be soloing today."

"I didn't want you to worry and not be able to sleep last night. I wanted you to be rested, but now that you have flown alone, without any problems, the remaining flights should be easy. You're a good pilot."

"Thanks, Vic. What are we working on today?"

Before the end of the month, Dan had his license. The day he demonstrated his flying skills to the examiner, Phil Langford, he drank nearly half a bottle of Pepto-Bismol to relieve his upset stomach. The last time Dan had been that nervous was when he took his driver's test when he was 16. So much depended on passing the flight test, he couldn't help having an upset stomach. When he got back to the maintenance area, he threw the remaining Pepto-Bismol in the trash. He shouldn't have been worrying, the flight test was a snap, and Dan had received the highest score on the written exams of all Vic's students from the past 15 years.

Dan quit working with Vic after the third week of February. He had to get the cabin cleaned and in the best shape possible for the Sterlings' return to Portland. The night of the 27th, Dan received a call from Terry Sterling; they would arrive in Portland on March 2nd and come out to the cabin the following day.

Dan had to get ready to fly to Anchorage with Nomah. He needed Nomah's weight, so he picked up his buddy and stepped on the bathroom scale. The scale indicated 249 pounds, so Nomah's weight was slightly over 50 pounds. Now, he had to contact one of the airlines that flew pets to Anchorage, leaving from Portland.

The next day, Dan checked out airlines, but found Nomah would be confined to a pet carrier, isolated from Dan for the length of the trip. Nomah's veterinary papers, including a record of his rabies vaccination, had to be available for the airlines and at the city of entry into Alaska. Dan wasn't sure what he was going to do. He decided to wait and talk with Terry Sterling. Terry had probably forgotten more about the airline business than Dan would ever know.

He began to think about Plan B—travelling roads through British Columbia. Dan knew he would be able to find a ride with someone. The only problem he could foresee was that Nomah might be quarantined when crossing from Washington to BC. Dan searched the Internet and found that all Nomah needed was to be with his owner and have a valid rabies vaccination certificate. Dan's imagined problem was not a problem at all.

The phone rang at 8:30 the evening of March 2. Both Val and Terry were on the phone. They had gotten back to Portland just after lunch and had spent the rest of the afternoon unpacking and getting their city residence in order. Terry and Val talked with Dan for about five minutes and then said good night. They would pick Dan up and take him to lunch tomorrow. They had much to talk about. Dan agreed; he had some important questions for them about traveling to Alaska with Nomah.

The Sterlings' white SUV pulled up at the cabin at 11:30 the next morning. Val was driving. She beeped the horn, just once, when she stopped in the driveway. Dan came to the door, greeted Val with a hug, and Terry with a handshake.

"Are you tired from your trip?" Dan asked.

Val replied, "We got a full night's sleep last night, so we feel pretty good." She looked at Terry for his approval. Terry grinned and nodded. "How have you been, Dan? You had quite an experience."

"Oh, I'm over that now. Guess what? I have my pilot's license."

Terry replied, "Wow. You really have been busy. The cabin looks great. I don't see anything wrong. And who is that over by the fireplace?"

Dan snapped his fingers and Nomah came over to Dan and sat beside him. Val and Terry sat on the sofa and Dan said, "I'd like you to meet Nomah. He is the son of Henry, the dog that got killed during the incident. His sister, Glittle, is with Susan Lawrence, one of the forest rangers."

Val smiled and said, "We know Susan—she's very nice. She works with Herb Edmond, doesn't she?"

"That's right. Herb's mother, Rochelle, adopted Duchess, the puppies' mother."

"Well, Dan, you found some nice people to care for the dogs." Val continued, "We thought we'd eat at the Green Garden restaurant. Have you been there before?"

"No, I haven't. I don't eat out very often. I'm not used to fancy places."

"Oh, don't worry. It's not very expensive or really fancy. It's just nice."

"Okay. Let me put Nomah in the garage and I'll be with you."

On the way to the restaurant, Dan told the Sterlings how he found the old miner's shack and the dogs, had the confrontation with the kidnappers, and how he rescued Ann.

Terry commented, "If we had been here, we'd probably be dead by now, and the cabin would be nothing but cinders. Who knows what would have become of Ann."

Val commented, "It sounds like you are fond of Ann. Where is she now?"

"She went back to Boise. I don't think she feels the same way about me as I do about her. According to her mother, Ann is attracted to a guy she knew in high school."

They got out of the car and started walking to the restaurant entrance.

Val remarked, "Well, Dan, you won't have any trouble finding a good woman in Alaska."

As they walked into the restaurant, Dan replied, "I don't know about that." He grinned and continued, "There are a lot more men in Alaska than there are women."

As they ate, Dan told the Sterlings about his tentative plans for returning home. Terry recognized Dan's uneasy feelings. The plane ride would be quick, but expensive; travelling by road was cheap, but time consuming.

Terry asked, "What about plan C?"

Dan frowned at Terry and said, "Plan C?" Dan laughed, "I don't have a plan C."

"*You* don't, but *I* do." Terry put down his fork, wiped his mouth with his napkin and pulled his cellphone from his jacket pocket.

Val swallowed some wine and said, "Terry, who are you calling?"

Terry's eyes sparkled and he grinned, "Hugh Inman in Seattle."

"Oooh. What a good idea, dear." Val looked at Dan and smiled.

Dan looked at Val, and then Terry. He had no idea what was going on. "Hughie?"

"Yeah. Who's calling?"

"Terry Sterling, in Portland."

"Well, you old dog! How's your beautiful wife?"

"She's just fine. She says hi. Say, I have a question for you."

"Shoot."

"Do you have a barge going to Alaska in the near future—like in the next week?"

"As a matter of fact, I do. My son, Jack, is taking some heavy equipment to Anchorage on the tenth of the month. You and Val want a ride?"

Terry laughed. "No, Hughie, but I have a friend, Daniel Newcomb, and his dog, a 50-pound German shepherd puppy that need a ride. Dan is an Afghanistan war veteran. He's smart and a good worker."

"No problem. He can pay for meals—unless he works, then the meals are free. He'll have a small berth to himself—the berths are a little cramped, but warm. The trip takes 14 or 15 days. He's got to have papers from a vet for the dog—rabies, you know. Can he get to Bellingham by the tenth?"

"Just a sec—." Terry looked at Dan and asked, "Can you get to Bellingham in a week?"

"No problem. Who do I report to?"

"Hughie? Who does he report to? Have you got a number?" Terry motioned to Val to give him a pencil. She extracted a pen from her purse and handed it to Terry. He jotted a name and number on a napkin and said, "Thanks, Hughie, I owe you one. Tell Pam hello for us, okay? We'll be up that way this summer. Save me a beer. Bye."

"We'll be watching for you guys, and bring some of that Oregon wine. Bye."

Terry closed his phone and dropped it into his pocket. "Well, Dan, you've got a ride to Anchorage. If you work on the barge, your meals are free, otherwise you pay for them. You'll have a small cabin—not much room, but it's warm. He said you have to have a statement from a vet about Nomah having been vaccinated for rabies. It will take you two weeks to get to Anchorage."

"That's fantastic! I can't thank you enough. You two have been very good to me. That's the best news I've had since I passed the test for my pilot's license."

CHAPTER 21

Back on the Freeway

That evening, Dan got his possessions together, but had to leave the crossbow in the Sterlings' garage. The weapon was too awkward to carry, plus he didn't think truckers would want to risk giving a ride to a man with a large dog and a dangerous looking crossbow. When he got home, he would send his address to the Sterlings and money to pay for shipping the bow to Alaska. He called Rochelle and Susan to say goodbye and left a message on Vic's answering machine thanking her for all the help with his training. He promised to get in touch with her when he got settled. He invited her to come to visit so he could show her Alaska from the air.

The Sterlings came to the cabin the next day to pick up Dan and Nomah. When they dropped Dan and the dog off at the Troutdale truck stop on I-84, Dan could see tears in Val's pretty eyes. She gave Dan and Nomah each a hug and walked back to the car, but she couldn't say good-bye. Terry wished Dan well and shook hands with him and Nomah. Dan thanked Terry for his help getting a ride back home. The Sterlings waved good-bye as they drove away.

"Well, Nomah, we've got to find a ride to Seattle. Let's go to the visitor center and see what we can scare up, okay?" Nomah gave a little bark and they walked to the truckers' diner. There was a sign on the door saying no pets, so Dan snapped a leash on Nomah's collar and tied the leash to a newspaper vending machine.

"Stay, Nomah. No barking. I'll just be a few minutes." Dan entered the souvenir/snack-area and made his way to the check-out counter. He stepped up to the counter and waited for the cashier to turn around. The slightly over-weight young man was engrossed with arranging candy bars and wasn't aware of Dan. Dan cleared his throat and said, "Could you please answer a question?"

The plump kid, holding a candy bar, turned around, and said, "Yes, sir."

"Do you know of anyone going to Seattle?"

The pimply-faced kid said, "Haven't a clue," turned around and continued arranging candy bars and other snacks.

Dan wanted to say something sarcastic, but instead, said, "Thanks." Dan scanned the area, but didn't see anyone that even looked like a trucker. Wondering where the truckers were, Dan joined Nomah outside and watched a few rigs depart and a few others arrive. A brightly-colored semi pulled into the parking area and stopped. The trailer was painted bright-yellow, adorned with large colored vegetables. It had Eat Your Veggies written with bright-red, script letters in an arch across the vegetables. As the driver climbed down from the truck and walked toward the dining area, Dan gave him a thumbs-up and said, "Nice paint job!"

The stocky driver approached Dan and said, smiling, "I just drive the truck. I didn't paint it. This your dog?" He leaned down and scratched Nomah's head.

"Yep. That's Nomah, my growing boy. We're headed to Alaska—going that way?"

"Never been there. I'm going north though—headed to Federal Way."

Dan frowned, "Where's that?"

"That's between Olympia and Seattle. I've got a load of canned vegetables and sweet onions from Walla Walla going to supermarkets in Federal Way. I've got to be there tonight. Can't farm during February, so I drive trucks for a couple of months."

"I've got to get to Bellingham. Could you give us a ride?"

"Does your dog bite?"

Dan laughed. "Not to my knowledge, but he's never been hungry."

The man stuck out his hand to Dan and said, "I'm Billy Farrand. Join me for a cup of coffee; we'll talk about it."

Dan shook hands and replied, "I'm Daniel Newcomb—we really need a ride."

Billy was at least a half-foot shorter than Dan, and wore blue-striped, gray work pants, and a yellow T-shirt. He looked like a farmer. He was husky, but not fat, and all the while Dan talked to him, Billy smiled. Billy, who looked to be about 50, ran his hand over his crew-cut graying hair and grabbed the door handle. "Let's go in and take a load off."

"Stay, Nomah. I'll be right back."

Billy hiked up his pants and climbed up on a bar stool at the counter. He took a brief look at a dog-eared menu and put it back between the metal napkin holder and the salt and pepper shakers. Billy looked like a kid at a 1950s soda fountain until his beard and the lines in is face were noticed. A frizzy-haired blond waitress, holding a pencil and an order pad, appeared and said, "What can I do ya for?"

Billy said, "Ham and eggs on whole-wheat toast. Don't spare the butter. Black coffee—make that two, please." He looked at Dan, who smiled and nodded. "So, Dan, you're going home?"

"Yep. My dog and I are hitching a ride to Anchorage on a barge leaving from Bellingham in a week. Where's your home, Billy?"

The waitress put the coffee in front of each man and said, "A couple of minutes for the food."

Billy said, "Thank you," and answered Dan, "Bonners Ferry."

"Bonner's Ferry? Where's that?"

"Idaho panhandle. Oh, that's right, you're from Alaska. Bonners is not far from the Canadian border. If we ever have an earthquake, the farm might be in Canada. Damn, I'd have to get a passport, wouldn't I?" Billy grinned, and leaned back from the counter to get a better look at the big plate of food the waitress slid across the counter. "Thanks. Got any ketchup?" He picked up a fork after tucking a napkin in his shirt. He waited for some ketchup, shook some on his eggs, and took a bite of eggs and toast. "I have a small farm, two girls, and a beautiful wife, named Mildred," he mumbled with his mouth full.

"When I saw you get out of your truck, it crossed my mind that you might be a farmer. What are your girls' names?"

"My gals are Sally and Meredith. They're the apples of my eye—or is it eyes? I'm not the greatest at English, but my girls are smart—get it from their mother, I guess, but I did finish high school. What are you doing in the lower 48, Dan?" Billy grinned and said, "Did you come down here for a warm winter?"

"Nope. I got shot when I was in Afghanistan. After I got out of the Army hospital, I was working my way across the states from one truck stop to another, and then I accepted a job cabin-sitting. While living at the cabin, I took flying lessons and got my license. I'm a pilot now. When I get back home, I'm going to get a plane." Dan skipped the part about the kidnapping. It wasn't necessary; telling the story just dredged up disappointment. Ann was history—like two trucks passing in the night, going in opposite directions.

"I'll bet planes are expensive in Alaska. Aren't there lots of bush pilots, and plenty of wrecks in the mountains?"

"Yeah. New planes are very expensive, but I'll look for a used one I can fix up. I'm good at repairing things. I'm going to work for my uncle Max for a while—until I can make a down payment on a plane. If I'm lucky, I should have enough to start buying a plane in a couple of years."

Billy put down his fork, took a last swig of coffee, burped into his napkin and said, "Get your stuff—Interstate 5 is waiting for us. Meet me at the truck with your dog. I've got to pay for this—be right along." Billy dropped from the chair to the floor, stood for a moment straightening his back and legs, and pulled his wallet from his work pants. He walked like an old man to the counter, and paid his bill, giving the waitress/cashier an extra two dollars.

"Thanks, mister."

"You're welcome. That was good eatin'. I'll come here again sometime." Billy reached into a jar of mints and took two, turned, and quickly left the diner. He smiled; his pretenses as an old man were gone.

As Billy was paying his invoice, Dan left the diner and untied Nomah. "Guess what, Nomah, we've got a ride." Dan walked over to the truck and leaned against the trailer.

Billy approached the truck, adjusted his pants, and climbed into the cab. Dan got Nomah settled on an old blanket behind the passenger seat. Billy said he used the blanket when he had to put on or remove tire chains.

Billy looked at Dan and said, "Ready for launch?"

"I thought you just ate—I'm ready," Dan answered and grinned at his joke.

Billy laughed, started the engine, checked his mirrors, and pulled his heavy load into traffic leading to I-84 west. As soon as the truck was up to speed, Billy said, "Tell me about your family. You can skip the bad jokes." Billy looked at Dan and winked.

Dan gave Billy the Newcombs' history, as he knew it, and concluded with, "That's all I know. The rest of the story still has to be written. I'm anxious to find out what the future as a bush pilot has in store. I like a little danger, makes me feel alive. I'd like to find out why and where my dad crashed with those hunters."

"Oh, I got something for you, Dan." Billy fished the chocolate mints from his pocket and flipped one to Dan. "That's courtesy of the diner." Billy unwrapped the chocolate, stuck it in his mouth, grinned, and nodded, "Not bad."

"Thanks, Billy. Got one for Nomah?"

"Nope. Dogs can't eat chocolate; don't you know that?"

"Yep. Just checking to see if you're really a farmer; all farmers know that, don't they?" Dan sat back, letting the mint dissolve under his tongue, and began to reflect on what had taken place in the past six months. As he recalled his activities, the truck transitioned from I-84 to I-205, and when north of Vancouver, Billy swung onto I-5. Both men were quiet as the scenery approached and then disappeared behind the truck.

"Hey, Dan, Nomah is whining. Is there something wrong?"

Dan heard a voice, but didn't react. All his concentration was devoted to flying the plane between two mountain ranges with a woman passenger beside him. He had to watch the gauges and be aware of sudden changes in the wind. What the passenger said was irrelevant.

Bill spoke louder, "Dan! Your dog is whining. What's the matter with him?" Billy was concerned, couldn't Dan hear him?

Dan blinked his eyes and looked at Billy. His eyes had been open all the time, he wasn't asleep. Was he dreaming with his eyes open? Dan glanced behind the seat at Nomah. "It's all right. Nomah has to pee, but he won't pee in the cab. Can we exit the freeway for a few minutes?"

"As a matter of fact, I could stand for an oil change myself. Coffee seems to go right through my plumbing. There's a rest stop a mile ahead. Can he hold it?"

"Yep. He'll be all right. He just gave us an early warning. Sorry, I was slow to react—I was lost in a dream, or something."

CHAPTER 22

North on Interstate 5

After the water pressure was released, and the three males were back in the truck, Billy took out a map and added the miles between markers. The truck had a flat-screen monitor and computer system, but Billy never used it. He had relied on his own methods of navigation for nearly forty years, so why change now?

"Two hours and we'll be in Federal Way. You want me to drop you somewhere? I don't think you want to go with me to my drop location."

"You can let us off at the nearest truck stop along your route. Don't go out of your way. We'll catch a ride to Bellingham, or thereabouts, easily enough. I certainly appreciate your generosity. I might have spent hours looking for a ride. It was supposed to rain in Troutdale this afternoon. I'm glad we got away from the rain."

Billy turned on the radio, and they listened to the weather report. Seattle was supposed to get at least an inch of rain in the next 24 hours. Within 15 minutes the drops began to strike the windshield, sporadically at first and then a constant splattering, accompanied by darkening, gray-black skies. The regular beat of the wipers was monotonous, so Billy found a radio station playing favorites of the 1970s. The music drowned out the metronomic sound of the windshield wipers.

It was a few minutes after 5:00 p.m. when Billy pulled into a Federal Way truck stop and let Dan and Nomah off. Dan thanked Billy, and wished him good luck with his return trip to his farm in Bonners Ferry.

Billy thanked Dan for the company and wished him good luck in Alaska. As Billy drove away, Dan and Nomah walked across the parking area to the visitor center at the well-lit Circle J Stop 'n Shop. The fluorescent lights were humming overhead, and the rain was dripping from the roof, which overhung the front wall of the cement-block building by six feet.

Out of the rain next to the windows, Dan took off his backpack and pulled his heavy coat out of the vinyl wrapping on top of the pack. It was getting cold; the moisture in the air made it feel even colder than the sign in the window indicated. He folded his light jacket, wrapped it in the vinyl, and inserted it in one of the backpack side-pockets.

"Are you hungry, Nomah?"

Nomah gave a little bark and sat down against the concrete wall below the big windows of the visitor center. Dan went in the center, picked up a small plastic shopping basket and headed for the pet foods. He grabbed a five-pound bag of dog food, a small box of plastic utensils, and continued on to the prepared food area. He picked up some potato salad, a chicken sandwich, and some bottled water. When he approached the counter, he grabbed a local paper, paid for the items, and joined Nomah outside.

Dan sat down next to Nomah and took out the newspaper. He took the sports section and folded it into a square box, added about two cups of dog food and slid it over to Nomah. While Nomah was attacking his food, Dan ate the entire eight-ounce container of potato salad and washed it down with bottled water. As soon as Dan finished his sandwich, he reentered the center and located the men's room. He washed the empty, plastic, salad container and filled it with water for Nomah. They sat on the concrete for about ten minutes watching cars, trucks, and the rain, listening to the rumbles of thunder. A few drivers and other travelers shook the rain from their clothes, stomped their feet, and entered the center.

"Hey, you can't hang out here. You and your dog have to move on."

Dan looked up to see where the voice had originated and saw a thin-bespectacled man of about forty leaning out the partially opened front door. He wore dark pants, navy blue or black; it was difficult to tell the true color in the fluorescent lighting. A black bolo tie with a silver clasp stood out against his white shirt. He must be speaking with some authority— probably a manager—so Dan got up and addressed the man, a couple of inches shorter than Dan.

"We'll be leaving shortly. I'm trying to find a ride to Bellingham. Can you give us some assistance? My name's Dan Newcomb and this is my dog, Nomah. We're on our way to Alaska."

The man stepped out onto the concrete, looking up to see where the rain water was dripping, and extended his hand. "I'm Stan Worley, night manager. I'll see what I can do for you. Let me call the service center. If anyone knows destinations, they will. Come on in—you can bring your dog, as long as he stays with you."

Dan and Nomah followed Mr. Worley to the counter, where he pressed a button on the intercom system console and spoke, "Bob, you got anyone going to Bellingham tonight?"

There was a pause and then a male voice answered, "Yeah, Stan. Brian Saletta is taking a load of motor parts north. He's leaving in an hour, after dinner. You got a rider?"

"Uh-huh. Man and his dog. They need to get to Bellingham— they're on the way to Alaska."

"Okay, send him over."

"Thanks, Bob."

"Not a problem."

Stan flipped a switch and looked at Dan. "Well, young man, you and your dog are in luck. Saletta is a private trucker and enjoys company; watch out, though, he'll talk your leg off."

"Thanks, Mr. Worley. Where do I go?"

"Out this door, turn to the left. There's an entrance to the repair center at the end of the building. Brian will be there shortly; he's eating dinner. He's about your size, but 20 years older. Oh, yeah, he wears a black cowboy hat and glasses; you can't miss him."

"Thanks again. Come on, Nomah, let's find our next ride." Dan opened the door and Nomah followed him out into the rain. They walked about 30 yards, opened a metal door and stepped inside the steel building. There was a noisy space heater in the shop near two tractors being repaired. One had the engine exposed with two men leaning over it and a young woman was changing a front tire on the other truck. She had just removed the last lug nut. She stepped back from the wheel and took a deep breath.

Dan looked at the girl, thinking she would have difficulty removing the wheel. She looked like she wouldn't have the muscle to lift the heavy wheel from the axle. Dan dropped his pack, started moving toward the girl and said, "Just a minute, I'll give you a hand."

The girl swiveled around and said, "That's all right, mister, I can do it." She picked up a hammer, hit the side of the tire, dropped the hammer, and wiggled the tire off the lugs and watched it fall to the floor with a thump. She stepped back, wiped her forehead with her shirt sleeve, and said, "See!" A smile appeared on her oval face as she turned to Dan and looked him in the eyes. Her face said a lot; she appeared to be a mixture of Chinese and Caucasian heritage. She was kind of cute; Dan guessed she was about 15 or 16, with a grease spot on her right cheek below her eye and another one on the tip of her chin. The grease spots matched her hair color. She pointed at Nomah. "That your dog?"

"Yes, ma'am. His name is Nomah. By any chance are you from Alaska?"

"Nope, Minnesota. Why?"

"Just curious. You resemble some of my high school friends."

"So you're from Alaska?"

"Uh-huh, on my way home. I'm waiting for Mr. Saletta to see if I can get a ride to Bellingham."

"He'll give you a ride."

"How do you know?"

The girl smiled. "He's my father. He'll do anything I say." She gave a little laugh.

"Hey, Leanne, who's that you're talking to?" A big guy wearing a black cowboy hat appeared from a door marked diner/gift shop. He walked quickly to the girl and stood between her and Dan. "Who are you?" he quizzed.

"Dan Newcomb. I assume you are Mr. Saletta. My dog and I would like to get a ride to Bellingham. Your daughter said it would be all right, but I thought I'd better check with you." Dan looked at Leanne and winked.

Leanne whispered in her father's ear, and they both looked closely at Dan.

Dan figured the ride was nixed. Mr. Saletta's body language said forget it to Dan. "Come on Nomah, we'll ride with someone else," and started toward the door.

"Hey! Hold on, Dan. Were you on TV a few months back? Did you save a kidnapped woman in Oregon?"

"Yeah. I thought everyone had forgotten about that. I just want to get back to Alaska. I've got things to do."

"You can ride with us to Bellingham. We'd like to hear your story of what happened. We weren't sure the TV reporters got it right. What do you say?"

Dan grinned and said, "Well, I guess I can tell the story one more time."

Mr. Saletta said, "I'm Brian, you've already met my daughter, Leanne. As soon as we get a new tire mounted we'll get back on the road. I expect we'll be in Bellingham by nine o'clock tonight, provided the traffic cooperates."

Dan shook hands with Brian and asked, "Can I help you with the tire?"

"We just have to roll it over to that cage so the new tire can be mounted. Leanne knows the procedure. We have to call for service—can't do it ourselves—against the rules."

Dan rolled the heavy flat tire over to the metal cage that protected the workers from an explosion. He watched Leanne press a red button which rang a service bell.

One of the men working on the engine climbed down, talked with Brian, and rolled a new tire over to the cage. Ten minutes later, Brian was rolling the new tire to his truck.

After the wheel was remounted, Brian drove the tractor out into the rain, backed up to the trailer and helped by Leanne's signals, rejoined the two units. Brian leaned out the window and shouted over the engine noise, "Permission granted to come aboard, sailors."

Leanne climbed in first, followed by Nomah, and then Dan. The rain and heavy traffic in the Seattle area slowed progress toward Bellingham. During the hour's travel to Snohomish, Dan found out that

Leanne's mother's name was Chunjing. She had grown up in Shanghai, but had gone to graduate school in New Mexico.

Chunjing had met Brian at a high school volleyball tournament. Brian had moved to Minnesota from New York to get away from the city life. Deep in his heart he wanted to be a cowboy, but the closest he was able to get to his life-long dream was wearing a black cowboy hat and boots. Brian had to laugh when he told Dan about his black Stetson. Leanne confessed that she was embarrassed when her dad wore the hat to one of her high school football games, but now she was used to it. Leanne had graduated a year early and hadn't made up her mind where she was going to college. She loved playing the piano and had composed several pieces of music.

Dan told the Salettas the story about the dogs and rescuing Ann from the three thugs that had occupied the Sterlings' cabin. Dan answered what seemed to be a thousand questions about his detour in Oregon. He told Brian and Leanne about getting his flying license and his desire to become a bush pilot. It was 9:18 p.m. when they arrived in Bellingham. After saying goodbye to the Salettas, Dan and Nomah walked two blocks to a motel and checked in for the night. Salettas left their trailer and headed back to Seattle after picking up a load for the return trip.

In the morning, a slight ocean breeze carried the smell of diesel and the sounds of tugs across the waterfront area, priming Dan's and Nomah's senses. Dan had left a wakeup call for 6:00 a.m. and when the phone rang, he nearly jumped out of bed thinking it was a fire alarm. He had been so fatigued, he had slept soundly all night. The life in the mountain cabin hadn't been much preparation for travelling on the freeways. Nomah, who had jumped up on the bed beside Dan sometime during the night, raised his head and looked up at Dan, but stayed on the bed. Dan dressed quickly and took Nomah outside to a park-like area for his number one and number two procedures. Dan had planned ahead, picking up the solids with a plastic bag taken from one of the motel wastebaskets.

The ocean air was chilly, the sky a uniform gray. According to the weather forecast, more rain was going to follow the drizzle from the previous day. After showering, Dan walked to a nearby McDonalds and bought breakfast, returned to his room and used the Styrofoam container as a bowl for Nomah. Dan packed his few belongings and found the note with the phone number of Inman Transfer Company.

His call was answered on the first ring.

"Inman Transfer, Jack speaking. How may I help you?"

"This is Dan Newcomb. Terry Sterling arranged for me and my dog to travel to Anchorage on your ship. I'm at the Driftwood Inn; how do I get to the ship?"

There was a pause and then Jack said, "That's over two miles from the supply boat. You'd better take a taxi."

"That's not bad. We'll walk. After riding in trucks all day yesterday, we need the exercise. Give me directions and we'll show up in about an hour."

"All right. Have the motel people tell you how to get to Wharf Street. Follow it south to where it crosses the Burlington Northern tracks; it becomes Pine Street there. Follow Pine to the end and continue across the unpaved area to the wharf. The Coast Hugger is blue and yellow; you can't miss it. We'll be loading equipment all day. We'll put you to work as soon as you get here."

"Okay, thanks. See you in about an hour. Bye."

"I'll be at the boat. See you later."

CHAPTER 23

Preparation for Sea Travel

Dan hung up the phone and said, "Ready, Nomah?" Nomah barked and moved toward the motel room door, waiting for Dan to shoulder his pack and put on his cap. They stopped briefly at the motel office to ask for the route to the wharf and drop off the key card. Nomah and Dan followed the directions, arriving at the wharf in just over an hour. Dan figured they had gone more like three miles than two, as was originally estimated. A few cars beeped at them when they crossed streets, but no policemen bothered to ask any questions. In fact, Dan hadn't seen any sign of law enforcement.

There were two ships at the wharf—a container ship about 800 feet long and a smaller ship, less than half as big. Dan was a little confused; neither ship seemed like it was a barge, certainly not the larger vessel. But the smaller ship was blue and yellow, so that had to be the one Jack Inman had mentioned. As he got closer, he could read the name on the bow, Coast Hugger. He had found the cargo ship.

"This is our ship, Nomah. We'll be aboard for two weeks. Then you will meet your Uncle Max. He likes dogs; you'll get along fine." Dan watched Nomah looking out at the large expanse of water giving a little whine. Dan looked down at him, smiled, and said, "Don't worry, you don't have to swim to Anchorage. We'll be on this ship. Let's see if we can find Mr. Inman."

Dan and Nomah started walking the length of the ship toward the stern, where a crane was lifting some containers from the wharf to the ship. The hull of the ship was below the height of the wharf, and a man wearing a hardhat was giving signals to the crane operator. He had a headset but was giving hand signals. Dan watched as a container was swung over the ship and lowered to the deck below. Dan stepped up to the man with the headset and said, "I'm looking for Jack Inman."

"You found him. You must be Dan Newcomb. You and your dog can wait over there for a few minutes; we've got one more container to load." Inman pointed to the far side of the wharf out of the way of the activity on the pier, where hooks on cables were swinging awkwardly in the air, ready to be attached to another container.

A worker on top of the container secured the cables and rode the container down to the deck of the ship. After the cables were unhooked, the crane swung back across the pier and was shutdown. The operator slid down the ladder to the ground and walked over to Inman. They shook hands, and the man walked away toward a warehouse. Inman motioned to Dan saying, "Follow me, I'll show you where you can bunk."

As Inman descended a pier ladder to the deck, Dan tossed his backpack to the deck and picked up Nomah. After a bit of a struggle carrying an extra 50 pounds down the ladder, he set foot on the deck and put Nomah down. He commented to Inman as they walked toward the bow, "I noticed you weren't using your headset when the crane was loading the containers."

"Yeah, that old fart operating the crane is a throwback. He's waiting to retire—he's almost 65. He doesn't like modern communication techniques, but he's union and we're stuck with him. Say, your dog is going to have some problems getting from one deck to the next. There's another place to sleep near the stern, but you'll have to put up with engine noise. It's only two steps down from the main deck; your dog can jump it easily enough."

Dan thought for a second, grinned, and replied, "Okay, I'll stay there. I can sleep through just about any regular noise. A gunshot or a loud noise, like a horn, will wake me up. Anyway, it'll only be for a couple of weeks."

Jack showed Dan where he would be staying for the trip, unless he and Nomah couldn't tolerate the throbbing of the dual engines. Jack shook hands with Dan and Nomah and said, "Glad to have you aboard. We'll be pulling away from the pier in a few minutes; better stay on the boat unless you want to take a long walk."

Surprised, Dan replied, "We're leaving for Anchorage right away?"

"Not yet. We have to move to a different location where we can use the stern ramp to load the heavy equipment. Any possibility you can drive dump trucks, tractors, or front loaders?"

"I can handle all of those. Learned how when I was in high school working for my uncle," Dan smiled, "and I can fly a plane."

"Good, I'll put you right to work. We'll need you after we move this clumsy hunk of steel about a mile from here. We'll be backing up to the dock, so stay clear of the ramp until we get ready for transferring the heavy equipment."

"You got it. Come on, Nomah, let's get our things stored." Nomah gave a little bark and followed Dan down two steps into a small room with a bed that folded down from the wall. The corresponding room on the opposite side of the stern was labeled fire equipment. When Dan had an opportunity, he wanted to check what extinguishers were available. Dan lowered the bunk and Nomah jumped up and lay down. Dan smiled and scratched Nomah's head. "Tired from all that walking, huh?"

Vibrations could be felt when the engines started, and the boat moved slowly out into the channel heading west. The throbbing of the engines stopped after a few minutes, and Hugger was bumped by another boat or a dock. Dan looked out the porthole and observed a tugboat guiding the stern of the boat until it had been turned 180 degrees. He heard and felt a sudden collision as the stern came in contact with something solid. Then a loud bang occurred as the ramp was released, striking the surface of a concrete dock near water level. Nomah looked a little nervous and whined, not understanding the motion and the noises.

"Okay, Dan, I can use your help now." It was Jack Inman calling from the deck.

Dan put a leash on Nomah and took him on deck and jogged toward the bow, where he tied Nomah. Dan wanted Nomah to see what was going on in order to associate the noises with the equipment being moved. Dan ran back to Inman and explained.

"Don't sweat it, Dan. Can you back that Caterpillar into the center of the hold as close to the superstructure as possible? My men will park the front loaders on either side of the Cat and then we'll line up the trucks across the beam. The grader will come in last. I'll handle it."

Dan checked the ramp orientation and said, "No problem, I'll put it anywhere you like. When I get close, guide me in."

It took about 45 minutes to get the equipment loaded and chained in place. Dan met three other crew members: Ross Watson, Frank Garver, and Sam Dowd. The names were difficult for Dan to remember, except for one, Ross Watson. Ross was introduced as the cook, one of the most important members of the crew, someone Dan would have to get to know. Dan was taking Nomah back to their berth when Ross, who was of slight build; sandy hair, about five-eight, walked with them and asked, "Where'd you get that nice looking dog?"

"Found him in the woods near Multnomah Falls. His name's Nomah."

"That makes sense. He's about a year old?"

"Seven months."

"Jesus! He's going to be a giant when he grows up."

Dan smiled, "He'll need to be big in Alaska—so the mosquitoes don't carry him off."

Ross thought for a second, grinned, and replied, "That's a good one. You should hit it off with Sammy; he's a real jokester. So you're going to stay in Alaska?"

"Yeah. I'm going to fly into the remote areas. I want to see if I can find where my dad went down, but there's one big problem; Alaska is more than twice the size of Texas, more mountains, and a whole lot more lakes, snow, and ice."

"Well, it's good to have you aboard and good luck." They shook hands and Ross commented, "After you put Nomah in your berth, join me on deck and we'll secure that equipment with chains. We'll check the chains every day; morning and evening. Say, what do you like to eat for breakfast?"

Dan answered without thinking, "Hotcakes with maple syrup and bacon."

Ross said, "You got it," and walked toward the bow.

As Dan was getting Nomah settled in the stern berth, Jack Inman stuck his head in the door and said, "I'm going to the supermarket to pick up groceries, you need or want anything special?"

"Sure do. I could use about five pounds of red delicious apples and a 25-pound bag of dog food, the best they have. Here's 20 dollars; that should cover it." Dan pulled a bill from his wallet, but Jack wouldn't take it.

"Keep your money, Dan. It's no good when you work for me."

"Thanks, Jack." Dan watched Jack walk down the ramp to the dock, get in an old, red, Ford pickup and roar off toward the downtown area, blue-gray smoke issuing from his exhaust pipe. Jack was about as tall as Dan but outweighed him by at least thirty pounds. He looked to be about 30, had a crew cut and hadn't shaved in a couple of days. Dan guessed that Jack wouldn't shave for the next two weeks; maybe not until he returned to Bellingham from Anchorage.

While Jack was shopping, Dan familiarized himself with the boat. It was explained to him that this was a supply boat, not a ship. Ships were much bigger and cruised the open ocean. This tub, as Jack called it, didn't sail far from shore. The shallow draft and low profile prevented open ocean excursions; the gunnels weren't far above the water. The Coast Hugger was 295 feet long with a beam of 56 feet, and including Dan, had a crew of five. Dan's meandering took him to the mess hall where he got a mug of coffee and a sweet roll. His stomach had been gnawing at his spine since arriving on the Hugger.

"I take it you're a landlubber, eh?"

"Almost, Ross. I've paddled around among ice flows and watched from a pontoon boat as glaciers calved, but this will be my first major trip on a boat. I'm looking forward to it."

Frank Garver, eating a heavily frosted doughnut, came in the mess hall and sat beside Ross. He started talking with his mouth full, bits of doughnut falling to the table top. No one could tell what he said until he swallowed. He ignored the napkin Ross shoved at him. "Hey, Ross, got any beer?"

"Are you kiddin' me? Jack would have my ass if I brought any booze on board, and he'd kick your ass for drinkin'. You know that!"

"I guess I'll have to celebrate with my wife tonight, then. I just turned 30."

"Shit, Frankie, you don't look a day over 19. I always thought you were a teenager that married an older woman." Sam had just joined the rest of the crew and was already picking on Frank—just like Ross had warned. An experienced seaman, Sam was about 35, muscular, built like a fireplug, and going bald. He had a tattoo of a toy tugboat on the crown of his head. He said the bargirls thought it was cute, they'd kiss the top of his head when he was drinking. He knew they just wanted him to buy more drinks.

Dan joined in the fun. "Gentlemen, this is just a warning, but don't make any quick moves near me when my dog is around. He'll take a piece out of your leg or ass, whichever is closer. Nomah is very protective. Happy Birthday, Frank."

"Thanks. I shouldn't have said anything. I knew Sammy would give me shit about it. Anyway, I'm leavin' for home. I'll see you boys tomorrow." He turned to leave, stopped, and then said, "Oh, when does Jack want to sail?" They all shook their heads, Jack hadn't commented to any of the crew about shove-off date or time. Maybe he was arranging for more cargo; the hold was only two-thirds full. "Well, he's got my number. I guess he'll call if he wants to leave early." He waved and said, "Later."

About five minutes after Frank had gone, Jack backed his pickup onto the ramp and called to the crew. "Hey, I could use some help."

Sammy, Ross, and Dan left the mess area, heading toward the stern where Jack was leaning against the pickup. The bed of the pickup was full of sacks and boxes of groceries. Each man carried two loads to the galley.

Jack brought in the last load, looked around, and said, "Where's Frank?"

Ross replied, "Today's his birthday, he left to celebrate with his wife. He said you'd call him if need be. None of us knew when we were shovin' off."

"Okay. We're leaving day after tomorrow around nine in the morning. Tomorrow we're getting a semi full of building materials to fill out our cargo hold. There will be about 50 pallets of shingles, metal siding, bolts, nails, and other crap. Call Frank and tell him to get his butt down here by 0800. He'd better not be drunk. Dan, you'd better get your apples and the dog food from the mess hall. You don't want Sammy to eat your dog food."

Sammy was the only crewman that didn't laugh. Jack was the one man on the boat that could pick on Sammy without starting a fight. An experienced seaman, Sam Dowd enjoyed ridiculing others, trying to make them squirm, something he began doing as he was growing up near the waterfront in Portland. He wasn't mean, just mischievous.

When he went too far, he'd apologize.

CHAPTER 24

Hugging the Coast

After 30 minutes of reading a book Ross had loaned him, it occurred to Dan that Nomah hadn't exercised since the long walk to the pier earlier in the day. The leash was coiled up on the bunk beside Nomah. Dan reached over and clipped the leash to Nomah's collar and said, "Let's go for a walk, buddy." Nomah jumped to the deck, tail wagging, and started out the door. Dan could hear rain drops striking the deck, so he pulled Nomah back inside while he donned his poly-raincoat. It was getting dark, but rain drops could be seen passing through the light near the dock. Fog was beginning to dim the dock lighting and the rain was letting up.

Ross was the only other crewman on the boat; the others had gone home for their last night's sleep on a soft bed for the next four weeks. After sleeping in one's own bed, sleeping on a bunk was more like staying in a cheap motel, very cheap. Dan and Nomah walked the length of the boat to tell Ross they were going for a ten minute stroll along the beach. Ross was still organizing things in the mess, trying to find space for all the provisions. He didn't ask for help—Ross wanted to know where everything was stored.

"All right, don't get lost. Let me know when you get back."

Dan answered, "Right." He and Nomah headed for the ramp. Off the boat, they moved down the dock toward a packed-gravel parking area illuminated by fluorescent lights shielded to cut glare from going skyward. They walked about a quarter mile in the sand and gravel, turned around, and started back. They hadn't seen a soul. As they approached the ramp, Dan glanced at his watch. They had been gone for almost 15 minutes. They climbed aboard on the stern ramp and moved toward the bow, walking slowly around the heavy equipment, avoiding the chains securing the big machines to the cargo hold deck. Dan wished he had a small flashlight, but they moved slowly and made it to the superstructure without tripping.

Dan called out, "Hey, Ross. We're back." There was no answer. Dan stood for a few seconds and then repeated, a little louder, "Ross, we're back." Still no answer.

Dan heard a voice from behind him. "Stick 'em up, mister." Surprised, Dan thought Ross was screwing around. He turned around to face a teenager holding a gun, so he raised his hands. An image of the three thugs in the Sterlings' cabin flashed through his mind. Was he going to kill this kid, or just disarm him?

"Take it easy, son. I'm not armed. What do you want?"

"Go up that ladder and join your buddy. Just a minute, turn around and put your hands on the wall. I'm gunna search you."

Dan did as he was told and felt a gun barrel pressed against his back. The kid said, "Stand where you are."

Dan let go of Nomah's leash and gave two short whistles. Nomah came out of the shadows growling. The kid looked away from Dan, who turned quickly and swatted the gun, which fired. The bullet ricocheted off the caterpillar tractor blade and whined through the air into the bay. Dan latched onto the kid's wrist and twisted his arm behind his back. The gun fell against the tractor blade with a clank. Dan pulled his throwing knife from behind his neck and poked the tip into the kid's neck above his Adam's apple.

"Ow! You're gunna break my arm. Hey, man—don't cut me."

"Shut up or I'll break both arms and cut your throat. Who are you and who are you with?"

"Tim Larson. My friend, Aaron. He's got a gun on your buddy up there. If I yell out to him, he'll shoot your friend."

"That's not going to happen." Dan held his hand over the kid's mouth and choked him until he passed out. Dan tied the kid up with

Nomah's leash, covered him with his slicker, and checked the gun. The clip was full. He shoved the gun in his belt and slowly climbed the steps to the galley. From the top of the steps, Dan heard a voice.

"Hey, Tim. You all right?"

Dan remained quiet as he sneaked through the passageway to the back of the galley. He could see another kid, bigger than the one tied up, holding a gun on Ross.

"Hey, Tim! I heard a shot. You all right?"

Dan moved the gun from the front of his belt to behind his back and stepped out so the kid could see him.

"Hey, Ross, what's going on? I heard some voices. You know this kid?"

"Nope. He just came aboard and pulled a gun on me. Said he wanted me to open one of the containers—supposed to be full of medical supplies. I don't have the keys to those containers. The kid wants me to get a bolt cutter and cut the lock off. You want to help me? I have to go below deck to get a cutter."

Dan responded, "Okay, I've got your six, make sure you've got mine."

Aaron said, "That's enough crap talk. You, mister, come over here while he goes after that tool."

As Dan passed Ross they slightly bumped each other. Ross looked at Dan's back and saw the gun in Dan's belt. Ross grabbed the gun, paused to steady himself, and Dan dropped to the floor. Ross pumped two bullets into Aaron, one in the right shoulder and one in the left leg. Aaron was so surprised, he dropped his gun. Ross watched Dan knock it out of reach and get up.

"Son of a bitch, you shot me!"

"No shit! You little asshole. I should've killed you, pulling a gun on me like that." Ross was really pissed off.

"Jesus! Call for an ambulance. I'm losing a lot of blood."

Dan replied, "First the police; we'll let them call the ambulance. What in the hell were you trying to do?"

"We just wanted to get some drugs so we could get high."

Dan looked at Aaron's eyes and said, "You mean higher, don't you?"

Aaron was silent. He looked away from Dan, probably realizing the stupidity of their plan. A call to the harbor police brought two squad cars and an ambulance, which arrived in ten minutes. A detective asked

Dan and Ross some questions, confiscated the guns, and took the two young men to the hospital. Ross and Dan had some coffee and talked over what had happened before retiring. They expected to be doing some hard work in the morning. The misty rain was still invading the harbor when they went to bed.

As Dan walked the length of the boat to his bunk, he wondered if there could be a reason he was involved in holdups and a kidnapping. Was he being prepared for some other, more complicated, illegal activities, or were these occurrences just a matter of probabilities? Dan climbed into his bunk and covered himself with a blanket. He was beginning to feel like he was back in Afghanistan.

Dan was fighting his way out of the cockpit of a plane, but this time his legs were being squeezed between the pilot's seat and the fuselage. As he broke the surface of the freezing cold water, he woke up. Nomah had been asleep against his legs, but had raised his head and was watching Dan. "It's all right, Nomah. I was dreaming again." Dan turned over and thought for a moment. *That woman beside me in the plane had great legs, but how could I see her legs, she should be wearing pants. Was it Ann? I couldn't see her face, the fur on her parka blocked my vision. Maybe it was someone I haven't met yet.* The gentle swaying of the boat helped him drift off to sleep.

Loud banging woke Dan in the morning. It was 0731. He dressed quickly and stepped up on deck. A semi had backed up to the ramp, and a lift truck was being lowered to the ground. The pallets were shrink-wrapped with black plastic and contained wooden boxes strapped together with nylon ties. A gangly stranger dressed in a gray jacket and black pants approached and said, "Anybody in charge here?"

Before Dan could answer, Ross yelled out from the bow, "I'm coming!"

Ross was out of breath when he reached the stern. He had rushed to get dressed and appeared from the deck hatch with his shirt half on. He stuffed his shirttail in his pants and asked the driver, "You going to operate that lift truck?"

"Hell no. Where's Jack? Ain't he in charge?"

"He'll be here at eight." Ross looked at his watch. "You're a half-hour early."

"Well, shit. Those office assholes tol' me to get over here ASAP. I got to waste thirty minutes. Got any coffee?"

"Yeah, come up to the galley. I just started the coffee. Come on, Dan, let's wait for Jack and the others. We can't do anything until we know how to place the pallets."

Ross and Dan introduced themselves to the driver, Mitch Ricchi, as they moved to the galley.

The three men had started drinking coffee when they heard a horn. Ross looked toward the stern and could see Jack getting out of his pickup. He was towing a trailer carrying a lift truck with pneumatic wheels. The big wheels allowed easy maneuvering over the boat's ramp. He released the trailer from his truck and drove the lift truck off the tilted trailer to the side of the semi.

Jack shouted toward the boat, "Hey! Where's the driver?"

Mitch came out of the galley carrying a mug of coffee and answered, "Right here, Captain. Are you Jack?"

"Yeah. How many pallets are on the truck?"

"That's what I want to tell you about. I brought 22 of 'em, the rest are goin' on another ship. They ain't ready yet."

"All right. Are they marked as to weight?"

"Uh-huh. Orange tags tell how many kilograms each one has; that's gross weight—includes the pallet."

Jack walked over to his pickup, reached in the back and grabbed a spray can of white paint. He climbed on the flat-bed and began inspecting the pallet tags, spraying numbers on the black plastic wrapping. After ten minutes, Jack came over to Dan and asked, "Can you run a lift truck?"

"Yes, but it's been a few years."

"Okay. Here's how I want the pallets loaded." Jack drew on a pad and showed the diagram to Dan."

"Got it." Dan climbed into the seat of the nearest lift truck, started it, and began removing the top layer of freight-containing pallets from the truck. Jack operated the other lift truck on the opposite side of the trailer. The flat-bed was empty in about 45 minutes. Dan drove Mitch's lift truck onto the elevator at the back of the flat-bed and let Mitch secure it to the trailer. Mitch waved, climbed into the cab, gave a toot on the horn, and drove away through a small cloud of black smoke.

The entire crew was on board now. They moved to the galley to discuss ship-out time. Ross had made breakfast while Dan and Jack were transferring the pallets from the truck to the cargo hold. Frank and Sam had finished breakfast and were drinking coffee as Dan, Ross, and Jack began eating. Ross had made pancakes for Dan in honor of his quick reactions to thwart the attempted theft of drugs from the containers.

Jack started talking, waving his fork toward Ross and Dan. "I want to thank you guys. If those containers had been opened, we would have been in real trouble. We'd have been tied up here for a week by the authorities. How'd you get the drop on that first kid, Dan?"

"Nomah distracted him and I disarmed him—tied him up, and then came up here. Ross took care of the other guy. If I have any more confrontations with gunmen, I might have to start attending church. I'm beginning to wonder if someone is trying to tell me something."

The guys all laughed and Jack told them the police had contacted his father late last night and explained what had happened. Jack only knew what Hughie had told him, but not any details. Jack went over the planned route to Anchorage and asked, "Are all of you ready to depart?" Everyone looked around and nodded. "Okay, you've got two hours and we're out of here. Take care of any last minute details."

Dan drained the last drop of coffee from his mug and went back to his berth, sat down and tried to think of anything he and Nomah would need in the next two weeks. Jack hadn't said anything about mid-journey stops, so he had to have all necessities with him. Two items came to mind; he needed toothpaste and Nomah could use some treats. As he walked toward a store on Marine Drive, Dan decided to get a ball for Nomah; confinement to the boat for two weeks might cause adjustment problems for Nomah and himself. Another activity would lessen the boredom. As he made his way toward the checkout counter, Dan realized he should have something to carry solid waste to the head. He bought a 60-pack of quart-size plastic bags.

When Dan returned to the boat, the crew had assembled, waiting for Jack.

They had talked for a few minutes before hearing Jack's pickup arrive. Jack boarded the boat and waved to his wife as the pickup moved away from the dock area. The ramp was raised and Coast Hugger began to drift away from the pier.

Jack looked at the crew and said, "Ready to start the engines, Frank?"

Frank grinned and said, "Yes, Sir—Captain."

"Okay. Get those screws turning."

"Aye, aye, Sir"

Dan had to smile at the nautical formalism of Jack and Frank. He imagined that would be the only such exchange he would hear during the next two weeks.

CHAPTER 25

Strait of Georgia and Beyond

Three hours later, Coast Hugger was entering the Strait of Georgia between Vancouver Island and mainland British Columbia. A cruise ship had passed the Hugger with people waving to the smaller vessel. Dan thought he saw a young boy give them the finger, but he laughed, waved back, and Nomah barked at the big blue and white ship, which dwarfed the cargo boat. It seemed to Dan the Hugger was trying to win the slow race. The bow wave from the cruise ship rocked the Hugger as the big ship left the supply boat in its wake. Dan climbed up to the bridge to investigate the controls of Inman's boat.

Jack looked up from a book when Dan stood at the bridge hatchway. "Come on in, Dan. You don't need permission to come on the bridge, come up here anytime you want. Have any questions?"

"Just one. What is the difference in speed between that cruise ship and the Hugger?"

Jack laughed and replied, "We're moving at a blistering 12 knots; that ship was going about 20, but they have lots of paying customers that bitch if they don't get to their destinations on time. Our cargo can't give us any shit, it arrives when we get there. Just relax, all that slow and steady do is strain our patience. This evening we'll be about a hundred miles out of Bellingham. You'll see the lights of Parksville, BC, to the west."

"When that cruise ship passed us, did you see a kid give us the finger?"

Jack grinned, "Yeah. Sometimes I wish I had a trained seagull that I could send to crap bomb the kid's hair. That kid wouldn't do that again— without looking around for birds first. Imagine, that kid pickin' on us."

Dan watched the radar and looked around the bridge for a few minutes. Jack had resumed reading his book. At the instant Dan had thought about returning to his berth Jack said, "Watch for obstacles while I go to the head. Yell at me if anything gets in our way."

Dan was taken off-guard, but replied, "Uh—okay."

Jack disappeared and Dan was left alone, very uncomfortable in an environment where he had no control. He thought he should have asked Jack more about what to do, other than yell, in case of an emergency. The boat was on autopilot; the radar and GPS systems were working fine, so what did he have to worry about? However, Dan was still nervous.

When Jack returned with two mugs of coffee, Dan started asking questions about the guidance system of the boat. Fifteen minutes later, Dan felt more secure. He now understood how the system functioned. No wonder Jack could relax and read a book— the boat could run itself. As Jack put it, the computer system was smarter than he was. Jack was just around for backup, software was not infallible. Frank would take over in about four hours, and Jack could eat dinner and get some sleep. Dan thanked Jack for the tour and went back to his berth.

Dan played ball with Nomah, reviewed some of the manuals Vic had given him when he obtained his pilot's license, and took a shower. After eating with the crew, he scanned the western shoreline and saw Parksville's lights Jack had mentioned earlier.

After checking the chains on the equipment, Dan sat on his bunk with Nomah and looked at coastline maps of British Columbia and Alaska, estimating the distance to Anchorage. If the boat covered 100 miles in seven hours, they would travel approximately 300 miles per day. That meant the trip should take only one week. As Dan was getting ready for bed, he had to wonder why it was going to take two weeks. Did he overlook something obvious?

The second day was all about establishing a routine; Dan assumed responsibility for cargo security twice a day. Nomah and Dan would make their rounds after eating breakfast and again after dinner. The regular crew kept the ship running, taking spells on the bridge and in the engine room. Ross kept coffee available at all hours and would prepare a meal anytime someone was hungry. During the daylight hours, Dan had established an exercise routine which included walking, playing ball with Nomah, and climbing ladders to all decks.

Day three started with two small floatplanes flying over about 30 minutes apart. They buzzed the boat and rocked their wings as they went north, disappearing over nearby islands. Dan imagined piloting those planes, delivering needed medicines, doctors, food, mail, and other supplies to the settlements that could not be reached by road or scheduled boats. Although Dan had never lived in the Alaskan panhandle, he knew of the rough interior country no more than a mile from the coast, where few people had travelled. Bigfoot would be at home there.

That evening, Jack came by Dan's berth to make an announcement, "We are now in southern Alaska—just thought you'd like to know. We're going to stop for a couple of hours in Juneau and top off our fuel tanks. We'll get there tomorrow morning. You can go ashore and let Nomah run around. I think he'll enjoy getting off the boat. Make sure you have his papers handy. We'll be there in about 12 hours. Oh, yeah, if you want to make a phone call back to Washington or Oregon; that would be a good time to do it. Our next planned stop will be Anchorage—in about six days; if the weather holds."

Dan smiled, "Thanks Jack. I'll see if I can find that kid from the cruise ship and paddle his behind, or maybe talk to his parents."

Jack frowned, squinting, "You're not serious, are you?"

"Nope—just a passing thought." Dan grinned. "How big is Juneau?"

Jack bit his lower lip and paused. He was trying to remember what he had read from a brochure he had from a year ago. "I think it's around 30,000—about the same as Fairbanks, a little smaller."

"Thanks. I thought it was smaller than that."

"Well, I'll see you in the morning. Have a good night's sleep."

"Same to you, Jack," Dan grinned, "if you're not reading."

Dan woke up a little earlier than normal. He sat up and realized the vibrations from the engines had ceased, but an occasional horn blast and some yells from the wharf could be heard. Nomah was standing on the deck two steps up from the floor of the berth watching some boat-side activity. The top of the wharf was nearly 15 feet above Hugger's cargo deck, and sporadically, someone would look down at the loaded boat. The Juneau harbor was fairly quiet, not much marine traffic was occurring. The Hugger was docked astern of a much larger vessel, the NOREG VI; the ship that had passed them days earlier. The top of NOREG stood nearly 50 feet above a three-story building next to the wharf. Dan dressed quickly and went to the galley where Ross was pouring a mug of coffee.

"Morning, Ross, when did we dock?"

Ross looked at his watch and replied, "Good morning—about 30 minutes ago. A pilot boarded and brought us to the cruise ship dock. No other ships are expected so we can stay here, at least for a few days. You want to eat here or on land? You might find service kind of slow in Juneau this morning—that cruise ship has lots of passengers."

"Yeah, I believe you. I'll eat here, unless you're busy with something else."

"Okay, have some coffee." He gave Dan the mug he was holding. "Hotcakes will be ready in a few minutes. Syrup and butter are on the table—real butter, not that imitation crap."

While Dan was eating, Jack came into the galley. He filled his coffee mug and sat down beside Dan. "You going ashore, Dan?"

"Yeah. I've got to make a call to Boise, and Nomah needs to get off the boat. You said we'll be here for two hours?"

"Your call will be longer than two hours?"

"No—just wanted to be sure of our timetable. I want to buy a few gifts for my relatives."

"Well, don't worry about the time. We're going to be here for at least two days, not two hours like I said. There's a storm front coming in. When it hits the cold air over land, it'll probably cause some rain or snow. I don't want to get caught out in the water during rough seas—we might take on water and have major problems. We'll ride out the storm here in the Gastineau Channel. There's little risk tied up to the dock."

"Okay. I was wondering the other night why it was going to take us two weeks to get to Anchorage, now I know. I should be back in about an hour, maybe a little longer. I need to make that call. I might walk around with Nomah for a while, too. See ya later."

Dan went back to his bunk, removed his knife and placed it under his mattress. He attached the leash to Nomah's collar, and they climbed the floating stairs to the top of the wharf, which Dan guessed was at least 50-feet wide. Dan and Nomah followed the wharf to the stern of the NOREG VI, towering above him, turned right, and walked to South Franklin St. behind a group of people from the cruise ship.

He stood watching the traffic and pedestrians, trying to decide in which direction to proceed. A man on a bicycle stopped beside Dan and asked, "May I help you?"

Dan looked at the gentleman and saw JPD on the back of his jacket. He was a policeman. "Yes. I'd like to buy some gifts to take to my relatives in Fairbanks. Can you recommend a store?"

"Are you from the cruise ship?"

"Nope, the cargo boat. We just arrived from Bellingham."

"You've been visiting and working in the lower 48?"

"Kind of. I was in Afghanistan. Got back about a year ago and spent some time in Oregon."

"It's good to have you back. Thanks for serving the country."

"No problem. I'm glad to be back, I love Alaska."

"You asked about shopping. Most of the stores along Franklin don't open until next month, but if you see something while window-shopping, knock on the door, they might open for you. There are some shops on the side streets, too. Money talks, but watch out for fake items. In one respect, you are lucky, there's only one cruise ship in town."

Dan frowned and looked at the officer. "Sir?"

"When several cruise ships are here, you'll need football pads to stay alive while moving along Franklin. It can be vicious when elbows start flying, but you look like you can take care of yourself, and you have a big dog to help out," he smiled. "What's his name?"

"That's my buddy, Nomah."

The officer leaned over his bike and scratched Nomah's head. "He's still growing, isn't he?"

"Yes, sir. Say, can you tell me where I can find a pay phone?"

"Sure can. Go to the Hook and Anchor restaurant. It's about 100 yards down the street on the other side. Tell them Clive sent you; you might get a free call." He smiled and whispered, "We have an understanding."

"Thanks for the help, Clive. Come on, Nomah, let's call Beverly."

Clive mounted his bike and merged into one-way traffic, moving north.

Nomah seemed to know where they were going. Pulling at the leash, Nomah headed down the sidewalk, passing one-, two- and three-story buildings, some new and some fairly old. Dan couldn't walk as fast as Nomah wanted; his land legs hadn't completely returned. He narrowly avoided bumping into a young couple strolling along looking into windows. They looked like tourists, maybe from the Norwegian ship.

Dan and Nomah stopped across the street from the Hook and Anchor restaurant. They crossed the street, entered the two-story, older building, and looked for a phone. Dan couldn't see one, so he asked a waitress as she walked by carrying glasses of water, "Is there a pay phone here? Clive said you had one."

"Just a sec." The young lady delivered the water to a nearby table of guests and returned to talk to Dan. "You probably don't recognize the phone booth. It's right over there—in the corner." She pointed to a box-like green booth that looked like it came from Europe before World War II. "Quaint, isn't it? Let me get you some quarters. Where are you calling?"

Dan answered, "Boise, Idaho."

"Oh, you'll need several quarters." She smiled and disappeared behind some swinging doors. She popped right back through the doors, hurried to Dan, and said, "Hold out your hand."

Dan cupped his hand and she dropped a roll of quarters into his palm. He closed his fingers around the quarters, smiled, and said, "Thanks, I'll pay you back after the call."

"That's not necessary; we like to help servicemen, especially when they are coming back from over-seas. Just a little thank-you."

"That's nice of you. I'll return the extra money. Thanks again. Come, Nomah. Let's call Beverly." Dan moved across the hardwood floor to the green box wondering if he would have to use Morse code. Would he have to text? He opened the folding door and was pleased at what he saw—the phone was a modern digital model. "Sit Nomah." The box felt like a coffin, or what he imagined one to be. He had never been in one, not even to try it on for size. A coffin wasn't like a suit. He stood in the box and dialed the Olsons' number, then sat down on the triangular seat and extended his feet out of the booth.

He heard Bev's voice after the third ring. "Hello?"

"Hello, Beverly. This is Dan Newcomb. I'm calling from Juneau, Alaska. I'm sorry I didn't call before I left Portland."

"Oh, my gosh. It's so good to hear from you. I thought we had lost contact and would never hear from you again. You're in Alaska? You sound far away."

Dan laughed. "I think it's this phone booth. It's very small. When I first saw it, I thought I might have to talk into a tin can hooked to a string. Now I know what a sardine feels like. How are you all doing?"

"We're fine, thanks, except Ben has a bad cough. I've been nagging him to go to the doctor. I have to tell you something. Ann got married—in January. I know you really liked her, Dan. I'm sorry things didn't work out. I would have liked you as our son-in-law."

Dan felt like he had been poked in the heart, even though deep down, he never expected to see Ann again. He didn't know what to say. He paused for a few seconds as he gathered his thoughts, swallowed hard, took a deep breath, and said, "Give Ann my blessings. I hope she has a wonderful life. Keep healthy, safe, and keep driving that big truck. Bye Beverly."

"You take care of yourself, Dan. Thanks for calling us. Bye now."

The phone went dead and Dan hung up. He stood looking at the buttons on the phone for several seconds. Three-one-two had been the number of Ann's hospital room. He wanted to tell Ann that he got his pilot's license, but it wasn't important any more. He sat down for about a minute before he stepped out of the box and returned the remaining quarters to the waitress and thanked her. "Come on, Nomah, we've got some stores to visit. I need some new underwear, you need a new leash, and we need to get some gifts for the Conleys. What else do we need?"

CHAPTER 26

Hello Anchorage

The first 24 hours of the storm contributed to Dan's initiation to a melancholic state. He didn't have an appetite and tried to read, but his thoughts about of the loss of both parents, his dog Henry, and Ann had so pervaded his mind, he couldn't recall what he had just read a few minutes earlier. He dropped the book to the floor and tried to sleep, but sleep evaded him. Nomah was sleeping peacefully on a rug beneath Dan's bunk. Dan leaned over the edge of his bunk and watched Nomah's shallow breathing movements, and then leaned back against his pillow and stared at the ceiling.

He recalled talking to his mother one evening when they were doing the dishes. She told him, at 12 years old, he could make decisions for himself, but he must consider the consequences. After his father's disappearance, Dan developed a fear of losing people he loved, so he avoided the company of others, and that was reinforced when he lost Henry and Ann. The bad dreams compounded the situation. Now, after being a loner for so long, he recognized his error in not having anyone to share his thoughts.

It had occurred to him that he might see a psychiatrist, but he laughed at himself when all he really had to do was trust in others. It was like playing a new game, losses at the beginning were to be expected until he gained some experience. Was there too much hope and not enough reality in what he had imagined in his relationship with Ann? He had only known her a short while, but he had truly believed she was the one for him.

But perhaps he had been correct about becoming established in Alaska before becoming serious about a life-partner. He couldn't blame Ann for finding someone else, nearly everyone will say one thing and end up doing another. The consequences of getting married at this stage of his life might prevent him from become a bush pilot and searching for his father's body, something he felt he must do. He had to be patient.

Dan got an apple from his pack and began eating. He found half an apple on the bed when he woke up in the morning.

After getting coffee and pancakes and talking with the Ross, Dan walked the deck in the rain and inspected the tie-down chains. Nomah joined him carrying the ball in his mouth. Dan hid the ball under the seat of the caterpillar tractor and went back to his berth to continue reading. Five minutes later, Nomah brought the ball to Dan, but it was raining too hard to play ball.

The storm cleared the coast after blustery winds and gray, wet weather were pushed inland by the sun. More than two complete days had been spent in Juneau, but the morning of the third day was going to be nice. The Hugger would only be presented with clear blue skies after 1100 hours, following four hours of rumbling motors. At two in the afternoon, Dan took Nomah on a walk around the deck, and they were standing at the bow looking ahead of the boat, watching the bow plow through the water.

Hugger had cleared Chichagof Island to the south and was pointed toward the open Pacific, but gradually began swinging to the northwest. Glacier Bay Park & Preserve lay to the Northeast with the dark-gray rock and snow-covered Fairweather mountain range pointing through wispy clouds into the blue sky. "Isn't that beautiful, Nomah? That's another thing I love about Alaska. I'm so glad to be going home with you. I'm going to show you some beautiful scenery: snow covered mountains, lakes, forests, and the aurora borealis." He looked at Nomah and said, "Aurora borealis, that's the northern lights. I sure hope you have color vision."

"Hey, Dan, you remind me of *Titanic*; you and Nomah standing at the bow of the boat, except Nomah isn't a woman." Jack was smiling as he walked across the deck toward Dan.

"Say, Jack, why are we so far from the coast? Aren't we usually within a mile?"

"Icebergs. Those glaciers in the park calve into the ocean. We don't want to tangle with any ice—not good for our little Hugger's hull. We'll sneak back closer to land in about three hours—after we're north of the park."

Dan nodded, grinned, and replied, "That's good to know. As long as planes are flying, they don't have to worry about glaciers,"

Jack smiled and said, "Yeah, but as long as ships are sailing, they don't have to worry about crashing into mountains."

Dan shook his head, smiled, and said, "Wise guy. Remind me to never argue with you."

"Since you're here, watch for ice. Give a yell if you see anything. I'm going back to my book. I've got another one to finish before we get to Anchorage."

"Okay. What are you reading?"

"It's an adventure story about a bush pilot that crashes in the mountains near Denali."

"Sounds interesting. Can I borrow it when you're finished?"

"Sure," Jack smiled. "I'll have Nomah deliver it, as long as he doesn't slobber all over it."

The sea air had claimed two victims. Dan and Nomah had gone back to their berth and fallen asleep. Dan woke up and looked outside. Ross was standing a few feet from the hatch holding two mugs of coffee. "Did the aroma from the hot coffee wake you up?"

"Maybe. I was dreaming about trying to get out of a plane that crashed in a lake. It's a recurring dream, but it's not always the same. I don't always have the same passenger. One had great legs though. Anyhow, I woke up because of the cold water in my dream."

Ross nodded, understanding Dan's dream. "Yeah, that cold water will shrink you up," he laughed. "We just cleared the northern edge of the park, so we'll be moving closer to shore. If we go down, you won't have so far to swim."

"Thanks, Ross. That's something you could have kept secret."

"Well, enjoy your coffee. Chow's in an hour."

"Thanks for the coffee. See you in an hour. I've got to check the cargo—make sure everything is lashed down tightly. Come, Nomah. Let's do something important today."

Six hours later, Dan was reading *Glacier Crash*. Jack had given Dan the book when the crew was eating. It was 2300 hours. Dan could feel the boat in a gradual turn to port. Curious about the maneuver, he went forward to the bridge. Dan stepped through the hatchway and stood watching Frank.

Frank was watching the radar intently. He didn't look up and said, "Aren't you usually in bed by now, Dan?"

"Uh-huh, but I felt the boat turn and I wondered what was happening. How'd you know it was me?"

"You're the only one that is light on his feet; the others walk like they're kicking rocks. We turned to avoid the calves from the Yakutat glaciers. This can be a dangerous area, especially at night. I was watching for ship traffic. From here to Anchorage we'll encounter a lot more ocean traffic to Seward, Homer, and Anchorage. Did you notice the increase in air traffic today?"

"I did. I didn't think much of it though, but now that you mention it, planes from Seattle, Portland, and San Francisco are probably coming into Anchorage."

"Yep. Hawaii, too. Everything here is under control. You can go to bed. And don't worry, we'll be in Anchorage in 54 hours. I'll bet you can hardly wait to get home."

Dan answered, "You've got that right. See you later."

The next two days were routine. If Dan hadn't had Jack's book to read, he would have been bored out of his mind. The book kept Dan's mind on flying and thinking about searching for his father's plane when he wasn't checking the cargo. Dan was pondering how to scrape up enough money to buy a plane. He didn't have any rich friends to put the bite on. Finally, he came to the realization it was going to take several years of work and living like a monk in order to put away enough money to make a reasonable down payment on a plane.

Hugger had rounded the southern tip of the Kenai Peninsula around 1800 hours the day before the boat was scheduled to dock in Anchorage. Dan was a half-day away from seeing his aunt and uncle and their two boys. When the boat was in Juneau, Dan had bought a couple of music CDs for Aunt Mona, a computer game for the boys, and a pen carved from ivory for his Uncle Max. The pen was expensive, but Dan had great respect for his uncle, so he didn't mind buying something extravagant.

Dan was in his bunk at 2300 hours, but couldn't go to sleep. He felt like a little kid on Christmas Eve, wanting morning to arrive quickly so he could climb out of bed and run in his pajamas to the lighted tree to find what Santa had brought him. Mom would be in the kitchen making pancakes, and Dad would be cooking bacon and sausage over the fire in the living room fireplace. The house would smell wonderful, even if the wind and snow were attacking the city of Fairbanks. But those remembrances were now food for thought, perhaps seasoned with more imagination than reality.

When in Oregon, Dan had created images of waking to Ann and some children, having them experience what he had as a child. But Ann was of the past; perhaps his visualization had become nothing more than smoke dissipating in the wind. He had to get on with his newest love, flying his own plane, and experiencing new adventures with Nomah.

Dan felt the boat bumping into something solid, heard noises from other ships and motors beyond Hugger's. He had slept through the night, and if he had dreams, he couldn't recall them. Nomah was already up and standing outside the hatch. Dan swung out of the bunk and pulled on his pants, slid into a long-sleeved, plaid, wool-shirt and went to the galley. Everyone was there except Jack. They were all eating and drinking coffee, planning the day's activities—off-loading the containers first, followed by moving the boat to another dock to off-load the pallets and heavy equipment.

"Where's Jack?" Dan quizzed.

Ross answered, "Went ashore to make arrangements for off-loading our cargo and picking up stuff for the return. He'll be back before long.

You taking off?" The men grew quiet and looked at Dan, expecting him to say yes.

"Just for a few minutes. I need to call my uncle in Fairbanks to let him know where I am. He's going to pick me up, but I'll work today."

Ross asked, "What do you want to eat?"

Dan smiled. "Do I need to say?"

Ross shook his head. "I shouldn't have asked. Griddlecakes in a few minutes, Dan."

After eating, Dan went ashore and called Uncle Max. Max said he would drive to Anchorage the next day; it would take a little more than six hours, provided the roads were open all the way. If he left early in the morning, he would arrive in Anchorage between noon and 1:00 p.m. As far as Max knew, there weren't any spring storms expected. His boys would be in school, and they would be checked on by a neighbor lady while Mona was working at the hospital as a laboratory technician.

"Dan, where can I meet you?"

Dan had checked a map of Anchorage before he left the boat and decided to meet Uncle Max at Gull Avenue and Tidewater Road. It wasn't far to walk and would be easy for Max to find. After Dan had given his uncle directions, he returned to the boat. Frank and Sam were working with a crane operator transferring containers to the wharf. Dan wasn't needed, so he went to his berth and tidied up, collecting all his things except items he needed for his last overnight stay on Hugger. He almost forgot to retrieve his knife from under the mattress. Nomah recognized things were changing so was sticking close to Dan, maybe worrying he was going to be left behind.

Dan sat with Nomah and reassured his closest friend that he wasn't forgotten. After an hour, the containers were off the boat and it was time to move Hugger to another section of the harbor in order to offload the pallets and heavy equipment. Jack was back on board and started the engines. Frank and Sam cast off and Hugger began to move. The boat inched away from the docking area and swung out into the harbor, moved forward about a quarter mile, and turned around, assisted by a harbor tugboat.

The tug nudged Hugger toward shore to a concrete dock where the stern ramp was lowered. Jack yelled at Dan from the bridge, "Ready to work, Dan? Two lift trucks are coming in a few minutes. We'll start transferring pallets to those railcars parallel to the dock on the other side. It's going to take a while."

While Jack and Dan drove the lift trucks, Sam and Ross fired up the engines on the heavy equipment, released the tie-down chains, and as soon as pathways were available, began driving the fuel-guzzlers off the boat to waiting flatbed railcars. Railway workers secured the heavy equipment and moved to other freight cars to secure the pallets. It took two and a half hours to transfer the cargo.

Dan parked his lift truck next to Jack's, turned off the engine, glanced at Jack, and said, "Is that it for today?"

Jack smiled and replied, "Nope, we're not done yet. We've got to load 20 tons of canned fish and 12 tons of minerals. Several semis will be over at the other wharf in about an hour. The fish is boxed and wrapped on pallets; the minerals are sealed in wooden boxes. We'll take the lift trucks on Hugger to help make the transfers. We should have it all loaded in about an hour. Let's drive these little guys on board. We'll go to another pier, not the where the cruise ship is."

Frank raised the ramp and Jack piloted Hugger back to a different, older wharf. A crane was used to lift the pallets from the flatbeds and lower them to the cargo deck. Dan and Jack used the lift trucks to move the heavily loaded pallets to optimal positions for securing. Jack had been right, it took a little more than an hour to complete the transfer. Dan got Nomah from his berth, and they went ashore for an hour's walk while Jack arranged for more cargo for the return trip to Bellingham.

When Dan returned with Nomah, a crane was lowering more pallets of canned fish into the hold. Sam and Frank were driving the lift trucks. Jack was on the bridge watching. Dan climbed up to Jack and said, "Sorry I'm late. Want me to take over for Frank or Sam?"

"No, that's all right. Those guys need to do some work. They pretty much sat around while we drove this morning. We'll be shoving off in the morning—about eight o'clock. You want to spend the night on board? You can have pancakes for breakfast, and, as Ross will tell you, with real butter, not that imitation crap." Jack laughed. "Ross is a good man and can be comical at times."

"Yeah, I know. I think I'll stay on Hugger tonight and take off in the morning so I don't have to do any work." Dan smiled and gave Jack a gentle slap on the back.

Jack put his hand on Dan's shoulder and asked, "How's that dog of yours?"

"He's getting tired of being restricted to the boat. He'll be happy to run around on land again when we get to Fairbanks. You own a dog, Jack?"

"Nope." He smiled, "I've got two kids and a wife to chase around—don't need a pet. Maybe I'll get a dog or cat when the kids are off to college."

CHAPTER 27

Fairbanks

Dan finished Jack's book just before 2400 hours, leaned back, and while thinking about seeing Uncle Max after four years, fell asleep after midnight. Nomah was curled up on the deck at the foot of the bunk when Dan woke up. Nomah must have gotten down from the bunk to avoid being kicked when Dan was dreaming—trying to escape from the airplane sinking into the water.

"Are you hungry, big guy?"

Nomah got up and came over to Dan, who scratched Nomah's neck and back. Dan gave Nomah the remainder of the 25 pound bag of food and some water, dressed, and headed to the galley. The four crew members were having coffee and talking about the return trip. When Dan arrived, Ross looked up at him and said, "The usual?"

Dan was pouring himself some coffee and answered, "Please, but make sure you put out some real butter this time."

"What? I always give you gents real..." Ross caught on almost too late, but he stopped talking, realizing Dan was yanking his chain. The crew, including Ross, had a good-hearted laugh. Everyone liked Ross and they rarely got him riled, especially about his food. Rarely had they eaten so well as on Hugger.

Frank was still smiling and said, "Good one, Dan. You got him on your last day."

After eating, Dan stood up and addressed the four men, "I'm kind of sorry to be leaving you and Hugger. I have enjoyed working with you and learning about ocean travel. I'm glad I was of some use during the trip. But, in another respect, I'm glad it's over. Now I'll be back with my family and will begin working toward getting an airplane. Maybe someday I will be able to fly you around Alaska—show you the mountains, glaciers, and herds of caribou. Good luck on your trip back to Bellingham. And Jack, tell your father thank-you for me." The crew shook hands with Dan and wished him good luck. Dan picked up his backpack, attached Nomah's new leash, and left the boat. As he walked down the pier toward Gull Avenue to meet Max, he stopped, turned around and saluted Hugger.

Dan had five hours to kill before Uncle Max would be at the meeting place, what was he to do? He was approaching an office building, located at the end of the wharf where it jutted out into the water. Dan decided to check the yellow pages for aviation supply stores, but he needed a phone book. After tying Nomah to an old bicycle rack, Dan entered Alaskan Ocean Freight through a big yellow door.

A woman, old enough to be his grandmother, sitting at a large wooden desk behind a computer screen, put down her coffee and asked, "May I help you?" She stood and moved to the counter opposite Dan.

"Yes, ma'am. May I borrow your phone book? I'd like to find an address."

"Sure. Just a moment." She turned, walked to her desk, and brought Dan the phone book. As she handed him the book, she said, "I assume you want the Anchorage book, we have lots more for different cities." She smiled, looking at Dan as if she wanted to read or turn the pages for him. "What address are you looking for, if I may ask?"

Dan answered, "An aviation supply store. Is there one nearby?" He looked at the lady, more closely this time. It occurred to him that she looked like Mrs. Santa Claus. She had a round face with rosy cheeks, curly grayish-white hair, and a pencil above her ear. Dan chuckled at his thoughts and said, "Has anyone ever told you that you look like Mrs. Santa? What does your husband do?"

"Well, dear, he's in the Los Angeles area recruiting elves." She started laughing. "My name's Mary, Mary Donaldson. Stu is in Seward today. He's inspecting a boat."

Dan was laughing with her and said, "You are a very funny lady. I'm Dan Newcomb. It's nice to meet you."

They shook hands and Mary said, "To answer your question, Huxley's Aviation is about five miles from here, near the airport. I can call you a taxi—it's quite a ways. You and your dog don't want to walk that far. Would your dog like a treat?"

"You saw my dog?"

"Yes, I was getting coffee and I saw you walking down the wharf. What's his name?"

"Nomah. He burns lots of calories; he's still growing. He'd like a treat. Can I bring him in?"

"Sure, we have four-legged visitors all the time —," she grinned, "reindeer and all, you know."

Dan brought Nomah in the office and over to Mary, who had come out from behind the counter holding a dog biscuit in her hand. Nomah had his eyes fixed on the treat, his tail wagging.

"Nomah, sit. You be nice to the lady."

Mary held the treat out. Nomah took it from her fingers very slowly, stretched out on the floor and started crunching the bone-shaped biscuit. Mary said, "Good boy, Nomah. You are a very good dog." Mary commented, "I'll call you a taxi, Dan. It will be about ten minutes. We're not on a regular city route."

When the taxi arrived, Dan thanked Mary for the help and the biscuit. As he put Nomah in the taxi, he saw Mary standing in the window, and waved goodbye. She smiled and waved back.

"Huxley Aviation," Dan said to the driver. Fifteen minutes later, the yellow SUV pulled up in front of a big, sky-blue, two-story, metal building about 300 yards from the airport entrance. Dan paid the fare, got out with Nomah, and entered Huxley Aviation. A new Cessna was parked inside between the door and a large circular counter. Dan hardly glanced at it, knowing it would be way above his price limit. A salesman, with Gary Upton on his name tag attached above his left shirt pocket, approached and asked, "May I help you, sir?"

"Just looking, thanks."

"Are you a pilot?" Gary asked.

"Uh-huh. Have any used Cessna 185s?"

"Looking for a tail dragger, huh? Last one of those made was in 1985."

"Yeah, but I can't afford it now. It will probably take me a couple of years before I can make a down payment. I just got out of the service, but I have a job waiting for me. How much would a 185 in reasonable shape set me back?"

"Well, those are in high demand as bush planes. One that needs some work will cost about 55 grand, maybe a little less, if you can find somebody that must sell. What you might do is look around for a fixer-upper, maybe one that has gone down. I'll give you my card. Call me every now and then and I'll tell you if anything has come to my attention. Why not give me your number? I'll call you."

"Wish I could, but I don't have a phone yet." Dan didn't want the guy calling his uncle's number, so kept it to himself. Besides, salesmen can become a pest if they think they can make a commission. Dan wanted to avoid the middleman if at all possible. The men talked about planes for nearly an hour; then Dan thanked Gary and moved toward the door. Nomah had been sleeping on the showroom floor beneath the new Cessna and was at the door ready to get outside before Dan could open the door. Dan found a service station phone and called for a taxi. It took 20 minutes to get to the intersection to meet Uncle Max.

Dan had bought three candy bars at the service station. He sat on a concrete bench at the rendezvous site, ate a Snickers bar, and talked to an elderly woman who had stopped to rest a few minutes. It was a little after 12:30 when a big black pickup stopped at the curb. Dan couldn't miss the slogan on the doors. It read Conley and Newcomb: You Break It, We Fix It. Dan smiled and quickly stepped to the passenger door and turned the handle. The window was open.

"Hey, sailor, want a ride?"

Dan swung the door wide open, urged Nomah into the back seat, and climbed in the big pickup. "Sure could use one, Uncle Max. How you doin'?"

"Just fine, and you?" They slapped hands together rather than shake.

"Trying to get my land legs back; ten days on that boat messed up my stability. How long have you had the beard?" Dan had never seen Max with a beard and wouldn't have recognized him had they passed on the street. But the voice was unmistakable, a rich tenor with a hint of gravel mixed in. If Max could sing, he could move to Nashville.

With his right hand, Max pulled at his chin whiskers and said, "Since Christmas. I thought I'd spend a year with a beard and shave it off on New Year's Day so I can see football better," he laughed. "Mona doesn't like it—says it tickles, but the boys get a kick out of it. They've come up with some funny comments. Duke calls me Max Bunyan. Earl says it won't be long 'til I won't need a shirt; the beard will keep me warm."

"How are the boys and Mona doing?" Nomah whined and sat up in the back seat.

"What's wrong with your dog, Dan?"

Dan thought a second and said, "I think he heard Mona and thought I said Nomah. If that isn't it, he has to get out and pee."

"I can't stop here. Let's get a burger, Nomah can get out and pee then."

"Sounds good to me. I could use something to eat. All I've had since breakfast was a candy bar."

"There's a McBou place about a mile from here, I saw it coming in."

"McBou—that something new?"

"A take-off of McDonald's, I guess. Caribou burgers and fries. Tell me about your trip on the water and your stay in Oregon."

As they ate burgers, Dan began reliving and relating his stay in Oregon and the trip on Hugger. Four hours later, they were approaching Denali Park. The last time Dan had talked as much was when he rode with Bert Sayers. They pulled over for gas and took a few minutes to stretch their legs.

"Dan, how would you like to take over driving? My eyes are getting tired, and so is my butt." Max was attempting to stand up straight but was having to stretch his lower back and thighs. He had been driving with little rest for more than ten hours.

"No problem, but my license has expired."

"Don't sweat it—no one will stop us near the park. I'll take over as we approach the city in case you've forgotten the streets. I'm going to use the facilities, walk for a couple of minutes and we'll go. Looks like we'll get home at eight o'clock."

"That makes it a long day for you, almost 14 hours on the road. I'd get tired, too, and I'm lots younger than you."

Max chuckled, "Don't start diggin' my grave yet, Daniel."

It was 8:17 p.m. when the pickup rolled into the driveway at 1112 Juneau Avenue. Max, Dan, and Nomah entered the ranch-style house and were greeted by Mona and the two boys. Mona threw her arms around Dan and said, "You look wonderful! You remember Duke and Earl?" She pointed out the boys and they shook hands. Duke had grown to nearly his father's height and had long, light-brown, almost reddish-blond hair.

Dan could tell the boys were a little nervous. They hadn't seen Dan for more than four years, when they were 10 and 12 years old. Fourteen-year-old freckle-faced Earl, with short reddish-brown hair, looked like he wanted to ask something, so Dan said, "Earl, have you got a question?"

"Ah—yeah. Dad said you got shot. Can I see the scars?"

"Sure, which wounds do want to see, the little ones or the big ones? I'll have to take my pants off; I don't want to embarrass anyone."

Mona, a tall red-head, had changed her hair significantly from the last time Dan had seen her. Her short hair and trim figure made her appear much younger. She wasn't Hollywood pretty, but nice looking—and Dan knew she had a heart of gold. Mona intervened, "Boys, leave Dan alone. He doesn't want to show you his scars. Maybe some other time. Isn't that right, Dan?"

"That's a good idea. When I was in Juneau, I bought you guys a computer game. It's a big-game hunt from snowmobiles." He opened his pack and handed a DVD case to Earl, who ran for the computer room with Duke close behind.

"Boys! What do you say?"

A yell came from down the hallway, "Thanks, Uncle Dan!"

Dan had to laugh, and Mona said, "Where do they get their manners?" She looked at Max. Dan laughed again.

"I brought something for you, too. Here you are." Dan gave Mona the music CDs and the carved ivory pen to Max. They were both very appreciative, thanking Dan with a hug, and in Mona's case, a kiss on the cheek. Dan went over to Nomah, dropped to his knees and scratched

Nomah's back and neck. "I need to feed Nomah. Mona, do you have a pie tin he can eat from—or a big bowl?"

"Oh, my! I didn't even see your dog. He must have been behind you when I rushed to greet you. He's beautiful, isn't he, Max?"

"Sure is. He's going to get bigger, too. Dan said he's still a pup. I'll bet Nomah is going to tip the scale at more than a hundred pounds. He'll be good to have at the shop for intimidation reasons. What do you think, Daniel?"

Dan was sitting on the sofa with his eyes closed, listening to the conversation.

He opened his eyes and glanced at Max. "He's a big teddy-bear, Max. He likes people, unless they act mean."

"Just what we need. A snarl and anybody that's obnoxious will mind their manners." Max stood up from his easy-chair and said, "I've got to go to bed, tomorrow's a work day for everybody. We'll get up at six, Dan. You'll have to sleep on the sofa; it's got a pullout-bed. I'll help you find a place tomorrow."

Dan yawned and said, "Sounds good to me. Come on, Nomah, let's go outside for a few minutes so you can pee." When Dan and Nomah came back inside, everyone had gone to bed. Dan moved the stack of blankets and pillows from the sofa, removed the cushions, and pulled out the folded bed. He didn't really make the bed, he just spread out a sheet and unfolded a blanket and comforter. He removed his shoes and pants and started to climb in bed, but first, he went to the front door and locked it.

Dan was sitting at a campfire with a woman, talking about a crash. She wore a parka, the hood pulled closely to her face, so he couldn't tell who she was. She got up from sitting beside him and poured some coffee. God that coffee smelled good!

"Hey, Daniel, time to get up. We've got to get to work. Mona's going to drop the boys off at school—they'll ride the bus home."

The dream was gone, but the smell of coffee was still present. Pants, clean socks, and shoes on, Dan folded the blankets and reassembled the sofa. He opened the front door and let Nomah out into the fenced yard. Dan didn't step outside—the temperature had to be below freezing. When he exhaled, the moisture from his lungs created a cloud about his face. A few minutes of being outside caused Nomah to bark at the front door. He preferred warmer temperatures after being on the mild ocean for nearly two weeks.

CHAPTER 28

The Airplane

Max and Dan opened for business at the shop at 8:03 a.m. The storefront's large, matching windows, separated by a setback of about four feet, led to a heavy, glass front door. The first-floor of the old, red-brick building covered 800 square feet, with a rear balcony half that size. Behind the building was a half-vacant lot of 800 square feet that contained everything that didn't need special protection from the elements. Dan rummaged around outside, getting an idea of what there was to work with among the piles of sheet metal under a lean-to. Heavy wooden boxes, and a half-dozen metal barrels of various sizes contained remnants of metal and wood; leftovers from various projects.

After ten minutes of exposure to the cold, Dan returned to the warmth of the building, went to the second floor balcony and looked over the ordered assemblage of bolts, nuts and washers, hinges, nails, and a disordered menagerie of odds and ends. He returned to the ground floor, where Max was waiting on a customer. The elderly man held a broken snow shovel; the handle had been snapped in two when he backed his car over it. Max asked him to come back in an hour to pick up the shovel. While Max worked on the shovel, Dan began checking for a place to live.

After 30 minutes on the phone, Dan was ready to start looking for roommates. Everything was too expensive or had requirements which Dan wouldn't accept. He wasn't a student or in the military, and he certainly would not give up Nomah. No pets was a deal-breaker. He was sitting at the counter thinking about alternatives, when a woman of obvious means came in the door. She wore a fur coat, lots of makeup, and approached Dan like she meant business.

"Hello, young man. Can you fix a microwave oven?"

"I'm not sure. Tell me what happened. Does it come on?"

"Oh, yes. It comes on, counts down, and turns off, but I can't get the door open. I tried to warm some soup but couldn't get it out of the oven. When I pressed on the thing that opens the door, nothing happened." She made a motion with her finger like she was pressing the opening lever. Dan couldn't miss seeing a large, sparkling, diamond ring on her finger.

Dan smiled and asked, "Where's the oven."

"Out in my car. The soup spilled all over the place. Can you clean that up too?"

"Let me get the oven so I can look at it. Show me where you're parked."

"Just follow me. What is your name, young man?"

"Daniel," he smiled. "What is your name, young lady?"

She began to laugh and replied, "Hah. I'm old enough to be your grandmother. Young lady, indeed. I am Madeline Cornell. My husband works for the pipeline company."

Dan carried the oven inside and in a couple of minutes had the top removed. As soon as he identified the problem, he asked her to come back in an hour. She said she had some things to do and would return. The plastic lift-arm was broken and had slipped out of position. It would take him 30 minutes to make another one. He repaired and cleaned the microwave and asked Max how much to charge.

"Well, 20 bucks an hour is my standard."

"So ten bucks then; it only took 30 minutes."

"Better make it $11.95, Dan."

"Why that amount?"

"Ten dollars is too simple; sounds like you rounded it up from less than ten. Parts never cost an even amount. She'll be happy with $11.95."

"I think I've got a lot to learn from you, Uncle Max. By the way, I haven't found an apartment yet, but I was thinking—there's enough room on the balcony for a bedroom. I just have to reorganize a few things, buy a mattress, and get a lamp. I can also be security for this vast wealth of equipment in the shop."

"Vast wealth?" Max laughed. "Well, if you want to do that, it's all right with me. Just don't have any sleepovers. I don't want the store to get a bad rep—women coming and going at all hours. Mona wouldn't like the boys to find out, either."

"Don't worry. I'm going to live like a monk. I'll go to the YMCA for showers."

Mrs. Cornell returned to the shop after 50 minutes. "Were you able to fix it, Daniel?"

"Yes, ma'am. It works like a charm. That'll be $11.95."

"Is that all? That's a real bargain. I was going to buy a new one if you couldn't fix it for less than $50. I'll pay you cash. Do you have a girlfriend, Daniel?"

"No ma'am, but I think I'm too young for you."

She started laughing, kind of a witch's cackle. "You aren't serious, are you?"

"Just joking, Mrs. Cornell. I'm not looking for romance, but I would go on a date. Do you have someone in mind?"

"Yes, my granddaughter. She's attending the university—studying architecture. Her name is Lisa Zorn. I'll tell her about you."

By the end of June, Dan and Nomah had adjusted to their new digs. Dan had a hot plate, a small microwave, some second-hand furniture, and a small refrigerator. Dan and Nomah would go for a run at 6:00 a.m., and Dan would shower in a makeshift, outdoor shower he had constructed from the backend of an old bus, frosting the windows to maintain privacy. His next plan, before the cold weather returned, was to add a heater to have hot water. He used the emergency exit door to enter and exit the shower. Nomah was also given a bath in the bus.

It was an early morning of the second week in July. Max and Dan were discussing business receipts for June when a man, easily over six-feet tall, entered the shop. He wore a sweat-stained white baseball cap, grease- and dirt-soiled blue-denim overalls, and sported a heavy black beard, but didn't wear a shirt. Both Max and Dan expected trouble. They could smell him from five feet away. Dan moved away from behind the counter so his movements wouldn't be restricted if a fight broke out.

"Howdy! Can you repair a front loader?" He placed a big fist on the glass countertop, looking at Max, and waiting for a reply.

Max answered, "Probably. What do you think is wrong with it?"

"Hell, I don't know. The damn thing just up an' quit on me. I've got a crew that needs it; we're gold mining about 40 miles northwest of here. We've got a small loader right now, but it can't move shit. We've got to process more dirt—fast."

"Where is it?"

"Outside on a truck. Can you take a look?"

"Sure. Come on, Dan, let's see if we can help this gentleman." Max grabbed his volt/ohmmeter and started out the door. The big man followed with Dan and Nomah close behind. Max tossed the meter to Dan and said, "Check the battery voltage first and then the starter wires." Dan climbed on the loader to use the meter. Max inspected the engine from top to bottom. "What do you think, Dan?"

"Voltages are fine. I think the filters are plugged or the gas is full of water or dirt, or both. Was the engine running hot, mister?"

"Ah—a little, but we was pushing it purty hard. The SOB just up and died."

"It's going to take us all day today to fix it, if it's what I think the problem is. How are you going to pay for it? We can't work on credit."

"Jesus! I've got all my cash sunk into the mining site. I can't pay you now. Can you wait 'til I got some gold?"

"I'm afraid not. We've got families to feed. I need $200 up front."

"How about if I got something to trade?"

Dan decided to help Max out. "You have something you can you trade or put up for collateral?"

"I got an airplane. Crashed in the timber near the mine a couple of years ago. Insurance people said I could have it. The body's in pretty good shape, prop's broke, and the wing come off, but I saved all the pieces." The big guy smiled, thinking he had a good trade for the work.

"Where is this wreck, Mr.—? Ah—what's your name?"

"Graves, Stu Graves. It's outside of town in a machine shed, about four miles from here. Drive me to it, I'll show ya."

Max tossed Dan the keys to the pickup, and with Stu in the front seat, Dan lowered the windows and followed the big man's directions. Fifteen minutes later, Stu was shoving a key in a padlock on an old, rusty Quonset building. The big metal door squeaked as it slid sideways on rusty rollers. Dan recognized the damaged plane immediately, a Cessna 185 tail dragger, blue and white. Dan couldn't have dreamed of a better find. It almost took his breath away, but he had to act like he had little interest in the wreckage.

Dan looked inside the cabin to see a large honeybee colony perched on top of the instrument panel; the pilot's door was ajar allowing the insects entry. He stepped back and said, "Well, Mr. Graves, we've got a deal, but my uncle has to agree. Let's go back to the shop and maybe sign some papers—after I talk with my uncle."

Dan couldn't believe the stroke of good luck. The Cessna needed major repairs, but the airframe was in good shape. It was going to require many hours of work, and a reasonable amount of money—several thousand dollars—to get the plane ready for flight. The 15 minutes back to the shop flew by, Dan was already planning the restoration.

"So you're going to cover the cost of the repairs to the loader?" Max quizzed.

"Uh-huh. I've got some money left from the reward I got in Oregon plus what I've earned here—about $3,500."

"You're sure you want to do this?"

"I'm sure, Uncle Max. I can fix that plane. It'll fly again. I've even got a name for it—The Glacier Phoenix."

"Okay, but where will you keep it? We don't have enough room here or at the house."

"I'll talk with Graves. Maybe he'll let me use his machine shed. I'll even pay him rent."

"Okay. Let's tell him we have a deal, provided you can use his shed."

"Thanks, Uncle Max. You won't regret it."

Max took a deep breath and exhaled, "I sure hope not."

CHAPTER 29

Coffee Date

Max and Dan were able to repair Stu Graves' loader in a day and a half. Graves gave Dan the key to his machine shed, and Dan worked on the restoration of the Cessna every chance he got. On the last Sunday in September, a black BMW sedan drove up to the Quonset hut. A girl with shoulder-length, light-auburn hair got out and slowly approached the open door where Dan was sitting, working on the engine. He had his back turned to the outside, was listening to a CD wearing earphones, and hadn't heard the car. Parts of the plane's engine were on the ground arranged on an old canvas and newspapers.

The girl spoke up, but not loudly enough to get Dan's attention. She picked up a wrench, thought for a moment, and struck the metal door, hard. Dan turned his head, looked up, and saw the attractive young woman. He reached for his CD player, pressed the off button, removed the earphones, and stood up, holding a greasy rag.

"Are you Daniel?" she asked, her car keys held with both hands at her waist.

"Yeah." He was a little irritated with the interruption. He had to make the best possible use of his few hours of free time. "What can I do for you?"

"My grandmother, Madeline Cornell, dared me to look you up. I'm Lisa. She challenged me to meet you. She was gushing about you, so I thought I'd better check you out, if nothing more than to stop her talking. You know how grandmothers are."

"Not really. I never met mine. They passed long ago."

"Oh, I'm sorry. You have a beautiful dog. What's his name?"

"Nomah. I got him in Oregon, where I learned to fly. He's going to fly with me."

When Nomah heard his name, he got up and walked over to Lisa, who knelt and scratched his ears. "God, you are a big boy, Nomah." Lisa looked up and commented, "Looks like you're working on an airplane. Do you think it will ever fly?"

Dan had scanned Lisa from head to toe. *This girl is a 10, but she obviously doesn't know anything about me.* He answered, "No question about that, but at the rate I'm going, it will be next summer before it will be air-worthy. I have to get the engine running and an inspection of the plane before I can get it registered and licensed. It's expensive and I'm short of funds, but it'll happen. What do you do? Your grandmother said you were in school."

"Yes. I'm in my fourth year of architecture school; it's a five-year program."

Dan grinned. "Going to design energy efficient igloos, huh?"

"Not quite." She frowned and replied, "How are you going to fly that plane without wings? Do you have an anti-gravity device?"

"Touché. The wing is out in back in two pieces. How do I get in touch with you at school, or would you rather I not? I've never been to college. I might not measure up to your academic standards."

"God, you must think I'm a real snob. I think I'd better go."

"Suit yourself. Tell Madeline hello for me. She's a nice lady. I hope her microwave is still working."

Lisa walked quickly to her car, got in, slammed the door and drove off. She spun the tires kicking up dirt and gravel.

Dan turned the music back on and resumed working on the engine. He thought about what he had said. *I guess I shouldn't have made that crack about igloos or never having gone to college. Maybe I'll go by the university and apologize for my comments. She had to have guts to come out here—and what's more, she's hot. I haven't gone on a date in a long time, I'll ask her out. If she doesn't want to, no big deal. I don't have much extra time anyway.*

It was nearly two weeks before Dan had an opportunity to visit the university in the early afternoon. He didn't know Lisa's schedule, but thought he'd take a chance and see if he could find her. The Architecture Department was on the second floor of a four-story, modular, concrete building called Aurora Hall, painted like curtains to resemble the northern lights so often observed in the northern latitudes. The fourth floor windows were shaped like igloos.

Dan took the stairs closest to the front entrance and saw a sign pointing to the opposite end of the hall where architectural exhibits were being shown. Curious to see what students had designed, he moved down the central hallway, which opened to a large area where students, family members, and faculty were gathered in groups socializing. There were punchbowls and cookies on a large table in the center of the room. Dan saw Madeline Cornell talking to an older gentleman wearing an ID tag on his suit pocket.

Dan walked over and said, "Hello, Mrs. Cornell, nice to see you again."

"Oh, Daniel! I heard that you and Lisa didn't get along."

"Yes, I came to apologize. I was trying to be funny and it was taken the wrong way, and then I made it worse. I have a tendency to put my foot in my mouth when I'm around pretty women. I suggested to Lisa that I lacked her education, so I would be below her intellectual interests."

"Uh-huh. That's what she said, but if you knew her, you'd know that would not be the case. There she is now." Madeline pointed to Lisa, looking at an exhibit with three young men. "Why don't you go talk with her?"

"Thanks, Mrs. Cornell, I think I will."

Dan walked over to Lisa, whose back was turned, and tapped her on the shoulder. She turned around and said, "Well, hello Dan. I didn't think I'd ever see you again."

"I seem to habitually say the wrong thing. I came to apologize. I didn't think you were a snob, it just sounded that way. My choice of words could have been better."

One of the three young men with Lisa stepped up and said, "You called Lisa a snob?" He attempted to push Dan back with his hand, but Dan didn't give ground.

Dan reacted, "Look, junior. That's not what I said—it's none of your business anyway. I was talking to the young lady."

"I'm making it my business. You don't talk to my friends like that."

Dan ignored the student and said, "Anyway, Lisa, I'm sorry for the way it sounded. Bye." Dan turned to leave, but he noticed in one of the display mirrors one of the young men was approaching with his fist cocked. Dan turned and ducked, the punch sailed harmlessly over his shoulder. He turned around quickly, shaking his head, and said, "You don't want to do that. If you want to fight me, you'd better come outside. I wouldn't want to damage any of these displays."

Dan left the room and the building. As he reached the parking lot, the three boys caught up with him. One boy grabbed his shoulder and spun him around.

Dan planted his fist in the young man's stomach, doubling him over. He was gasping for wind. The other two boys attacked, and Dan quickly dropped them to the asphalt parking surface. None of the three wanted any more. Dan got in the company truck and left the campus.

The company phone rang at 2:30. Max answered and said, "Hey, Dan, it's for you." He covered the phone with his hand, grinned, and said, "It sounds like a young lady."

Dan wondered who would be calling him, surely it wasn't Lisa. "Hello?"

"Hi, Dan. This is Lisa. I heard what those guys did. I'm sorry—I didn't know. I wonder if we could start over, but I know you work a lot. Could we meet for coffee after dinner sometime?"

"That sounds good. How about next Monday at Hobo's, seven o'clock?"

"Okay. I know where that is. See you at seven. Bye."

"Bye." Dan hung up the phone and looked at Max, who was smiling. "It's just a coffee date, Max. No big deal."

"Dan, if that was the coed that was looking for you a couple of Sundays ago, it *is* a big deal. She is choice!"

Dan grinned and replied, "I can't disagree."

Max shook his head and offered one of his proverbs, "I've always said you can never tell what will happen after you fix an old lady's microwave." They both laughed as they got back to work.

Hobo's Java House wasn't very busy Monday evening. Dan arranged to be there five minutes early and was waiting outside the entrance. Nervous about the meeting with Lisa, he looked at his watch repeatedly, wishing time would move faster and hoping Lisa would show up at 7:00 p.m. as planned. At five minutes after, a sedan pulled up and stopped, motor running, and Lisa got out of the passenger side. She gave a little wave to the driver, who slowly drove away.

"Hi, Dan. Have you been waiting long?" She had a cheerful voice and smiled as she approached. "Sorry, I'm a bit late. Grandma doesn't like to drive downtown—too many lights and reflections bother her. She's developing cataracts."

"No problem, a few minutes never bother me, especially when I'm looking forward to seeing someone. I probably would have waited an hour if I'd known you looked so nice."

"Thank you. I'm impressed. How *long* would you have waited tonight?"

Dan smiled. "Oh, at least an hour, maybe longer."

Dan held the door for Lisa and escorted her to a table in the back. He helped her remove her jacket, held her chair, and removed the reserved sign from the table for two.

Lisa smiled and said, "I didn't know they had reserved seating."

"They don't, but I helped repair Tony's refrigerator on Saturday. I asked him to reserve a table in the back where we could talk."

Lisa looked around and commented, "This is nice."

They ordered coffee and began talking. Some topics were intense but many were comical. Lisa and Dan had grown up under very different circumstances, but opposites were attracting that evening. Dan noticed, when Lisa talked, the tip of her perfectly straight nose moved, almost imperceptibly. He only noticed it when he looked into her pretty blue eyes. It was after nine o'clock before they realized nearly two and a half hours had gone by.

Lisa glanced at her watch and said, "Oh, nuts. I have to go. I've got some studying to do for tomorrow. Could you please take me home?"

"Sure. I've enjoyed your company. Maybe we can do this again."

"I'd like that, Dan. I think you have had a fascinating life. I want to hear more about your job in Oregon. I've never been there. Thank you for tonight."

Following Lisa's directions, Dan dropped her off at her parents' house. He walked her to the door and they said good night. Dan turned to walk toward the truck, but Lisa ran up to him and planted a kiss on his lips. She spoke with a sexy whisper, "Good night, Dan."

Dan had not anticipated the kiss and said, "Thanks, Lisa. G'night." Dan continued toward the pickup and almost fell over the mailbox near the curb. He hadn't noticed it before. He looked back to see if Lisa had seen his clumsiness, but she had gone into the house.

CHAPTER 30

Preparation for the Mountains

Lisa came over to the Conleys' for Thanksgiving dinner. The boys stared at her while they ate, finishing the meal last, which was very unusual. Dan noticed their behavior and gave Mona a wink. When Lisa said good night, she gave the boys a kiss on the cheek.

Between Thanksgiving and Christmas, Dan purchased gifts for all the Conleys, and he didn't forget Nomah. The Conleys gave Dan a scarf and sweater; deficiencies in his wardrobe. After spending most of Christmas Day with the Conleys, Dan joined Lisa and her grandparents for Christmas dinner. Following dessert, Dan and Lisa played bridge with the Cornells, unfortunately, Dan hadn't played in several years, and the younger pair lost miserably. A second bottle of wine was emptied as the two couples watched a Christmas movie. A few minutes after eleven o'clock, the Cornells retired.

Lisa asked, "Shall we watch another movie?"

Dan looked at his watch and said, "Sure, why not? I'll get back to the shop at 1:00 a.m., but Nomah won't mind."

Lisa laughed, "So Nomah won't ask where you've been?"

"He'll know as soon as I get home, he'll smell your perfume."

Lisa stood up and walked toward the guest room. "What type of movie do you want, mystery or romance?"

Offered those two choices, Dan answered, "Mystery."

199

Lisa had hoped for the romantic movie, but chuckled and said, "Okay, I'll be right back."

Dan looked around the room at all the Christmas decorations. He had never seen a room with so many elaborate ornaments adding to the beauty of the rich, home furnishings. He wondered if he would ever make the kind of money it would take to run a home like the Cornells'.

Lisa came back from her room carrying several compact disks. Her hair had been pulled back into a bun at the back of her head, but was now loose, hanging down to her shoulders. She had changed from her Christmas sweater to a yellow and green University of Oregon sweatshirt. She sat next to Dan and showed him the movie covers. "Which one?"

Dan pointed at a Tom Selleck-Jesse Stone movie and then asked, "Where did you get that sweatshirt?"

"The bookstore on campus. It was a special order—you said you were a fan of the Oregon Ducks. I actually ordered it for you, but they sent this one. It's too small, but it's just right for me. I'll get you another one, okay?"

"Sure. Thanks for thinking of me. I have something for you—it's in my coat. Dan started to get up, but Lisa said, "Stay here, I'll get it."

He leaned back into the soft sofa and said, "It's in the right inside pocket." Dan watched Lisa pick up his coat, reach into the pocket, and retrieve a small jewelry case.

As she walked toward the sofa, Lisa inspected the little box, wrapped in shiny green paper with a silver ribbon, trying to find a clue as to its contents. She sank down onto the cushion and leaned against Dan, looking up at his smiling face. "Can I open it?"

"Sure, I got it for you. I waited until we were alone, I didn't get anything for your grandparents."

"You brought that bottle of wine. That was enough. They didn't expect anything." Lisa cautiously removed the wrapping, trying not to tear the paper. She wanted to prolong the anticipation, wondering what Dan had given her. Surely, it wasn't a ring, Dan wouldn't make that leap before he knew their feelings were mutual. She didn't know if Dan was seeing someone else, his emotions were veiled behind humor and his quiet demeanor. She rarely knew what he was thinking, and that bothered her. She tilted back the lid to expose a pair of stud earrings, aquamarine stones set in gold.

"They're beautiful, Dan. Oh, thank you so much. How did you know my birthday was in March?"

Dan kissed her and said, "I asked your grandmother. She was very helpful, even recommending a jeweler, after I mentioned how much I could spend. Madeline is really nice, you're lucky to have her as a grandparent."

Lisa held out the box to Dan and said, "Help me put them on."

Dan lacked dexterity with his big fingers and he struggled to free the earrings from the box. He noticed Lisa's blue eyes following his fingers and her broad smile, as he wrestled with the delicate jewelry, but he didn't give up. He moved the stud toward Lisa's left earlobe and asked, "Can you move your hair back so I can complete this maneuver?"

She laughed, "Military talk, huh?"

"Uh-huh, but just a small skirmish. There, one down, one to go."

After the second earring was in place, Lisa said, "Well done, Captain."

"Thanks, but I was never an officer, just a grunt."

"Yes, but as soon as you are flying, you will be a captain. Correct?"

Dan grinned, "Well, I guess you could say that. I could have five passengers—actually four plus Nomah."

They started the movie, and as the actors' names began flashing across the screen, Lisa put her head in Dan's lap and stretched out on the sofa. She reached for Dan's right hand and clasped it between hers. "Your hand is cold, are you chilly?"

"Not now. I was a little nervous about the earrings—afraid you wouldn't like them."

"I love them, Dan. They'll go with so many of my things." Lisa raised her sweatshirt several inches and placed Dan's hand on her stomach. "I'll get your hand warm for you."

"I think that should do it. I might have to take off my shirt if I get too warm," Dan grinned and then more seriously said, "My hands are very rough; I don't want to irritate your soft skin."

Lisa moved Dan's hand upward, under her shirt and placed his hand over her right breast. "I don't think your hand is too rough. How does this feel?"

Dan could feel Lisa's erect nipple in the palm of his hand, her firm breast fitting into his hand almost perfectly. He squeezed her breast slightly and then moved his index finger around the areola, barely touching Lisa's delicate tissue, the nipple extending further from her breast. Dan looked at Lisa's pretty face, her eyes were closed as she took a deep breath and then slowly exhaled. It was obvious that he wasn't hurting her.

Lisa whispered, "There's another one," as she turned so Dan could have complete access to both breasts. She raised her shirt to her neck so he could see her exquisite charms.

Dan whispered, "God, you are so beautiful," as he moved his hand to her left breast to continue the touches that both were enjoying. He had a desire to kiss both mounds and explore her nipples with his tongue and lips, but Lisa's and his positions prevented access. He would have to experience those gentle touches some other time.

Lisa whispered, "Your touch is magical, Dan. You make me feel wonderful."

She paused for a moment and then said, smiling, "Do you have some of my grandmother's silverware in your pocket?"

Dan grinned, knowing what Lisa was referring to, and said, "I came here with a teaspoon, but I think it's a serving spoon now. We'd better slow down, it might spill over."

Lisa ran her hands over the bulge in his pants, got up quickly, grabbed Dan's hands, and pulled him up from the sofa. Lisa removed her shirt, started to loosen her pants, but suddenly grabbed Dan's left hand and moved toward her bedroom. Dan picked Lisa up and carried her into the room, dimly illuminated by a nightlight.

Dan got back to the shop at 2:00 a.m. He checked Nomah and crawled into bed, exhausted. He couldn't remember a time when his mind was so untroubled. New Year's Day was spent visiting friends with Lisa. Wherever there was mistletoe, Dan and Lisa were close by. Lisa had become an important part of Dan's life. Even though they were both extremely busy, they found time for each other, if only once or twice a month, sometimes just for coffee, other times for dinner, a movie, and intimacy.

Lisa began a master's program in the spring, planning to go to Portland for an internship during the summer. Dan called the Sterlings to get information on rentals near Lisa's workplace, but Val and Terry said that wasn't necessary, inviting Lisa to stay with them during the summer. Val and Lisa had exchanged a number of emails, becoming good friends during the spring.

When Lisa left for the summer, Dan felt like he had when Ann left for Boise. What if Lisa found someone else, decided to stay in Portland, or somewhere else in the lower 48, never to return? He worked feverishly on the plane, pouring every penny he could scrape up into the repairs. Dan needed to be making some money from flying to pay off a bank loan. He hated paying interest.

Parts were expensive, and Dan knew he could only make some of those necessary for the wing. The wing had suffered major damage when the plane went down in the forest. The strategic pieces would have to be purchased or he would have to find an intact wing. He had finished with the motor, a 300 horse-power beast; the fuselage, and the entire tail assemblage had minimal damage, requiring a few minor patches and upgrades. Dan was able to get the bees removed from the cabin; selling the hive provided partial payment for a new prop. The cabin interior looked new when it was restored.

The second week of June had been tough. Work at the shop with Max had consumed most of the week, requiring two 16-hour days for repairs the customers had to have, but they were charged for the extra hours of labor. Dan felt he could invest a few bucks, so he called Huxley Aviation in Anchorage.

"Hello?"

"May I speak with Gary Upton, please?"

"Speaking."

"This is Dan Newcomb in Fairbanks. Have you heard of any 185s going down recently? I need some wing parts."

"Hi Dan. I remember you. Do you want the good news or the bad news first?"

"Any news would be good. What have you got?"

"The good news is a 185 crashed; the pilot and two passengers were okay and hiked out. The landing gear, the engine, and the right wingtip are damaged. The bad news is that they crashed into timber at about 2,000 feet. The plane is leaning against some trees. However, the Park Service is willing to pay to have the plane removed—$2,000 max. I can give you the coordinates. Sorry, that's all I can tell you."

"That's all right. Give me the position." Dan scribbled the position on a pad next to the phone, and said, "I owe you one for this, Gary. Thanks a bunch."

"You're welcome, Dan. Good luck! Bye."

"Bye." Dan memorized the numbers, tore off the page, and stuck it in his pocket.

He stood for a moment thinking. *How am I going to recover that plane? I can use the wing, sell the instrument panel, the engine, and the wheels. The rest of the plane is scrap. How am I going to get through a forest at 2,000 feet and carry the wreckage out? I'm going to need some major assistance. Who can I call?*

Over the weekend a tentative plan was devised. First: get maps from the Park Service office in Fairbanks. Second: get in touch with Stu Graves to borrow his small front-loader; he could probably part with it for a couple of days. Dan had promised Stu fast delivery service once the plane was ready to fly. Third, and perhaps most important, was man-power. He called all his friends from high school and explained his problem. Three former classmates volunteered to join Dan on the following weekend. He told the guys they could split the recovery money three ways.

Simeon Ervette was a daredevil on a four-wheeler during the summer and on a snowmobile during the winter. He kept in top physical shape, was a health-foods fanatic, except once a month he got out of his gourd drunk. Simmy was five-seven, weighed about 170 and sported long black hair which he occasionally braided. He was single and managed a pizza joint. He loved country music and played the guitar, but he couldn't sing.

Roy Riggins taught high school physics and math. He bleached his dark-brown hair white, stood six-two, wore glasses, and weighed about 220 pounds; he was not in the best of shape, but was smart and could be counted on in a pinch. Rigs worked on computers for the Park Service during the summers. In high school Rigs had worked in the forests; he possessed a lot of chainsaw experience.

Curtis Conrad worked at Fairbanks Trust as a loan officer, perhaps the youngest man ever to occupy that position at the bank. He had played football as a wide-receiver and could out-run anyone on the team, but he didn't like being tackled. Nicknamed Fear, Curt was blond, five-nine, and a snappy dresser. The girls loved his blue eyes. He was engaged to Shelly Sandler, from Anchorage. Shelly ran a daycare for preschoolers; all the kids loved her.

The four young men gathered at the repair shop on Wednesday night to go over the plan. Dan had soft drinks, coffee, chips, and dips to keep everyone in a semi-festive mood. They talked over old times for a few minutes and then got down to business. Rigs was first to speak, a coke in one hand, the other clutching several chips.

"Guess what, Dan? That crash isn't at 2,000 feet, it's at 1,200 feet, between Starvation Creek and Goose Creek. That initial estimate was from a low resolution map. I entered the coordinates at my workstation yesterday and here's what came up." Rigs gave printouts to each of his friends.

Simmy was wide-eyed and said, "Shit, Rigs, how do we get to that? No roads up there. Wait, I can get in there on my four-wheeler, at the confluence of Moose and Starvation, then swing west about two miles." He pointed to a narrow valley between the two creeks.

Dan commented, "Look, there are trees up there. We'll have to clear a path to get the plane down to Starvation Creek where it's fairly flat. That's about two hundred feet lower. We're going to have to be careful. I don't want anyone hurt recovering a dead airplane."

Fear chimed in, "But your future business rides on whether we're successful or not, doesn't it?" He chugged down half a coke and let out a loud belch.

Dan laughed and said, "You all right? Well, I don't know if we'll have another downed plane this close to us, ever. I'm wondering why the pilot went down there. The Quail Creek and Minto landing strips are both about ten miles away. Something must have occurred all of a sudden."

"There might be other wrecks—easier to get to," Rigs stated, as he stuffed another chip into his mouth. "I read the pilot's report. He stated the plane unexpectedly lost power, but he was too low to make either landing strip." He stuck another chip in his mouth, crunched it, and said, grinning, "Maybe that's an area like the Bermuda triangle."

Simmy couldn't stand what he was hearing. "You guys are a bunch of pussies! Let's do this! This could be the most fun we'll ever have in our lives. Something to tell our kids and grandkids about—how we recovered a plane from the mountains and fought off bears and wolves."

Rigs replied, "Yeah, if we live through it."

Dan took over. "Okay, how many of you dudes are with me?"

Everyone except Rigs raised his hand. Simmy looked at Rigs, as did Fear, and Rigs reacted, "All right, you got to me. I'll do it. Damn peer pressure."

"That's great. Let's meet here again tomorrow night at seven o'clock and go over the equipment we'll have. So, get to it tomorrow and see what you can come up with. I'll get the food, a tent, and other necessities. Don't forget your suntan lotion. Nights are cold in the timber area, so wear your long johns. If you want, bring a few beers."

Simmy smiled and said, "Okay, Dan. Let's do what we can tonight, dudes."

As the three men stood and began leaving, Rigs came back, grabbed a handful of chips, and followed Dan down the steps to the first floor. As Rigs went out the door to his car, Dan grinned and said, "Why didn't you take the whole sack?"

Rigs grinned, "I didn't know if you had dinner yet. I didn't want to deprive you of grease, salt, and carbs."

Dan tried to kick Rigs in the ass, but he missed when Rigs zigged out of the way. Laughing, he said, "I'll get you tomorrow night, Slim."

The group of four met the following evening as planned. They piled into the company pickup, and Dan drove them to see his plane. He wanted them to see what they would be dealing with for the recovery. They each planned to take Friday afternoon off, which would allow them time to bring materiel to Graves' metal building. The early Saturday morning adventure was to start at 5:00 a.m.

Friday, Dan ate lunch with Max and they talked about the expedition. Max didn't have much to contribute except to tell Dan to remember sunscreen, mosquito repellant, and toilet paper. "Are you going to take Nomah with you?"

"You bet. He's got to come along and start getting accustomed to the mountains. I think he'll like to get out in the open, away from the city, and he'll have plenty of trees to pee on. I think he'll adjust very quickly to the environment, including my partners. They all like dogs."

Dan put his hands on his knees and stood up. "I've got to get the flat-bed trailer and front loader, fill up the 100 gallon tanks with gas and diesel and take it to the building. The others will be showing up with their equipment. We'll load up so we can move out early tomorrow. I hope you don't mind me being gone from work for a day. We should be back Sunday night—or early Monday, but those guys have jobs, so Monday won't be in the cards."

Max shook hands with Dan and said, "Good luck and have a nice trip. I'll see you Sunday. Make sure you call or come by the house when you return. I want to hear all about it."

"Thanks, Max. Later."

It was a few minutes after 3:00 p.m. when Dan arrived at the corrugated metal building. Fear and Rigs were there with all their equipment. Fear was drinking coffee from a Thermos cup, and Rigs was tipping up the Thermos bottle getting the last dribble.

"Hey, guys. Where's Simmy?"

Rigs answered, "Said he'd be here with his wheels—didn't say when. He was going to get 200 feet of nylon rope and some boards in case we need to build a sled."

Dan responded, "Damn, that's a great idea! I should have thought of that, or Rigs should've."

"Hey, don't blame me. I don't think there's any snow there now, anyway. It's almost July."

"Not just snow, Rigs, rocks. That empty plane weighs about 1,800 pounds."

"No kidding? We're gunna bring the whole thing back?"

"If we can. We'll each make about a grand from selling the instruments. I don't need them."

Fear and Rigs gave each other a high-five as they heard the sound of a motor approaching. It was Simmy, coming in hot. He hit the brakes at the last second and did a 180 ten-feet in front of the others, who were scattering out of the way. He cut the engine and swung off his ATV as the dust settled. "Hi guys! I brought some more towing equipment—just in case."

Rigs said, "Jesus, Simmy. You could've killed all of us."

"Nah, you're my buds. I wouldn't hurt you, unless of course it was for a lot of money." He started laughing. Fear tossed the rest of his coffee at Simmy's feet, but missed.

CHAPTER 31

The Dead Bird

The recovery team hit the road at 5:37 Saturday morning. Dan was driving Stu Graves' truck, pulling a flat-bed trailer with the equipment secured to its surface. The front-half of the trailer was fully loaded, the back-half empty, leaving enough space to transport the plane. If more space were needed, Simmy's ATV could be put in the back of Rigs' pickup. Nomah was caught up in the excitement, watching from the passenger window as Dan drove the Elliott highway toward the Forest Service road near Moose Creek. Driving his pickup, Rigs followed the trailer. Simmy and Fear napped, trying to catch up on the sleep they had missed, having gotten up at 4:00 a.m.

Just as the map indicated, the FS road diverted from the highway 93 miles from Fairbanks. After four miles of unimproved road, the grade increased, Dan down-shifted and slowed to about 15 mph, sometimes even slower. The forest road narrowed and began to twist and turn as thickly forested areas and large boulders had to be avoided. As suddenly as they had entered the trees, they emerged from them. They had only travelled a few hundred yards through the forested area. Dan was forced to stop; the road ended at the confluence of Moose and Starvation creeks. The FS sign read 1,217 ft. Dan glanced at his watch. It was 7:49 a.m.

Dan sat in the cab, his eyes scaling the surrounding trees from trunks to tips and blue sky. Checking the map, he estimated the position of the plane was 3.7 miles up Starvation Creek to the west-southwest.

There was no way the truck could proceed; turning around would be hell, but he could do it with patience and signals from the others.

"Hey, Dan. Where the hell are we? I can't see a plane anywhere." It was Simmy, standing on the running board of the big old truck, yelling through the window.

Dan lowered the window and said, "Hey, take it easy. Ask Rigs what his GPS says. Let's compare it with the position of the plane marked on our maps."

Simmy walked over to the pickup and talked with Rigs, who opened the door and got out. He looked around and then walked over to Dan, who had climbed down from the truck. "According to these coordinates, we're off by two to three miles, maybe a little more."

Dan turned around and looked upstream. "I'm thinking the plane is in those trees on the right bank, maybe three miles from here. Let's make camp near those trees and plan the next step." He pointed at the edge of the forest 50 yards to the north. "Hey, Simmy, get on your whatsit and take a ride to the west. Follow the stream. Got binoculars?"

"Nope, just got eyes." He was smiling, pointing at his eyes with two fingers.

"Never fear, men, Fear is here." Fear opened his coat, released his binoculars from a neck cord, and handed them to Simmy. "Don't break 'em."

Rigs commented, "Way to go, Fear."

Simmy stored the binoculars in the travel compartment at the back of the ATV and yelled some orders. "Pull out the ramps at the back of the trailer so I can get my wheels down." No one moved. He shook his head and said, "Please?"

Dan smiled and replied, "Gee, Simmy, you asked so nicely. What happened to your four-letter words for us?"

"All right. You horses' asses, extend the ramps so I can get my Pinto off the trailer." He grinned, thought for a second, and said, "Huh, no four-letter words."

Fear grinned, "That's more like it, a little gusto."

Before the ramps were extended, Simmy was revving the ATV's engine, waiting to roll to the ground. When the ramps dropped, Simmy shot off the end of the trailer and was almost out of sight in ten seconds, riding while standing to keep his butt from flying off the seat as he skipped over rocks, occasionally splashing water up from the creek.

"Okay. While he's gone, we'll set up camp. You guys grab one of those wooden boxes and carry it over to that flat spot next to the trees, I'll get the other one." The wooden boxes were inside the scoop of the front-loader, tied so they couldn't escape while on the road. Dan and Rigs erected the tent, and Fear established an area for a campfire. He man-handled some large rocks for seats and made a circle from smaller rocks to surround the fire. As they were admiring their work, they could hear the ATV engine noise growing louder. Simmy came into view, slowed down, and when about ten yards away, shut off the engine and bumped to a stop.

"I found the plane. It's leaning against some big-ass trees. I think we can wrestle it out of the spot it's in. We'll have to remove the wing to get it out from the trees, and if Fear can make a skid, I can tow it out of the trees and back here. We'll have to chop down a few small trees. Dan, can we take the engine out to lighten the load? With a few trees removed, you can haul the engine in the front-loader scoop. This is a sure thing, gentlemen."

"From what you say, removing the engine might take longer than getting it back here, but we can cut it out of the plane. Good work, Simmy." Dan continued, "Let's get something to eat, and then we'll hike up to the wreck. Besides the tools we can carry in our pockets, we'll haul everything else we'll need on the ATV."

An hour later, the team set off to determine to best route to drag the plane from the trees to the creek bank. Having to travel over the rocky creek bank took over two hours to cover the more than three mile distance. Using the ATV and nylon ropes, the plane was lowered to the ground. Dan put Rigs to work designing a skid to replace a blown tire. Fear and Simmy starting cutting wires from the console to the engine and removing bolts from the engine mounts. Dan began the long walk back to camp to get the loader. As he walked, he made note of a pathway for Simmy to drag the fuselage out of the ravine with his mechanical horse.

After three hours of dismantling the plane piece by piece, the engine was on the ground, and the wing was disconnected from the fuselage. Since they didn't want to damage any parts they could resell, they worked carefully. Progress had been agonizingly slow in some cases, but they saved every part they detached. The three men rested their fatigued arm muscles and sore fingers as they sat on the ground next to the fuselage. Simmy had brought some drinks, but no beer, and Rigs had a bag of cookies in his backpack. Fear leaned back against the fuselage, which had been turned on its side to facilitate removal of the blown tire. As they snacked, they talked about how much work remained to be accomplished.

Simmy was the first to hear the engine of the front-end loader as it moved slowly toward the wreck. Dan had to push over small trees and dig boulders from the ground, filling in cavities in order to construct a relatively smooth route. It was four in the afternoon, and the area was in the shadows of the western ridges. The mosquitos were beginning to be annoying, the swarms getting larger as the evening approached. The bugs seemed to constantly form little clouds around their heads. Having decided to quit for the day, they began walking toward the sounds of the loader, waving the mosquitos from their faces.

Rigs and Fear rode back to camp in the loader scoop, a new experience for them, feeling like they had to hold on with white knuckles or die. Simmy rode his ATV slowly, marking trees that might have to be felled to create a path for the plane. Nomah jumped over rocks, in and out of the creek, keeping up with the loader as it bounced and swayed over the tumbled-smooth rocks near the creek. When Dan stopped and lowered the scoop, Nomah barked at the men as they tried to regain their equilibrium when stepping onto solid ground.

Rigs was elected cook, the others made a fire and coffee. While eating, Dan was apprised of the dismantling of the aircraft. After eating, they moved into the tent to get out of the chill and mosquitos. The men talked for about an hour about Sunday's plans, swatted a few mosquitos, slipped into their sleeping bags, and slept soundly all night.

Nomah woke Dan early Sunday morning in order to water some trees. Dan opened the tent, stuck his head out and surveyed the landscape. No bears were in sight.

"Okay, Nomah. I'll come and get you if you're not back in a couple of minutes. It's damn cold this morning." He could see his breathe condensing when he exhaled.

"Ahhh. What's goin' on?" Rigs was waking up, yawning, stretching. "How's the weather?"

Dan was pulling on his pants, looked at Rigs and said, "Just let my dog out to pee. Cold this morning—in the 40s. I'm gunna start a fire—make coffee."

"Make mine black, one lump." Fear chimed in.

Dan grinned, "Sorry, my ears are plugged. I can't hear anything."

Rigs asked, "We have any toilet paper, Dan?"

Simmy answered, "Just use a rock, there's got to be a soft one out there—or maybe a pinecone that has just dropped."

Fear added, "Back up to a small tree, part your cheeks and rub—up and down, not sideways."

Dan shook his head. "Yeah. There's paper in that wooden box in the corner." Dan pointed with one of his shoes.

"Thanks, Dan. You're the only civilized man here, except for yours truly." Rigs had pulled on his pants, put on his coat, and was opening the box.

"Rigs—don't forget to put your shoes on, and be careful where you step. We don't have enough water to wash both your shoes." Dan laughed as he joined in the joking.

Rigs replied, "You serious? We're short of water? What about the creek?"

"Just joking, Rigs. Just not enough water for you to take a bath, unless you want to bathe in the creek." Dan pretended to shiver, slipped into his heavy coat, and went outside. Nomah wasn't back yet, so he whistled twice. Nomah came running, panting, and his breath condensing—looking like a werewolf chasing down a man in the moonlight, but it was already light outside; there were twenty hours of light each day during June in Alaska. "There you are. Good boy!" Dan put Nomah in the tent and unpacked utensils and food for breakfast; bacon, eggs, and oatmeal.

Rigs, gripping a roll of paper, left the tent saying, "I'll be back in a few."

Simmy yelled after him, "Watch out for butt mosquitos. Don't let the bears steal your paper!" Everyone had to laugh.

"I didn't know you guys were comedians." Dan smiled as he struck a match and lit a wad of paper. For starting fires, he had brought the wood from a broken pallet. The slivers of dry wood started burning immediately. He tossed a log on the rapidly burning dried wood. The pop and crackle of the fire always added a bit of enjoyment to the camping experience, even if it was a work detail.

They didn't have to clean up much—the used paper plates and plastic utensils were tossed in a bag destined for the garbage dump in Fairbanks. It was time to get the plane back to camp so they could pack-up and get the hell out of the mountains—away from the tormenting mosquitos. Simmy took his ATV with Fear bouncing on the seat behind him hanging on for dear life. Dan powered up the loader, and Rigs climbed onboard carrying a chainsaw. Nomah followed behind the diesel-powered workhorse. When Dan reached the next boulder to be moved, Rigs jumped off and cut down some small trees as they cleared a path the remaining distance to the plane.

After half an hour, Dan and Rigs reached the wreck. Dan used the scoop to move the engine and turn the plane around, assisted by the others, and the nylon ropes. Rigs had constructed a wooden skid from a small misshapen tree, which he mounted on the axle of the blown tire. They had to remove the elevator so they could secure the plane's tail to the four-wheeler. The team lifted the tail off the ground so Simmy could tie it to the ATV. After lashing the elevator to the side of the fuselage, Simmy started pulling the fuselage along the pathway to the creek. Rigs walked alongside to keep the structure from slipping sideways into the trees or the stream.

Dan removed the broken prop so the engine would fit snugly in the scoop. Then they wrestled the two wing portions onto the sides of the loader and fastened them with nylon ropes. The contraption looked like a giant insect with its wings folded against its body. Two hours of sweat and strained muscles were invested getting the plane to the flatbed. Their major goal achieved, the four men and Nomah had lunch and rested for an hour before loading the plane on the trailer. Before starting the return trip to Fairbanks, the team went back to the crash site and cleaned up, minimizing the environmental impact of the recovery.

When the guys got back to the Quonset building, it was 6:40 p.m. It took them half an hour to unload the truck, storing the recovered plane behind the building, out of sight from the road.

As Dan was thanking Simmy, Rigs, and Fear for their assistance, he asked, "Rigs, where did you put that roll of toilet paper?"

Rigs smiled, "I donated it to the bears; there wasn't much left."

Everyone was laughing as they climbed in their vehicles to go home for Sunday dinner.

CHAPTER 32

Bullet Holes

Max let Dan get in some extra sleep Monday morning, opening the shop a half-hour later than normal. Max had unlocked the shop and was trying to be as quiet as possible. He started some coffee and refrained from his morning whistling. He had discussed the Cessna 185 recovery with Dan Sunday night, and Dan had fallen asleep talking on the phone. When Max got no response to his questions, he hung up. Max knew everything was all right when he heard Nomah coming down the stairs from the loft. Max whispered to Nomah, "Are you hungry, big boy?" Max gave Nomah a dog biscuit.

"That better be you, Max." Dan was awake but still in bed when he called out.

"I'll be ready to go in a few minutes."

"Don't bother with coffee, Dan. I just started a pot down here."

"Thanks, Max. Sorry I fell asleep on you last night. I was really draggin'. I woke up trying to stick the phone in my mouth."

"Don't sweat it, but I'll need your help today. We've got a truck to work on. Old man Betz is bringing it in at nine o'clock. Needs brakes and headlamps. You can do the brakes." Dan couldn't see Max's smile. Brakes were the difficult part of the job.

Dan didn't give the assignment a second thought, he had to work his normal shop hours before he could put any more effort into rebuilding the plane.

"Okay—be right with you, after I eat an egg sandwich and feed Nomah."

The whole day went that way, with a few knuckle-buster jobs that were time consuming, and a few over-the-counter sales of spark plugs and oil filters. Dan couldn't wait to get out to the Quonset building and work on the wings they had recovered. He bought a Coke and two cheeseburgers for dinner and drove out to work on his plane. As he neared the rusting metal building, he couldn't miss seeing a dark-blue SUV parked at the side of the building. "Who do you think that is, Nomah?" Dan let Nomah out of the pickup and stepped out of the cab.

Nomah had run behind the building and was barking, but the barks weren't in anger, they were for excitement. Dan rounded the back corner of the building, and to his great surprise, Simmy, Fear, and Rigs were sitting on the ground petting Nomah. Nomah made his way from one man to the next, receiving hugs and pats.

"What are you numskulls doing here?" Dan smiled and shook hands with the guys. "Did you come to bug me, or do you just want a ride in my plane? I think I'll have to sell tickets."

Rigs spoke, pointing at Simmy and Fear, "These nitwits thought you might need some help getting the wing on your plane. I borrowed my mom's car, and we came out to see if we could help you get the Glacier Phoenix into the air. I want to offer our superior construction and inspection services."

Each night for the next week, the team worked on the plane following Dan's detailed instructions. The work Dan had thought would take him a month took only eight days. During the last day of work, his three friends gathered all the parts Dan thought could be sold. The next weekend, Rigs and Simmy were going to take the items to Huxley Aviation in Anchorage. Fear couldn't go with them—his fiancée was coming to Fairbanks for a family dinner and she was going to stay for the weekend.

The plane was ready for inspection and recertification, but Dan thought he'd better get a set of service manuals from Cessna. He called the home office and had the manuals shipped by air to Anchorage in care of Huxley Aviation. Rigs and Simmy would pick them up. Dan knew he should have gotten a set of manuals sooner, but he had been devoted to getting the plane repaired and hadn't taken the time to order manuals until he considered he might have overlooked something. He might have been over-confident knowing Vic had taught him everything she knew. Vic had told him about over-confidence and flying, the combination could be disastrous.

While Dan waited for the manuals, he inspected every remaining piece of the wreckage. He kept asking himself why the engine lost power. The engine cowling was badly damaged, but his close inspection disclosed a hole concealed in a crease. When he straightened the metal out, it appeared the opening was a bullet-hole. No wonder the plane had lost power: a bullet had entered the engine compartment. Dan went through the bag of miscellaneous plane parts from the wreck and found the badly damaged ignition harness. Some of the clustered wires had been severed. He wondered how thorough the crash investigation had been. An investigator should have determined that someone on the ground had shot at the plane.

It was the middle of July when Dan was cleared to fly. He made a crude airstrip next to the Quonset hut, loaded Nomah into the cabin, taxied down the strip, and lifted into the air. Finally, he was flying again.

"Nomah! We're back in the air!" Nomah approved with a bark. Dan stayed close to the landing strip, flying in circles, building his confidence in both the plane and himself. After a week of trials, each day venturing farther from Fairbanks, he was ready for passengers and cargo. Max and Dan began advertising air delivery service to points within a radius of two hundred miles. Glacier Phoenix's first notable flight went from Fairbanks to Minto, then to Livengood and back to Fairbanks. Dan spent most mornings flying and the afternoons working with Max in the shop.

Lisa returned from her Portland internship at the end of August, excited about her last year of school. By Christmas, Lisa and Dan were planning a June wedding. Dan was too busy to get involved in the details of getting married, but Lisa had accepted the responsibility for all the particulars.

Dan's flying had become an important part of the Conley and Newcomb business, generating about forty percent of the company's revenue. Dan invested in skis for the plane and was now equipped for the winter season.

Each morning, when Dan got up, he hoped the phone would ring by mid-morning to charter his plane to fly cargo or passengers. There was no denying it—he loved to fly, and so did Nomah. When a morning call concluded, Nomah seemed to know if they were going to fly, but it was probably Dan's enthusiasm Nomah sensed. The second week of March, a call came in from Anchorage. Dan was to take a three-man film-crew to the Allakaket landing strip close to the Arctic Circle. The crew was going to hike about 90 miles to Coldfoot on the Winter Trail, shooting background pictures for a movie. The three men were experienced mountaineers, having spent three months in the Antarctic with an adventure group going to the South Pole.

Dan and Nomah picked up the men at the Fairbanks Airport at 10:00 a.m. Wednesday. Cruising at 160 mph, Dan's plane landed in Allakaket at 11:35. The temperature was 12 degrees Fahrenheit. Dan shut the engine down for about ten minutes while he helped the film crew unload their gear. He wished them a safe trip, good luck, climbed back in the plane, and left on the return trip to Fairbanks.

An hour into the return flight, Dan received a radio message from Fairbanks that a plane was overdue from a pumping station on the Alaska Pipeline. Pilot Nathan Burke and an Emergency Medical Technician (EMT) were on their way back from Station #6; 42 miles Northwest of Livengood. Dan was acquainted with the area, so when he was about 20 minutes out of Fairbanks in the vicinity of Livengood, he descending to about 500 feet and began a slow circling pattern, watching for a downed plane. He theorized a plane on the snow-covered ground should be fairly easy to spot unless it had crashed in the trees. Dan flew over Brown Lake just south of Elliott Highway, continued turning to the left and passed over Livengood, then increased his radius by about a mile. Two more circles were made without any luck. He was beginning to think the missing plane was not in the area, or it was out of sight in the trees.

"Well, Nomah, one more pass over this area and then we've got to go home, okay, buddy?" Nomah wagged his tail and yawned, making a little squealing sound. Dan grinned, "I guess that was a yes." The last pass was taking Dan and Nomah over a lake about a mile long and a half-mile wide, north of Brooks Creek. As Dan watched the lake come into view, he saw it—a plane, upside down at the southern edge of the lake. He dropped down to two-hundred feet, cut his speed to 85 mph, and looked for survivors.

Two figures, one prone, were at the edge of the frozen lake. Both were waving as he flew over. He wiggled his wings, made a second pass and looked for a place to land. As he scanned the area for a level landing site, he informed the Fairbanks Airport that he had found the plane. He gave the coordinates and landed Glacier Phoenix about a half mile southwest of the wreck in a flat, snow-covered area.

"Okay, Nomah, we're going for a walk." Dan packed some blankets, a first-aid kit, and some food onto a small sled and started trudging through the foot-deep snow. At first, Nomah followed in the tracks made by Dan and the sled, but as they got closer to the pilot and passenger, Nomah bounded through the snow, barking. Dan yelled, "Nomah! Quiet! You'll scare them."

When Nomah reached the two figures, he raised up, placing his front paws on the standing figure's chest and began licking the person's face. Dan was still too far away to see the features of the individual standing, but as he got closer, the fur-lined hood fell back, exposing the person's face. The woman looked like Ann Olson.

"Ann, is that you?" Dan couldn't believe what he was seeing. He had to ask— maybe the woman just resembled Ann.

Ann opened her arms and hugged Dan, saying, "It's me, Dan. I'm so glad to see you! Nomah has gotten really big! I thought I recognized him. I saw the name on his collar, but then I thought it would be crazy for you to be rescuing me again."

Dan looked down at the pilot who he recognized, and asked, "How's Nathan doing? Did he break something?"

Ann responded, "He's been shot, Dan—his left thigh. The bleeding has stopped, but he needs to get to a hospital to have the bullet removed. His wound is much worse than the ones we had. He's going to freeze if we don't get him someplace warm. He has been inactive for nearly two hours."

"Damn! Some lunatic is shooting at planes." Dan knelt beside Nathan and asked, "What happened to your plane, Nate?"

Nathan was beginning to shiver, so Dan and Ann wrapped blankets around him. In a quivering voice, Nate replied, "The surface of the lake looked smooth, but the left ski hit a rock sticking above the ice and we cartwheeled—flip…flipped over."

"Hang in there, buddy. We'll get you to the hospital in Fairbanks. They've got great doctors. They tell me surgical equipment is left inside their patients, ready for the next operation. Have you been there before?"

Ann reacted, "I know you're kidding, but what a thing to say!"

"Don't worry, he knows I'm joking. Let's get him on the sled and back to my plane. It's only about 12 degrees out here. None of us needs hypothermia. Are you warm enough, Ann?"

"I'm okay, but my face is cold. Let's get to your plane, make Nate comfortable, and deliver him to the hospital. We have lots to talk about on the trip back to Fairbanks."

After reaching Dan's plane, they loaded Nate, and then the equipment. Ann climbed in without assistance after Nomah had been lifted into the cabin. Dan made sure everyone was buckled up, started the engine, and swung the plane into the light wind. As soon as they were airborne, Dan looked at Ann and asked, "When did you come to Alaska?"

"About five months ago. Mom, the baby, and I are living in Anchorage."

"And your husband?"

"I divorced him and took back my maiden name. Josh turned out to be a control freak—wanted to know what I was doing every second. He almost hit me once, and that was the end. I took the baby and moved in with Mom and Dad. About a month later, Dad had a massive stroke, picked up an infection, and passed away about six weeks later. Mom and I had a long talk and decided to start over in Alaska. Mom sold the trucks and the house and we made plans to move to Anchorage. She thought it would be a good place to start a new life—you had told us your wonderful memories of Alaska. But I didn't think I'd ever see you again, Alaska is awfully big. I was astounded when you appeared with Nomah, I couldn't believe it."

"I'm sorry your marriage didn't work out. How is Beverly, and what is your baby's name?"

"Mom is fine. She's been wonderful. She was devastated when Dad died, but when I joined her with the baby, she took over like a drill sergeant leading a bunch of recruits. She's taking care of Larry Daniel while I work as an EMT."

"You gave your baby my name as his middle name? I'm honored."

"Well, without you, he would never have been born. I would have died in that cabin."

"So you didn't finish your nurse's training?"

"No, I couldn't. Josh wouldn't let me go back to school. He had to know where I was all the time. I should've seen it coming. When we started dating, he called me all the time. I thought he was just wanted to be with me because we were in love." Ann turned to look at Nate and felt his face. He was asleep. "Nate's warming up." She looked out across the snow-covered landscape and asked, "I can't see through your gloves. Are you married, Dan?"

"Not yet, but I'm engaged to a very nice young lady—Lisa Zorn. She's an architect. We're getting married in June."

Ann didn't want her disappointment to be evident in her demeanor so she looked out the window, glanced at Nomah, and at Nate before she said, in a cheerful voice, "That's nice. I hope you will be happy. Will you live in Fairbanks?"

Dan hadn't thought they would live anywhere else. Why would he want to move away from where he grew up and had a lucrative business? But he began to think, *would Lisa be happy in Fairbanks? How would she be able to practice architecture here?* He didn't have time to think of those things right now, they were approaching the airport; landing the plane took all his concentration. He called the tower and asked for an ambulance to meet the plane at gate 22, where emergency medical cases were whisked off to the hospital.

As soon as Nate was on his way to the hospital, Dan turned to Ann and asked, "Do you want to stay over at my uncle's place tonight? I'll bet you don't want to do any more flying today. I'll get you on a commercial flight to Anchorage tomorrow morning. It's only an hour away."

"Can you take me to Anchorage?"

Dan thought for a moment and answered, "I have a company flight tomorrow. A round trip to Anchorage would take me five hours. I'm sorry, but I can't afford the time. If I were the sole owner of our business, I would do it, but I have to consider my uncle's family. He has two boys and a wife to provide for."

"I understand. I'll stay overnight though; I need to relax. I'll call Mom from your uncle's. In the morning, I'll check on Nate before I get on the plane. Thank you, Dan."

"Anytime, Ann, but let's not do this rescuing thing too often." He smiled and gave her a hug.

CHAPTER 33

More Gunfire

It was April 7 when Dan received a message to fly to the Porcupine Creek Landing Strip near Coldfoot to return the three film makers to Anchorage. The trip was approximately 640 miles, one of the longest flights for Nomah and Dan, taking over four hours. When Dan dropped the three men off at Anchorage, he had lunch and called Ann. Dan wanted to talk with Beverly again, see Ann's baby, and find out if Ann had experienced any more problems flying. He was also curious about Nate's recovery; Ann should know the details.

Dan took a taxi to the Olsons' apartment, paid the driver, went up to 200C, and tapped lightly on the door. The door opened, and Beverly rushed into the hallway to give Dan a bear hug. Bev was so excited, Dan almost lost his balance, but he grabbed the door frame to keep from falling.

"Take it easy, Bev. Don't kill me! I'm not the enemy!" He laughed as he regained his balance.

"Oh, I'm sorry, but it is so good to see you, Dan. I thought we would never see you again. Ann told me you are engaged. Please come in and tell me all about your fiancée." Bev pulled Dan into the apartment from the hallway and said, "Let me take your coat."

As Dan removed his coat, he saw Ann sitting on the sofa bottle-feeding the baby. The little boy had short orange-brown hair, wide-open brown eyes and smiled when Dan approached. The baby reached out as if to shake hands. Dan took his tiny hand in his and said, "You are a handsome little man, Larry. Your mommy should be very proud of you." Dan looked at Ann and could see tears in her eyes. He placed one hand on Ann's shoulder and she reached up, placing her hand on his.

"I'm so glad you came to see us, Dan. You mean so much to us."

In spite of what had happened, Dan realized he still had feelings for Ann, but how could he be in love with Lisa and still have strong feelings for Ann? How was he supposed to react to these conflicting emotions? He knew for sure that he had to be careful and not make any stupid comments or rash decisions. He didn't want to hurt anyone, including himself.

The phone on the end table beside the sofa rang three times before Ann could reach the phone. "Hello. This is Ann. Yes, I can be ready in an hour." She looked at Beverly and Dan and continued, "Just a minute, I'm talking to a pilot right now." Ann looked up at Dan and said, "Could you fly me to Pumping Station #6—right away?"

Dan didn't have to think and answered, "Sure, I'll take you wherever you need to go. I just have to fuel the plane."

Ann spoke into the phone, "Okay, Mr. Dietrich, I have a flight arranged. We'll be in the air in an hour. Good bye." Ann put down the phone and said, "Please hold Larry for me." Ann put the bottle down and gave Larry to Dan.

Dan was nine years old when he last held an infant, Duke, his cousin. All he could remember was to support the head, or was that just for babies? He wasn't sure, so he carefully transferred the infant to Beverly, who had sensed Dan's uneasiness.

"I'll take Larry, Dan. Why don't you call the airport and get the plane refueled?"

It only took Ann a couple of minutes to get on her ski-boots, a sweater, and her down-filled fur-lined parka. She checked her pockets to make sure she had gloves and her ID. In the meantime, Dan had made a call and ordered his plane refueled. Ann kissed little Larry and Beverly and headed out the door. Beverly had called a taxi which was waiting outside the entrance to the building.

When Ann and Dan reached the airport, Dan picked up Nomah from Jerry Talbot, the AVIS rent-a-car dealer who was a good friend of his uncle Max. Dan helped Ann load her supplies into the plane, gave her and Nomah a boost into the cabin, and climbed into the pilot's seat. Ten minutes later, they set off on the 395-mile trip to Station #6. Dan expected the flight to take about 2 hours 40 minutes. Following Ann's treatment of the worker's infected finger, they would fly back to Fairbanks, where Ann would get a flight back to Anchorage the next morning.

Ann inspected the worker's hand, gave him a shot of antibiotics, pills for ten days, and was ready to fly to Fairbanks. They left the pumping station at 5:13 p.m. and were approaching Livengood, near the site of Nate Burke's downed plane. Dan veered to the southwest to see if Nate's plane was still there. It was only a couple of minutes out of the way. Glacier Phoenix began descending from 3,000 to 500 feet.

"Okay, Ann, see that lake on the left? That's Brown Lake. I'll fly over the lake west of here where I picked you and Nate up. It's about four times the size of Brown Lake—it's not named on the map. Maybe it's called West Brown Lake," he smiled. "About 20 miles west of here is where my friends and I recovered that wrecked plane. I used some of the parts to rebuild Glacier Phoenix."

Ann was looking down to see if she could spot Nate's plane before Dan could see it when she heard a snapping noise. "What was that? Did something break?" Her eyes opened wide as she looked at Dan. Then they heard it again.

Dan said, "Someone's shooting at us. We're going down."

"Are we going to crash?" Ann started to reach for Dan, but she realized she might interfere with him flying the plane. She reached toward Nomah and grabbed his collar. Holding on to Nomah reduced her anxiety. Nomah shoved his nose under her arm so she could scratch his head and neck.

"We're okay, Ann. We're not going to crash. I want to go after the SOB that is shooting at us. We're going down on the other side of the trees we're over right now. Hang on tight—we might hit some rough spots when I set the plane down."

The landing was fairly smooth until the plane had nearly come to rest, a few bumps rocking the wing up and down. Dan shut off the motor and turned to Ann, "I'm sorry—I should have asked you if you wanted to do this. I was so pissed, I let emotion take the place of reason and caution. I can turn around and take off if you'd rather not wait for me to find the shooter, but someone has to put a stop to it. I think I'm as qualified to track him down as anyone."

"I'm tired of being shot at, Dan. This is the second time and it's scary. One of us could have been killed by a bullet, or if you had been hit, the plane could have crashed, killing us both. I'd like to be around to raise my baby. I don't want Mom to have to raise Larry alone, so go after the scumbag. Do you have any weapons?"

"No problem. A rifle and two knives are more than enough, and it will be dark before long—just the conditions I like. Stay in the cabin with Nomah. When the sun goes down, the temp will drop into the 20s, so stay warm. Use blankets and Nomah to keep warm. There are some sandwiches and juice in the cooler behind the seats. Help yourself. I should be back in a couple of hours—if I'm not back in two hours, send Nomah after me."

Dan pulled his rifle and a dozen rounds of ammo from behind the back seats, took some energy bars from the cooler, and descended into the foot-deep snow. He quickly shut the cabin door, waved to Ann, and began hiking a gradual uphill slope toward the forest. Nomah barked and moved to the cabin door, wanting to go with Dan.

Ann understood that Dan didn't want to risk Nomah getting shot. She put her arm around Nomah and talked quietly to him until he relaxed and looked away from the window. After seeing Dan disappear into the trees, Nomah moved to the back seat of the plane. Ann held out a treat for Nomah. He sat up and took it gently from her hand.

When he reached the trees, Dan began ascending the northern slope of the hill they had just flown over. He reached the top as daylight was nearly gone. The shadows were getting darker gray as was the sky. Dan carefully made his way through the trees, watching for the gunman's footprints. He crossed tracks in the snow, but looking closely, he realized they were bear tracks. Dan knew that both black and brown bears might be in the region. He would have to listen closely as he moved in the dark. Bears would probably be moving about the forest at night; they didn't need keen eyesight; their senses of smell and hearing gave them an advantage over humans. Nomah would have been of use, but Dan didn't want another of his dogs shot.

The snow on the southern side of the hill was melting during the day when the temperatures were above freezing, but an icy layer formed on the surface of the snow when the thermal readings dropped into the 20s at night. His footsteps were noisier now, thin patches of snow and bare ground didn't mute the sounds of his movement as effectively as the deeper snow had on the northern slope. Dan would move a few yards, stand silently and listen. He emerged from the trees, checked his watch, and decided to return to the plane. Ninety minutes had passed since he had set out looking for the shooter.

Dan stayed at the edge of the forest, skirting the trees, the moon giving him enough light to see an unrestricted route. He was trying to avoid the rocks that seemed intent on tripping him. He almost fell once but caught himself with his rifle butt as if it were a cane. Circling to the left, he came to a small stream which he was able to jump over. Unable to see any tracks made from boots, periodically Dan illuminated his path with his pocket flashlight for a few seconds. The brief intervals of light allowed him to check for tracks paralleling his own.

Back at the plane, Ann worried as the minutes passed. When the two-hour time expired, she opened the cockpit door and urged Nomah out. "Find Dan, Nomah." Nomah jumped to the ground and without hesitating, ran for the trees. Ann slammed the door and wrapped up in the blankets, her foot-warmer gone.

A few minutes later, Ann heard noises outside the plane. *Was Dan back?* She looked outside, and in the dim moonlight, saw a strange figure approaching the plane. She wasn't sure it was a man. Could it be a bear? Its motion was erratic, but near darkness prevented her from getting a clear view. Without Dan or Nomah, she was scared that something bad was about to happen. She wanted to look for a gun, but didn't know where to turn on the cabin light. Images of the three kidnappers came into her mind. *Where was Dan?* She could hear footsteps and then a tapping on the cabin door.

A deep gravelly voice said, "Anyone in there?"

"Go away! I've got a gun. My husband will be coming back in a few minutes. If you try to open the door, I'll shoot you in the face."

"All right. I'm not here to hurt you. I'm going to make a fire and wait for your man. I thought you were some dirty hunters."

Ann heard steps in the snow as the stranger moved away from the plane. A minute later she saw a flicker of light and flames beginning to grow from a small pile of branches. She could barely make out the dark clothing the man was wearing. His rifle was pointing up like a post, sticking out of a small pile of snow. Ann noticed the unknown visitor had a pronounced limp as he moved to the forest to obtain more wood. She couldn't see his features. His hair was shoulder-length and hung limply about his face. Ann relaxed a bit, feeling that she was not in immediate danger, but time appeared to pass slowly; five minutes seemed like an hour. She kept thinking, *when will Dan be back?*

Watching for human tracks and trying not to stumble were consuming most of Dan's concentration, but when he felt he wasn't far from the plane, he began to hear an animal approaching rapidly from behind. He stopped, turned toward the sound, and flipped on his flashlight. For a second, Dan thought a wolf was in the beam. He raised his rifle but a split second before he pulled the trigger, he recognized Nomah. Dan lowered his gun and glanced at his watch. He had left Ann two and a half hours ago. Dan hugged Nomah and said, "Good boy, Nomah. We'll rest a minute while you catch your breath."

Dan turned off his flashlight and stood with Nomah in the dim moonlight, looking where he expected to see the plane. Light-green auroral curtains danced across the sky. At ground level, a flicker of light appeared in the distance. Dan worried that Ann had somehow started a fire on the plane. He had to get there to help. She might get burned, the plane could explode, and they would be stranded. "Come on, Nomah. Ann's in trouble!"

To move faster, Dan turned on the flashlight and saw tracks in the snow. He ran toward the growing, dancing flames, following the tracks. Someone else was at the plane! It had to be the gunman. Nomah ran ahead through the rocks, bounding through the large patches of snow. Dan called, "Nomah! Come back!" A few seconds passed and Dan heard a rifle shot. Dan yelled, as loudly as he could, "No! Don't shoot my dog!

I'll kill you! Hide, Nomah! Hide!" Dan pointed his rifle toward the trees and squeezed off a round, hoping to discourage the gunman from taking another shot at Nomah, assuming the first shot had missed. The report from Dan's gun echoed across the valley; the gunman had to have heard Dan's gunshot; more than once.

No more shots came from the direction of the plane. As Dan got closer, he could see the fire was near the trees, ten yards from the Cessna. Dan, now 50 yards from the plane, moved into the trees and whistled twice. He paused next to a large tree and listened. After a few seconds, Dan heard panting behind him—the light from the fire was enough to see Nomah's glistening eyes. Dan removed his gloves and ran his hands over Nomah, but no blood transferred to his hands. Nomah wasn't injured. Dan whispered, "Good boy."

Dan worked his way through the trees until he was 20 yards from the fire. He could see a large man sitting on a rock, his back to the trees, warming his hands over the flames.

"Come on out, I won't shoot. My gun's on the ground." The man's gruff voice wasn't reassuring. He stood and turned toward the trees, raising his hands to show he had no weapons. The man, about Dan's size, wore fur-trimmed boots, leather pants, and a bearskin coat. He hadn't shaved in months. His beard extended to his waist; his foot-long, shaggy, brown hair hanging down around his neck made Dan think he was looking at Big-Foot.

Dan, a little wary, stepped out from the trees with his rifle ready. He spoke, "Who the hell are you?"

"I'm Stan Hanks. Who the hell are you?"

"Dan Newcomb." Dan watched the man turn his head and move his hair away from his right ear, apparently to improve his hearing.

"You said Dan Newcomb?"

"That's right."

"What was your mother's name?"

"Jean. She passed away eleven years ago."

"Eleven years?"

"Uh-huh. Did you know her?"

"Maybe." Stan exposed his right forearm. "See, I've got the name Jean on my arm. Jean was my wife. She had cancer—died nine years ago."

Dan couldn't believe what he was hearing. The light was too dim to make out the tattoo, so he moved closer. He looked at the tattoo; it was just like the one his father had, and in the same place. Dan paused for a moment, thinking. Part of him wanted to hug his father and part wanted to knock him on his ass. *Could this—creature—be my father?* This man had to be his father. Dan looked into Stan's eyes, and said, "You're not Stan Hanks, you're Henry Newcomb, my father. We all thought you were dead."

Stan thought, *this kid knows my real name, maybe he is my boy.* "How old are you?"

"I'm 25."

"You're not my son, you're too old, and my son can't fly a plane. My son would have finished high school three years ago and is probably in the army. I can't figure out how you got the name Dan Newcomb—must be a coincidence."

Ann opened the cockpit door and said, "Is it all right to come out, Dan? What are you talking about? Who is that man?"

"Come out, Ann. I know this man is my father, but he doesn't think I'm his son."

"Oh, my God, are you kidding me? Are you sure he's your father?"

"Yes. My dad had a tattoo—Jean is written on his right forearm in fancy lettering." Dan looked at his father and asked, "Will you let the young lady verify it?"

"Not necessary. I have Jean written on my skin like I showed you—but she died nine years ago, not eleven. She was real sick."

"Jean was my mother's name, your wife, but she died of cancer eleven years ago, not nine. For some reason, you're missing two years. Where have you been? What have you been doing?"

The bearded man, surely Hank Newcomb, was frowning, confused, and said, "Eleven years? I don't understand." He limped toward the fire and slowly sat down where he had been before. He stared at the ground, shifted his eyes toward the fire, and rubbed his forehead with the fingers of his right hand. He appeared to be a defeated old man, out of touch with reality.

Ann came over to Dan and whispered, "Where's Nomah?"

Dan answered, "He's hiding. I'll call him." Dan whistled and Nomah came out slowly from the trees, watching the man covered in animal fur and human hair. Nomah stood beside Dan watching every motion of the man. When Hank turned his head toward Dan and Ann, Nomah growled.

"Tell your dog I won't hurt anyone. I'm sorry I took a shot at him. At first, I thought he was a wolf, but they usually don't attack straight on when they're alone. Can you come over by the fire? I think we need to talk."

Dan crouched and rubbed Nomah's back. "He's okay, Nomah. Let's go over to the fire. Ann, please bring those blankets. This might take awhile."

Dan put his arm around Ann's shoulders and whispered, "I know he's my dad, but his time frame is out of kilter. He's lost a couple of years." Dan rubbed his chin, frowning, still retaining some disbelief. Dan spoke, nearly in a whisper, "How strange is this? We've got some things to straighten out. Maybe you can help."

CHAPTER 34

A Long Talk

Hank snapped his fingers, trying to summon Nomah, but Nomah stayed with Ann, closely watching the unkempt intruder from across the fire. Dan moved closer to his father and they shook hands vigorously. Dan said, "God, Dad, I'm glad you're still alive. It's so good to see you again. Come, Nomah. See, it's all right." Nomah remained beside Ann, his eyes still locked on the stranger, watching every move Hank made. Dan joined Ann and Nomah and sat down cross-legged next to the fire, his father at arm's length to Dan's right.

"I think I know why your dog is wary of me. I haven't had a bath since I visited the hot springs 40 miles west of here a couple of weeks ago. He probably doesn't like my smell—or the way I look. I don't blame him. If you stay upwind where you are, you won't be offended by my stench," he smiled. "Tell me what you know about me, Dan. Maybe it'll help me remember more about the passage of time. I seem to have lost a couple of years."

Dan began talking about his high school days and how one day his father was flying two hunters into the back country to hunt bear and caribou, but didn't return. Dan told his father about going to Afghanistan, staying for the winter in Oregon, and meeting Ann. Dan traced his return to Alaska and starting into business with Max. When Dan mentioned Max, Hank perked up significantly.

Hank commented, "Max is Jean's brother. Right?"

"That's right. He's probably wondering where Ann and I are. We were supposed to be back in Fairbanks about three hours ago." Dan continued his story about fixing Glacier Phoenix and routine flying— until someone started shooting at the plane.

Hank sat quietly, staring into the fire, listening to Dan recount his activities since Hank disappeared. The fire consumed the bark of a log like time had taken Hank's life for eight years, the wood converting to smoke and heat. Hank could only account for six of the eight years.

"Dad, are you hungry? I have some things in the plane we can eat. I'll get some juice and sandwiches." Dan started moving toward the plane.

"Uh—all right. I ate yesterday— or was it the day before?" Hank looked at Ann and asked, "Are you Dan's wife now?"

Ann smiled and replied, "No. We're good friends. I was married to another man but I got a divorce. I have a son. He's with my mother in Anchorage. Dan and I were returning from a medical trip when you shot at the plane. I'm an EMT."

"Sorry about that, young lady. I figured you were hunters—shooting wolves and bears from the plane with shotguns. I was wrong. I guess people in low-flying planes aren't always doing rotten things."

Dan returned from the plane with the food container and let Hank pick what he wanted from the sandwiches and bottles of juice. Dan asked Hank what he remembered from the trip with the two hunters.

"I remember a lot. I've gone over it in my mind many times. It was overcast. We left Fairbanks in the early afternoon and flew north to Fort Yukon, about 170 miles. I landed, and while the two hunters talked, I gassed up the plane. When we were back in the air, they told me to fly toward Arctic Village, another 100 miles farther north. They wanted to fly low, so that's what I did, just over the trees, but high enough to be safe."

Ann asked, "Who were those guys? Where were they from?"

"I remember their first names, because they were odd: Knox and Bank. They were from some little town in Pennsylvania. I don't remember the name. They had rifles and shotguns. I thought the shotguns were for birds, but it turned out they wanted to shoot wolves and bears from the plane with the shotguns. I said I wouldn't do it; it wasn't right. They said if I didn't do what they said, they would track down my son and kill him." Hank paused and looked at Dan. "So, I took them on a joy ride up a valley, and when I got to the end of the valley, I crashed into the side of a mountain. I figured I had a better chance of living than they did; I was belted into my seat, they weren't."

"Jesus, Dad. That took a lot of guts."

"They saw what was coming. We were climbing out of the valley and they were looking ahead and yelling, 'Pull up! Climb!' But I wanted to hit near the summit of that peak in front of us, and I did. I don't know how long I was out, but when I woke up strapped in the wreckage, those bastards were dead. Then I felt the pain—my left leg was broken and my left shoulder was badly bruised. It was nearly dark and getting cold. The wind was blowing snow into the smashed cabin."

Hank poked the flickering flames with a stick, tossed it and some branches on the campfire, and continued. "I took the coats from the bodies and used them like blankets until morning—can't remember sleeping. I tried to move, but my leg was stuck. When it was light, I used a bungee cord and stocks from the shotguns to make a splint. I used a rifle as a lever to move the instrument panel off my leg. Crawling out of the wreckage into the snow wasn't easy. I took everything I could carry that I might need for survival, and started down the mountain. Slipping and tumbling a few times, I made it to the trees where I built a lean-to and set some snares."

The flames were dwindling, so Dan left to gather more firewood. When Dan moved toward the trees, Ann said, "Mr. Newcomb, would you like me to trim your hair?"

"No thanks, but you can cut my beard. It's getting longer than I like—and my eyebrows. They're interferring with my vision."

As Ann began shortening Hank's beard, Dan returned with enough firewood to keep the fire going for a couple of hours. Dan asked, "Dad, why have you stayed out here so long?"

"I figured since I killed those men, I'd end up in prison and embarrass you and Max's family. With the plane wrecked, I had no way to earn a living. The insurance wouldn't pay—the crash wasn't accidental. I didn't want to be dependent on others. Was I wrong?"

Ann responded as she snipped off a six-inch chunk of matted beard, "I don't think anyone would have known you had crashed on purpose;

you could have worked at Max's shop." Ann looked at Dan for reassurance and saw Dan nodding. "Mr. Newcomb, under all that hair, I'll bet there's a handsome man some lady would latch onto. I can think of one lady right now." Ann smiled, looked at Dan again, and whispered, "Beverly."

Hank overheard Ann and asked, "Who is Beverly?".

"My mom. My Dad died about a year ago. I think it's about time she moved on with an honest, dependable man. I think you qualify and I'll bet she'd like you. She has a lot of guts, too. She used to drive semis for a living."

Dan grinned and added, "She's a great cook, too, Dad. She'd fatten you up in no time."

Ann finished clipping Hank's eyebrows and brushed off the hair she had removed from his face. "There, you look like a new man."

"Funny, I don't feel very new, just old and worn out," he replied. "But thank you, Ann." Hank felt his beard and ran his index finger over his eyebrows. He smiled. "I guess I look a little more civilized."

"How long did you stay in the lean-to, Dad?"

"Three or four days, until my arm didn't hurt so much. I whittled a cane from a branch and made my way to a creek and followed the water until I got out of the deep snow regions. I've been wandering around Alaska and the Yukon all this time. When I met up with people, I gave them an alias, like I told you. Each time, I made up a different name so no one could track me. Most everyone I met was nice. I bummed food and coffee from people I met. One day, about a year ago, I watched a plane flying low— somebody was shooting at a bear. They landed, cut off the bear's head, and flew away. That's when I decided to shoot back when planes were low enough. I guess I hit a few of 'em."

"Yes, you did. One of my pilots was shot in the leg, but we took him to the hospital. He's going to be all right."

"That's good. I didn't mean to shoot any innocent people. Why were those planes flying so low?"

Dan replied, "We're between two landing strips, each one about ten miles from here, so the planes are descending, getting ready to land."

"Huh, being a pilot, I should have known. I was pretty upset when I saw that bear killed. It didn't have a chance. That bear was in agony until they shot it at close range to kill it. That incident really pissed me off. Oh! Sorry, young lady."

"Don't worry about your language, Mr. Newcomb, I've heard a lot worse than that. Should we try to sleep a few hours, Dan?"

"I guess so. Why don't you climb in the cabin and wrap up with Nomah and the blankets. I'll talk with Dad a little longer."

"Okay." Ann stood and said, "Good night, gentlemen. Come on, Nomah, let's go to bed."

When Ann was out of earshot, Hank commented, "That's a fine woman, Dan. She really likes you. I've been watching her when you're talking. I think she's in love with you."

"Well, I'm engaged to another woman, Lisa Zorn. She's an architect, smart, and pretty. I was interested in Ann about two years ago."

"Does Lisa like to fly?"

"We tried it once, but she didn't like it. We took off, and in a few minutes, she barfed, so I turned the plane around and landed. I never asked her to go up with me again, and she has never asked to fly with me." Dan tossed another log on the fire and looked at Hank. "I have to ask you something, Dad. Would you like to come back to Fairbanks, live with me for a while, and work with Max and me? You could update your pilot's license, and we could do a lot more flying—maybe get a second plane. We could have quite a business; Conley, Newcomb, and Newcomb—or maybe Conley, Newcomb, and Son."

"Well, I'll have to think about that, Dan. Why don't you get some sleep? I'll rest beside the fire for the night. If I'm here in the morning, I'll go with you. Good night."

"I hope you'll come with us, Dad. I'd like you to be around for my children. You could tell them some fantastic stories. See you in the morning."

"Dan, wake up. Your dad's gone." Ann was looking out a cabin window and shaking Dan's shoulder. There was disappointment in her voice. "I guess he's not going with us. I'm sorry. I know you wanted him to come with us."

"Are you sure he's gone?"

"The fire's out, and I can't see him anywhere. Maybe you should get out and check."

Dan stretched his legs and wiggled his arms, yawning. "I need a good night's sleep. Sitting up to sleep is lousy. That's a good idea. I'll look around to see if he's really gone." When Dan opened the cockpit door, Nomah jumped out and ran for the trees. Dan looked around but couldn't see his father. He stood next to the plane for a moment and then directed his eyes to the plane's ski tracks. Apparently, Hank had walked the depressions in the snow and cleared any obstacles that might hinder takeoff. He must have done that at first light.

Dan could hear Nomah barking from the forested area, and when Dan knelt to look under the plane in the direction of the barks, Nomah was running toward the plane. "What is it, Nomah? Did you see a bear?" Nomah joined Dan, turned toward the trees, and barked twice.

Ann called out, "Why is Nomah barking, Dan?"

"I don't know. Hand me the rifle; it might be a bear."

They didn't have to question the barking for long. Hank suddenly appeared from the trees pulling a sled carrying several large leather bags.

Dan yelled to his dad, "We thought you were gone for good."

Hank smiled and replied, "Nope. I've had enough of this life. It's about time to make some changes. I had to get my suitcases."

"I'm glad you're coming with us. I've got to turn the plane around. Leave your things there until we're ready to take off." Dan got in the plane and started the motor, but when he revved the engine, the plane wouldn't move. The skis were frozen to the ground. He shut off the engine and got out of the cabin with two metal containers, usually used for cooking. Hank was starting a fire, knowing they needed some hot water to melt ice and snow attached to the skis. Dan grinned and said, "Way to go, Dad. You've had to do this before, haven't you?"

"A few times, but it's been awhile."

It took about 30 minutes to free the skis. Dan turned the plane around and with the engine idling, they loaded Hank's large bags into the plane. Dan helped Hank into the cabin and made him comfortable in the back seats next to his baggage. Dan climbed into the pilot's seat and looked at Ann, Hank, and Nomah. "Everyone ready?"

Two yeses and a bark signaled Dan to rev the engine and start moving the plane through the snow. With the throttle wide-open, Glacier Phoenix picked up speed, rose above the snow, turned to the south, and in 25 minutes, Glacier Phoenix landed at the Fairbanks' airport.

Ann ran to the terminal to phone her mom so Beverly wouldn't continue to worry.

Dan asked Hank to stay in the plane and watch their belongings while he called Max.

"Hello?"

"Hi Max. We just got back from the pumping station. We had to set the plane down overnight. We picked up a hunter, Stanley Hanks. Could you bring the pickup over and get him? He's going to stay with me for a while."

"Yeah, okay. I'll have to close the shop—be there in about ten minutes or so. Bye."

"Bye." Dan smiled and walked back to the plane. Ann was talking to Hank when Dan returned from calling Max.

"Hey, Dad, Max is coming over to get you. I told him you are Stanley Hanks, a hunter. He's going to be shocked. After he recovers, he'll take you to the shop, and you can get cleaned up. You can shower, shave, and change to some of my clothes. I fixed the loft into an apartment. I'm going to fly Ann back to Anchorage and should be back in time for dinner. I imagine we'll eat at Max's place."

Hank wrestled his bags from the back of the cabin and handed them to Dan. When he climbed down from the cabin, Dan noticed Hank's rifle was missing.

"Dad, where's your rifle? Did you break it down?"

"Nope, I buried it back there in those trees—just a precaution."

Dan smiled, "Smart, Dad; very smart."

The two men carried Hank's bags over to the parking area, but didn't have to wait long. Max drove up, stepped out of the truck and waved to Dan and Hank. Dan shook hands with Max and said, "Uncle Max, I'd like you to meet Stan Hanks. We picked him up near Livengood. He was on his way back to Fairbanks."

Max stepped up to Hank and shook hands. "Glad to meet you, Stan."

"Likewise, Max, but we've met before. You don't recognize my voice?"

Max frowned, a little puzzled, and replied, "I don't think so."

"Well, Max, I married your sister."

"What! Is that you, Hank? We all thought you were dead." Max gave Hank a bear hug, stepped back and said, "God, it's good to see you, but you could smell better. How did Dan find you? Was it an accident? Where have you been?"

"Whoa! I'll tell you all about it after I clean up. Maybe you'll recognize me after I get most of this hair cut off; I won't need it any longer. Dan said I can clean up in the loft of your shop."

"Hell, Hank, you're coming home with me. Mona can give you a haircut and I'll give you some clothes to wear. Mine will fit you better than Dan's; we're more the same size. Let's load your things and I'll take you home. God, I'm glad you're back among the living." Max and Hank tossed Hank's bags into the back of the pickup and climbed in the truck. Max rolled down the window and yelled at Dan, "Oh! Dan—Lisa called me last night. She wondered where you were. You'd better give her a call. She expected you to call last night." Max waved and said, "Better not forget."

"Thanks, Max. I'll take care of it." Dan waved at the truck as it moved away toward the highway. Dan told Ann it would be a few minutes—he had to call Lisa. He jogged over to the terminal and made the call. Ten minutes later, he was back in Glacier Phoenix talking to the tower. They waited for two other planes to take off before they lifted off and headed toward Anchorage.

CHAPTER 35

Trips to Anchorage

On the way to Anchorage, Dan asked Ann what her wedding had been like. He wanted to find out more about the ceremony from a bride's viewpoint. Knowledge about how Lisa felt was going to be useful. The wedding was going to be much more emotional for Lisa than it would be for himself, but that might be a big assumption. How happy would they be when married, and where would they live? However, now that a member of his immediate family would be present, the ceremony was going to be more important than he had previously thought it would be. Hank appeared to like Ann and Dan hoped his father would like Lisa even more.

When they landed in Anchorage, Ann called a taxi and Dan ordered fuel for the plane. Dan escorted Ann to the taxi where Ann kissed him on the cheek and said, "Have a nice wedding. Good luck. Send us an invitation." Although Ann appeared to be happy, when she turned away from Dan, tears began to flood her eyes. As she rode home in the taxi, all Ann could think of was what a huge mistake it had been to marry Josh Springer. Why couldn't she have finished school and kept in touch with Dan?

Dan drank two cups of high-test coffee before paying for the fuel and climbing back into the Phoenix for the return to Fairbanks. He hoped the coffee would keep him wide awake for the trip. Twenty-four hours without sleep was not good preparation for flying an airplane. He landed at the private airstrip at 7:08 p.m. Dan saw Lisa waiting, leaning against her car, as he taxied up to the old metal building. As soon as the prop stopped spinning, she ran over to the plane to greet him. When he stepped down from the cabin, they hugged and kissed, and she pulled at his hand, backing toward the car.

"I'm so glad you're back, Dan. I hate for us to be separated for so long. You said you wanted to introduce me to someone. Is it an old girlfriend?" Lisa grinned and said, "If it is, I'm not going to like her."

"It's a surprise. Let's go over to Max's house—I'll introduce you. I can't wait to see your face when you meet him." Dan glanced at Lisa and grinned.

"So, it's a man. Hm-m-m. Now I'm confused. Tell me more, Dan, please!"

Dan smiled, "No begging, Lisa. We'll be there in a few minutes."

"I'll do something special for you."

"Uh, you'd better not come over to the shop at night any more. I'm going to have company."

"What? I don't mean that! I'll make you some cookies."

"Nope. Park over there next to the pickup."

They went to the Conleys' front door and Dan knocked. They only had to wait a second and Mona opened the door. "Hi guys, come in and join in the fun."

Lisa said, "Hi Mona. Dan wouldn't tell me what's going on. Please tell me!"

Mona looked at Dan and replied, "I think Dan should tell you. Right, Dan?"

They stepped into the living room and Dan, holding Lisa's hand, walked up to Hank, who was standing next to the fireplace holding a drink.

"Lisa, I'd like you to meet my father, Hank Newcomb. Dad, this is Lisa Zorn, my fiancée."

"What?" Lisa looked at Dan in disbelief. "You told me your father was dead."

Hank smiled and extended his hand toward Lisa and said, "Dan thought I was, but as you can see, I'm not dead—yet. I'm happy to meet you, Lisa. Dan has told me all about you. I hear you're an architect. That's very impressive."

"Thank you, Mr. Newcomb. It's so nice to meet you. My god! What a surprise!"

After eating, everyone sat around the fire and listened to Hank tell stories of his exploits above the Arctic Circle. It was nearing 10 p.m. when Dan fell asleep. Lisa roused him and said, "Dan, I've got to take you home so you can get some rest. Come on." Lisa grabbed Dan's hand and pulled to help him stand.

Dan was zombie-like, but stood, slipped into his coat, and followed Lisa to her car. When they arrived at the shop, Dan unlocked the front door, kissed Lisa good night, stepped inside, locked the door, and joined Nomah on the bed.

It was late morning when Dan woke up and looked around. He didn't remember getting onto the bed. He still had his clothes on. When he first woke up, he thought it had all been a dream—meeting his dad, flying Ann to Anchorage, and eating dinner at Max's home. He sat on the bed for about five minutes, letting the facts fall into place. Realizing it was all true, he decided to take a shower and put on clean clothes. As he descended the steps to the ground floor of the shop he heard Max say, "So, you *are* alive. I've been as quiet as possible to let you sleep. You were really beat last night when you left with Lisa."

"I've got to shower, eat something, and get back to work."

"Lisa called—wants you to call her back. Here's the number." Max put a post-it next to the phone.

"Thanks, Max. How is Dad today?"

"He's trying to adjust to his new environment. I think he slept on the floor last night. It's going to take awhile for him to get used to a regular bed."

"Thanks for putting him up last night, and thanks for the dinner. You guys did a great job of welcoming him back."

"You're welcome. I talked to him about working here. He said he had to take care of some things downtown. He wanted to set up new bank account."

"With what? I don't think he has any money. Well, I guess we'll find out before long."

After Dan called Lisa, he showered, got into clean clothes, fed Nomah, and ate breakfast. He was going to meet Lisa for lunch at 12:30 at the Mountain Vista Hotel, four blocks from the shop. Dan left for the hotel at 12:25, walking slowly, watching people shopping at stores he had ignored for a long time. He was surprised to see some of the items that were advertised on the Internet displayed in storefront windows. He smiled as he thought about how Fairbanks had emerged from the 1950's dark ages. His mom and dad had told him of how his grandparents had reminisced about things around the time of the 1964 earthquake.

Lisa was waiting for Dan at the dining room in the hotel. After they were seated and had ordered, Lisa said, "I have something to tell you. You know the company where I did my internship?"

"Yeah, I remember. Pacific Northwest Builders, wasn't it?"

"Uh-huh. They offered me a job in Portland. I'll be working with one of the senior partners for six months, and then they'll let me work on my own projects. Don't you think that's awesome?"

"That sounds great, Lisa. If you go to Portland, when do you start? And what about us?"

"They want me to start next week, and I want you to come with me, of course." Lisa smiled and reached across the table to touch Dan's hand.

Dan tried to adjust his sitting position to get more comfortable, pausing before replying. "Lisa, I can't go to Portland with you now. I just got my father back. He has no way to earn a living right now, and we need some time to get reacquainted. He has to reapply for a pilot's license and explain what happened to the two passengers. I hope he doesn't have any problems, but I'd like to be here if he has any trouble. I can't run out on Max, either. My flying is keeping our business in the black. My whole life is in Alaska. I was hoping you would find a job in Anchorage, or even here in Fairbanks."

"But, Dan, think of *my* opportunities. And you could fly in Oregon and Washington. Wouldn't that be all right? We'd be together, and your father is a pilot. He could fly for Max after getting a new license." Lisa withdrew her hand from Dan's and sat back in her chair, crossing her arms in front of her chest. "Dan, do you *want* to get married?"

"I've been thinking a lot about that in the last week or so. Have you sent out invitations?"

"Not yet. I was going to mail them this weekend. What are you thinking?"

"Maybe we should wait. You can go to Portland and see how the new job works out. See if you really fit into the position. Find out what is expected of you. If we are really meant to be together, then everything will work out all right. In the meantime, we can get adapted to our new situations without the additional stress of adjusting to being married. That alone will be a big change for both of us."

Lisa smiled, "I should have known you would have something logical to say. I wasn't sure of what to do, but I think that's a good plan. I love your idea and I love you, Dan."

"I love you, too, and I'd love to have another dinner roll. Toss me one, please."

Lisa didn't hesitate, she picked up a roll, laughed, and threw it at Dan. He reached for it, but missed, and tipped over his water. Fortunately, the glass was almost empty. The roll hit the floor, but Dan picked it up, smeared on some butter, and ate it. Then he said, "Good throw, bad catch, good roll. I'm out of water. Can I have yours?"

"You can have my water, but not my dessert."

The waiter arrived with their food and poured Dan a fresh glass of water. Lisa talked about her plans to find an apartment in Portland and mentioned some of the renowned architects with whom she might be working. Dan had to smile when he considered the differences between Lisa's job and his.

Lisa noticed his big smile and turned serious. "Dan, what are you smiling about? Did I say something funny? Are you happy I'm leaving?"

"No, I'm not happy you're leaving. I was thinking that I will be flying around Alaska delivering people and cargo while you are designing buildings for corporations—very different types of work."

A week later, Lisa was settled in Portland. Lisa and Dan talked every day for a week, then every other day for about ten days; then they exchanged emails once a week. After six weeks, the communications stopped. One night at ten o'clock, Dan's phone rang.

"Hi Lisa. How is everything going?"

"This isn't Lisa, it's Ann. I'm really mad at you, Daniel. Why didn't you send me an invitation to the wedding? Mom and I wanted to come."

"Lisa and I haven't gotten married, Ann. Lisa took a job in Portland. I sent her an email last week, but she hasn't replied. I'm going to call her earlier in the day. It's too late tonight."

"I guess I have no reason to be mad then. How are you and your dad doing? Is he adjusting to city life?"

"We're living together in the loft above the shop. He got a cot for sleeping, but I think he'll be getting a regular bed before long. When the weather gets cold, he'll want a mattress for more insulation."

Ann commented, "He probably needs something soft to cushion those old bones."

"He's a lot tougher than you might think. He's been working with Max and me in the shop and getting ready to reapply for his pilot's license. He'll probably want to get a plane of his own, but I don't think he can afford it now. I'm pretty sure he doesn't have any money. Anyway, we'll both be flying Glacier Phoenix for a while. How are you, Beverly, and the baby doing?"

"Oh, we're fine. Remember, when you and your dad come to Anchorage next time, call us. I want Mom to meet your dad. They might hit it off."

"Will do, Ann. Say hello to Bev for me—thanks for the call. Take care."

"Bye, Dan."

Dan hung up the phone and sat on the bed looking at it for about a minute before he heard footsteps on the stairs to the loft.

"Hi, Son. Are you off the phone?"

"Yeah, Dad, come on up. I was talking to Ann. She wants you to meet her mom. We're supposed to call them next time we go to Anchorage."

"Sounds all right to me. We could take them to dinner. Let's go down there after I get my plane."

"You're going to get a plane? How are you going to pay for it? Do you have enough money to start making payments?"

Hank pulled his check book out of his left rear pocket and tossed it on the bed next to Dan. "Take a look."

Dan reached over and opened the blue-vinyl cover and saw the balance: $192,000. "Holy—." Dan leaned back against his pillows and said, "Where did you get that much money? Did you rob a bank and keep it a secret?"

Hank had a broad smile. "What do you think I was doing all the time I was in the Yukon—twiddling my thumbs? I had my hands and feet in cold water and dirt."

"You found that much gold?"

"That's not all of it. That's the total for the nuggets—the high grade stuff. I've still got another five pounds of dust."

Dan paused a few seconds as he was calculating, and replied, "Geez, Dad, that's another $100,000."

"Uh-huh. That's about what I estimate. Altogether, I think there's enough for a plane and a house, don't you think?"

"Ah, yeah. That should do it." Dan laughed and said, "Boy, I've underestimated you, Doctor Newcomb. You seem to be able to cure just about any problems that arise."

Hank smiled, "Please, not Doctor. Dad is fine. Let's hit the sack, Dan. We can talk more tomorrow. I've run out of steam for today." Hank kicked off his shoes and went to bed with his clothes on. He didn't need a blanket.

When Dan woke up Saturday morning, he found a note on Hank's cot. It said he was at the airport checking out a plane. He should be back by 10 o'clock. Max wouldn't be in 'til nine o'clock so Dan decided to call Lisa. On the fourth ring, a male voice answered.

"Yeah? If you want Lisa, she's in the shower. Is this Dan?"

"Yes. Who are you?"

"I'm Lisa's boyfriend."

"Oh, really. Let me talk to Lisa, please."

"Just a minute."

Dan could hear the male voice call out, "Lisa—it's that dude from Alaska. You want to talk to him?"

Lisa answered from the background. "Yes, I'll be there in a sec. Have him wait."

Dan heard what was said, so he spoke into the phone, "I'll wait. Thanks." Dan heard a clunk as the phone was laid on something hard, probably a countertop.

Lisa's voice came on, "Hi, Dan, I was going to call you. I've been really busy. I have a new boyfriend—we're living together. I hope you understand."

"Oh, I understand. Bye, Lisa." Dan hung up the phone, but after what he had heard, he didn't feel bad at all. The short conversation had confirmed his suspicions; people were throwaways to Lisa. It was time to move on.

He needed at least one positive thing for the weekend, so he quickly showered, dressed, and drove to the Joe and Hotcakes restaurant for a pancake breakfast. When he returned to the shop, Max was talking on the phone. Dan saw Max motion for him to come to the phone.

Max gave the phone to Dan and said, "It's Hank."

"What's up, Dad?"

"Can you drive over to the airport? I bought a plane, and you have to fly it to our landing strip. I'll drive the truck back and pick you up. See you in ten minutes."

Hank hung up before Dan could say "Okay."

Dan looked at Max and said, "Dad bought a plane, and he wants me to fly it to the landing strip. He'll pick me up and we'll be back here in about 40 minutes. I'm sure glad he isn't crazy, or we'd be in real trouble." Dan hung up the phone and called out, "Come, Nomah, we're flying."

Nomah ran down the steps from the loft and went to the door. Dan looked at his watch, grabbed his keys, and as they ran to the pickup, he said, "We have ten minutes, Nomah, no rush." Nomah barked and jumped in the front seat when Dan opened the door. Nomah whined when he didn't see the regular sites on the way to the airstrip. Dan pulled into the airport parking lot and made his way to the terminal. Hank was waiting outside, and they walked toward a red and yellow Cessna.

Hank said, "This is it. I'll meet you at the landing strip."

Dan was surprised; it was a Cessna 185, the same model as the Glacier Phoenix. The two men exchanged keys, and Nomah followed Dan to the cockpit. Hank walked toward the parking lot twirling the keys on his finger without saying anything more.

Dan taxied Hank's plane to the runway and in five minutes, he was parked at the company landing strip. He waited about 10 minutes for Hank to show up. While waiting, Dan checked the plane, inside and out. He was happy his dad had the foresight to get the same model as the Glacier Phoenix. The parts were interchangeable, so they would only have to have spares for one model. Dan was wondering when his dad had gotten so smart. When Dan was in high school, he recalled that he and all his friends thought their parents seemed pretty dumb. Dan smiled and laughed at himself.

A month later, both Hank and Dan were flying two to three times a week. Their reputation for dependability drew more business for Conley, Newcomb, and Son, which was painted on the fuselage of both planes. Occasionally, both of the planes were in the air simultaneously, but usually when one Newcomb was flying, the other was working on a project with Max.

One morning toward the end of August, the three men were sitting in the shop drinking coffee and shooting the bull. Nomah was half asleep on the floor next to the heat register.

Max asked, "Dan, whatever happened to Lisa? Did you guys brake up?"

Dan had never discussed what had happened, so he related the Lisa story to Max and Hank.

Max and Hank didn't comment, thinking Dan had handled things very well. Hank refilled his coffee mug and said, "You know what they say, Dan. When you fall off a horse, you've got to get right back on and ride."

Hank added, "That's right. Say, have you thought about that EMT, Ann? She struck me as being level-headed and happy with her position in life. She seems to enjoy her job—caring for others. I'm sure she likes you. Why not call her and set up a date?"

Dan nodded and went upstairs to his phone, wanting some privacy. He dialed Ann's number, not sure of what to say; he was a little nervous. But the worst case would be if she said no about going on a date. Dan would see if any of his female classmates from high school was still available if Ann didn't show any interest.

After the third ring, Dan heard Ann's voice, "Hello."

"Hi, Ann. How are you?"

"Hi, Dan. We're all doing fine. What about you, Hank, Max, and Nomah?"

"We're fine. I'm calling to ask if you would like to go out with me for dinner this Saturday."

"I'd like that very much." There was a short pause. "Can you bring your dad?"

"No problem. I'm sure I can get my dad to come along. We'll arrive at the airport at 5:00 p.m. and drive to your apartment. We'll see you around 5:30. Is that all right?"

"That's great. We'll be expecting you. See you Saturday, Dan. Thanks for calling. Bye."

"Bye, Ann." Dan smiled as he hung up the phone. He thought, *that was easy, and painless.* Now he had to convince his dad to fly with him to Anchorage on Saturday afternoon. He descended the steps and saw Nomah still on the floor, and heard Max and Hank talking about a job coming up the following week. Dan filled his coffee mug and sat opposite his dad.

"How about flying to Anchorage with me on Saturday? I've got a dinner date with Ann. I think she wants you to meet her mother." Dan expected an argument and an excuse from Hank.

Hank gave a hint of a smile and said, "Okay. When are we supposed to be there?"

"You'll go?"

"Sure. Why not? I don't have any hot dates planned." Hank smiled, took a big drink of coffee, and said, "I've got some work to do on a snow blower, I'd better get busy."

The rest of the week passed quickly. Dan bought some new clothes to go with the sweater he had received at Christmas from the Conleys and made reservations for four adults and a toddler at a nice restaurant, not far from the Anchorage airport. Saturday afternoon was a blue sky day, great for flying. Dan felt bad about leaving Nomah at the shop with Max, but he didn't feel right about leaving Nomah in Ann's apartment either. When Dan and Hank left the shop at 2:30, Nomah whined and barked when he realized he was being left behind.

Dan was a passenger on the flight to Anchorage, Hank piloting his own plane. They arrived a few minutes before 5:00 p.m. Dan rented a four-door sedan and made sure there was a seat for Larry Daniel. They drove to Ann's apartment and went inside to wait for the ladies. Ann greeted the men at the door and said, "Mom's almost ready, she'll be out in a minute. I'll take care of some finishing touches." Ann smiled and asked, "Do you gentlemen want something to drink?"

Dan looked at Hank and said, "We're good. Go ahead and put on your war paint."

"Okay, I'll just be a sec." Ann disappeared into the bedroom. Bev came out of her bedroom and joined the men. Dan introduced Bev and Hank.

Bev was beaming. She glanced at Hank and then Dan. "How was your flight, Dan? Is your dad as good a pilot as you are?"

"The trip was fine. Dad's flying is better than mine, but he has 20 years more experience than I do." Dan looked at Hank and grinned. "I wouldn't want to go into a competition against him."

Hank smiled and replied, "Don't lay it on too thick, Dan."

"Ta-dah!" Ann came out of her bedroom and did a pirouette holding Larry in a car seat. "We're ready."

Dan commented, "Boy, you ladies look great. We don't need the car seat, Ann. I had one installed when I picked up the rental at the airport."

"That's great. Thank you for doing that. We won't have to fasten this seat in the car. I'll leave it here." Ann held LD while Dan undid the straps.

It took about ten minutes to reach the restaurant. Hank helped Bev out of the car and the older couple walked toward the entrance holding hands. Ann had removed Larry from the car seat and saw Dan frowning, watching Hank and Bev. Ann grabbed Dan's arm, stopping for a moment. Ann spoke softly, almost a whisper, "Your dad has been seeing Mom for nearly a month. Didn't you know?"

"Not a clue. That son-of-a-gun! That's why he didn't object to coming here for dinner. He wanted to see Beverly. Boy, am I going to give him a bad time. You could have told me about them the other day. You sure can keep secrets."

"I thought your dad had told you." Ann laughed and gave a tug on Dan's jacket. "Come on."

Bev and Hank were waiting inside. Bev was seated on a bench against the wall in the waiting area. Ann, the baby, and Dan approached the bench and Ann sat down beside her mom.

Hank and Dan got in line behind a young couple. The young man turned and looked at Dan, "They're busy tonight. We've been waiting for 30 minutes, but it's worth it. The food and service are really good. Aren't you Dan Newcomb?"

"Yes. Should I know you?"

"Probably not. I was a sophomore when you were a senior in high school."

The couple talked with Dan and Hank for a couple of minutes until someone tapped Dan on the shoulder from behind. Dan turned around and saw Mrs. Cornell.

"Hello, Daniel. How are you?"

"Hi, Mrs. Cornell. It's good to see you again. I'd like you to meet my father, Henry Newcomb."

Hank and Mrs. Cornell shook hands. Mrs. Cornell said, "I drove down from Fairbanks to pick up my granddaughter, Lisa. She just got in from Portland about an hour ago. We thought we'd have dinner before driving back home. When I saw you, Dan, I had to say hello."

Dan responded, "Is Lisa here?"

"Yes. She's freshening up a little after the trip. She'll be here in a minute or two. I thought I'd better get in line—they're busy this evening."

"You said you drove down from Fairbanks?"

"Oh, I didn't drive. We have a chauffeur, Eduardo; he's Italian. Heavens, I don't know the roads except around our area of Fairbanks. I'd get lost in Anchorage, everything is so much bigger." She smiled and turned, looking for Lisa, who was walking toward them, smiling. "There she is."

Lisa saw Dan and skipped ahead, throwing her arms around him. "It's so good to see you, Dan. I've missed you."

Dan gave Lisa a brief hug and said, "Hi, Lisa. There is someone I want you to meet." Dan took hold of Lisa's left arm and escorted her to the bench where Beverly and Ann, holding Larry, were sitting. "Lisa, I'd like you to meet Beverly, Ann, and Larry Olson. Beverly is Ann's mother. Ann is my fiancée."

Ann was surprised, but knew Dan had a reason for saying she was his fiancée. She accepted it, even though it had nearly taken her breath away. Dan was apparently telling Lisa their relationship was over.

Lisa looked at Dan in disbelief. She was shocked, but looked back at Beverly and said, "How are you, Mrs. Olson? Dan has told me all about you. It's a pleasure to meet you."

Beverly replied, smiling, "It's nice to meet one of Dan's former girlfriends." Beverly had heard the whole story about Lisa and Dan from Hank.

Ann stood up and said, "I'm glad to meet you, Lisa. Dan has told me so much about you." Ann had heard all about Lisa from her mom. Dan had talked a little bit about Lisa back in April, but nothing since.

Beverly said, "We have to go, Dan. Hank is motioning that we're going to be seated. It was nice to have met you, Lisa. Maybe we'll see you at the wedding."

Lisa let the words sink in and replied, "Ah, enjoy your meal."

Dan picked up Larry and walked with Ann over to Bev and Hank who were standing with a hostess. Dan looked back at Lisa and said, "Have a good trip back home, Lisa. Bye."

After the dinner party was seated and they had ordered, Ann put her hand on Dan's, smiled, and said, "Yes."

Dan took her hand, looked into her eyes, smiled and said, "Yes, what?"

Ann smiled, almost laughed, and then her eyes began to fill with tears. She blotted her eyes with a napkin and said, "Yes, I will marry you."

Dan got up, pulled Ann to her feet and kissed her. As they hugged, they both said, "I love you." Dan got the attention of a nearby waiter and said, "I'd like to order some champagne." When Dan and Ann were reseated, Hank and Beverly were still applauding, as were several patrons at adjacent tables.

Dan wasn't completely satisfied with what had taken place. He was grinning and nervously aligning his silverware when he said, "I must ask you, Ann, will you marry me?"

Hank, Bev, and Ann all laughed, but Ann answered, "Yes!"

Hank said, "Congratulations, Dan and Ann! You have both made excellent choices."

Bev couldn't keep tears from rolling down her cheeks. She was so happy that Ann and Dan were finally together, something Bev had hoped for nearly three years ago. Bev had only one disappointment, she was sorry her husband, Ben, had not lived long enough to meet Dan and witness his daughter's marriage to her soul mate.

Bev was watching Dan as he fidgeted with his keys. She asked, "Dan, what *are* you doing?"

Dan smiled and replied, "I'm getting something from my jewelry store." Dan had removed his truck key from the smaller of two rings that retained all his keys. He separated the smaller, now empty, ring from the larger, reached over to Ann's left hand and slipped the small key ring on her finger. "There, now it's official."

Ann had been smiling ever since Dan had asked her to marry him. She held up her hand, looking at the ring, and said, "This is the nicest ring I've ever had."

Everyone laughed, but they all understood what she meant.

Beverly invited the men to stay overnight in the living room at the apartment. Dan and Hank flipped for the sofa: Dan won. Bev gave Hank several blankets to cushion the floor, but even after Hank said the blankets weren't necessary, he relented and slept well on the makeshift bed; the champagne had helped relax his body and mind.

Early in the morning, Dan woke suddenly after fighting his way out of the cabin of his plane as it sank into ice-cold water. This time, he had seen the face of his passenger: it was Ann. She was terrified. Dan guided her to the surface, made sure Nomah was out of the sinking plane and struggled upward, breaking the surface of the water gasping for breath.

Dan sat up for a minute, blinked his eyes a few times, and looked around. He saw Hank asleep on the floor. Realizing everyone was all right, he went back to sleep.

A week later, Dan was sitting on his bed scratching Nomah, assessing his life since returning to Alaska. He hadn't had the throat-cutting dream in months, and the last dream about escaping from a submerged airplane wasn't very alarming.

He had fallen in love, fallen out of love, and fallen in love again, this time with the right woman. His father had returned to his life, and within a few months he would have a wife, a son, and a mother-in-law. He was enjoying all aspects of life, even his job, doing what he loved— flying with his pal.